HIDE AND SEEK

John Darnell and Sergeant O'Reilly resumed their patrol through Whitechapel with Constable Fenham pacing along in front of them. The night deepened, and a light fog obscured their vision beyond a few yards ahead.

At close to eleven, O'Reilly choked on the words she was saying and pointed to an alleyway. "He's there! I saw him!"

Darnell turned and looked in the direction she pointed, seeing a small alley between two three-story, clapboard buildings. "Let's go," he said.

He ran into the alley with the constable and O'Reilly close at his heels. The alley opened into an unlighted courtyard and then into another alley at the far end of it. Darnell ran through the yard and out the other alley and stopped, looking both ways on the far street. He could see no one in either direction.

The three stood looking at each other for a moment. Darnell said, "He's been watching us, stalking us. Waiting for just the right time to show himself when he could then seem to vanish."

"But will he kill again?" O'Reilly asked.

Darnell's face was dark. "He will, if he's copying Jack the Ripper. He'll kill again within two days."

O'Reilly looked at him. "How do you know?"

"The Ripper's second victim was found in the early morning hours of September eighth. It's just past midnight now. The sixth of September."

THE CASE OF THE RIPPER'S REVENGE

A JOHN DARNELL MYSTERY

Sam McCarver

A SIGNET BOOK

SIGNET
Published by New American Library, a division of
Penguin Putnam Inc., 375 Hudson Street,
New York, New York 10014, U.S.A.
Penguin Books Ltd, 80 Strand,
London WC2R ORL, England
Penguin Books Australia Ltd, Ringwood,
Victoria, Australia
Penguin Books Canada Ltd, 10 Alcorn Avenue,
Toronto, Ontario, Canada M4V 3B2
Penguin Books (N.Z.) Ltd, 182–190 Wairau Road,
Auckland 10, New Zealand

Penguin Books Ltd, Registered Offices:
Harmondsworth, Middlesex, England

First published by Signet, an imprint of New American Library,
a division of Penguin Putnam Inc.

First Printing, November 2001
10   9   8   7   6   5   4   3   2   1

Ⓟ   REGISTERED TRADEMARK—MARCA REGISTRADA

Printed in the United States of America

PUBLISHER'S NOTE
This is a work of fiction. Names, characters, places, and incidents either are
the product of the author's imagination or are used fictitiously, and any
resemblance to actual persons, living or dead, business establishments, events,
or locales is entirely coincidental.

For Joe Pittman and Genny Ostertag

Author's Note

On August 31, 1888, in the dark, dangerous streets of the Whitechapel District of London, the most famous serial killer in the annals of crime committed the first of five vicious murders that kept London alarmed, enraged, and fearful for months. Scotland Yard made supreme efforts to apprehend Jack the Ripper, but he dropped out of sight after his last murder on November 9, 1888, and was never heard from again.

In this story, women see a ghostly figure with a pasty-white face, top hat, and cloak appear and then seemingly disappear in 1917 in that same Whitechapel District. Again, London is shocked by a series of killings remarkably resembling those perpetrated by Jack the Ripper twenty-nine years earlier. The first of the new unfortunate victims is similarly discovered in Whitechapel on the morning of August 31.

Incorporated into this tale are certain real-life persons of the era, most prominently the eminent playwright George Bernard Shaw. However, except for their involvement in historical and documented events, their participation in this story derives from my imagination, since this book is a work of fiction inspired by real situations and people.

I'm grateful to my former editor, Joseph Pittman, and to my new editor, Genny Ostertag—to both of whom I've dedicated this book—for their advice and perceptive editorial comments. I appreciate the excellent scrutiny of manuscripts by NAL's copy editors and the striking and classic book cover rendered by NAL's design artists. I thank Donald Maass, my literary agent, for his continued valued support and guidance.

Chapter One

London, Thursday night, August 30, 1917

The woman gasped, grabbed her friend's arm, and pointed at the dark, caped figure faintly visible through the fog at the end of the street. "It's the ghost again, Bessie!" she shrieked. "Second time I seen 'im. My Gawd!" She looked sidelong at the woman standing beside her, who was staring where she had gestured. She released her arm, but urged, "See?"

"I don't see nothin', Sadie. Where?"

"There! Oh, 'e's gone." She leaned against the lamppost, shuddered, and fanned her face with her hand. "We got to find the constable." She turned and ran back toward the opposite corner, her friend's heels clattering behind her. Rounding the corner, they ran into Constable Burt Fenham.

"Thank the Lord you're here," Sadie Latkins blurted out, breathless. "I saw 'im again, Burt! The ghost!"

The constable pushed the women back. "Now, now, Sadie. Calm down. You say you saw him again? The same man?"

"Man? I don't know if he's a man. Spirit or ghost, more like. You're the law, you tell me who he is, what he is. 'N' tell me 'ow he just disappears into thin air."

Fenham turned to Bessie Morton. "Did you see him too, Bessie?"

She shook her head. "No. I ain't seen nothin'. But I'm sure Sadie did. I guess, like she says, the fog swallered him."

Sadie grabbed the constable's uniform. "Look 'ere, there's others as can tell you. Ask Pearl. Or Hannah. They seen 'im, too. 'E's been about here for two weeks now."

"Then why haven't I come across him? I walk these streets seven hours a night. Aren't you imagining all this?" Fenham took off his hat and scratched his balding head. The corners of his mouth turned up as he studied the two women.

"Tell you what," he said, "*show* him to me, and I'll warn him to leave off scarin' such poor women as the likes of you. Women just tryin' to make a decent livin' on the street." He smacked his nightstick into his big palm and smiled. "I'll put the fear o' God into him."

"Put fear in a ghost?" Sadie sniffed. "Not bloody likely."

Constable Fenham pulled his hat back on and said, "Well, get on with you, and don't bother me no more with such tales."

The constable walked away a few steps and turned back to them. "And lay off the ale. Next thing, ye'll be seein' the Loch Ness monster paradin' about."

Poppy Nellwyn began the last night of her life in her usual fashion. After freshening herself with the bowl of water and cloth her landlady provided, she pulled her black stockings on all the way up to their tops, then carefully rolled them back down to just above her knees. She smoothed her stockings and admired her trim legs, smiling.

She slipped on the best of her three dresses, the long flowered one, and stepped into black, high-button shoes. She bent over and buttoned them. The black shawl with only one small tear in it completed her night's ensemble, except for her dark blue hat with an artificial flower. Poppy glanced in the stained mirror fixed to the wall and turned to the right and left.

She tossed off the one large swallow of whiskey in the pint bottle on her dresser, pulled the door closed behind her, and walked down the three flights to the street below. Poppy needed some coin to pay her rent.

She hoped she could find some good customers this night, those who had not just drink to offer for her services, but hard cash. She looked up and down the street, noticing Sadie and Bess walking toward Whitechapel Road in animated conversation. She turned and sauntered in the other direction toward her usual spot, swinging her hips from side to side, humming a dance-hall tune.

How Poppy came to be a streetwalker in the Whitechapel District of London at only nineteen was a not unfamiliar story in that area at that time. The man who fathered her was killed in a street fight when Poppy was but a year old. Her mother plied the trade that later become Poppy's livelihood. Beginning as early as her twelfth year, Poppy had been raped by men who first used her mother and then, when the mother collapsed into a drunken stupor, turned to the frightened girl huddled on her cot in the alcove. In the three years since Sarah Nellwyn's death, Poppy Anne Nellwyn had made her mother's pattern of existence her own desperate means of survival. She knew nothing else.

Down on the dark street now, Poppy asked a man walking by, "Make you feel good?" She stood on the street corner out of the bright glow of the street lamp but with enough of the ambient light falling on her so men could see her face.

Her countenance brought her more than her share of street business. Few prostitutes had the pleasant, even features that Poppy boasted, the milk-white skin of youth, the soulful black eyes, and the long dark hair. Yet in recent months even her fresh looks had begun to show facial lines and darkening circles under her eyes.

The man glanced at her, about to go on, then halted his stumbling stride as he heard her voice and saw her face. "Well, dearie," he said, "depends on what it costs now, don't it?"

She named a figure and added, "I like to see the coin first."

He laughed and pulled out several coins. "You got a place?"

Poppy shook her head, but took his arm and led him to a dark courtyard bordered by lodging houses, the few windows of which emitted little light. The moon provided the only slight illumination. She pushed the man against the side of a building and wrested the coins from his hand. "You won't be needin' these." She dropped them into the large pocket of her dress, which she then hitched up, revealing her nakedness underneath. She felt the man's warm whiskey breath on her face. "Well, lovey, it's up to you, now. How do you want it?" She smiled as he reached clumsily for her.

Ten minutes later, Poppy entered The Three Hares pub and marched to the bar. She plunked a coin down on the bar and said to the red-haired barkeep, "Whiskey, neat, and keep the bottle handy." She tossed off the first small glass, then nodded at the bottle. The barkeep filled her glass, and she sipped it slowly as he watched. In a few moments, she said, "One more, Rusty, 'n' be generous this time."

Poppy put a second coin on the bar. As he refilled her glass, she took his wrist and tipped a bit more into it, laughing.

The barkeep jerked away. "Don't you think you got enough there?" He replaced the bottle on the back counter. "If you keep that up," he said, "by the time you're twenty-one you'll be a sodden drunk." He added with a frown, "Or dead."

Some time after midnight, after talking and laughing with several friends and finishing her last drink, Poppy stepped back out on the street. She looked one way, then the other.

She walked, somewhat unsteadily now, to her regular spot once more. Knowing she had spent half her money, she needed to replenish it before the night was out. Several men passed, ignoring her invitation. It was getting late, and some had no money and were heading to their lodgings to sleep off their drunks. She turned her collar up in the sudden cool breeze.

In the distance she saw a man who looked like what she called "a proper one." It might have been the top hat that made her think it, or the cape and vested suit, shabby as they were. It could have been just the way he swaggered as he walked, or her sense that he seemed older, perhaps in his fifties. What it was, she didn't know for sure, but when she had this feeling about a man, she knew she'd get her rent money that night.

"Want to feel good, lovey?" she asked him in her most enticing voice as he approached. "Real good?" She was pleased when he stopped.

But when the man looked into her eyes, Poppy involuntarily shivered. Something about his eyes, cold and hard, made her catch her breath. Yet she had seen that kind before, and knew that in a few minutes she could make those cold eyes turn soft and moist.

"Name your price," he said, his eyes still boring into hers.

She named it, and he laughed. "All right, ducky. I'll pay your price this one time. But I'll want the lot for it."

She nodded, tucked her arm into his, and managed to talk him into extracting coins from his pocket and showing them to her as they walked on. The next dark alleyway seemed as good a place as any, the man apparently relaxed from drink, and eager.

She led him into the alley and was pleased that he made jokes and laughed as they walked. Maybe he was a nicer bloke than she thought.

Poppy relaxed, thinking this would be the last of the night, and there'd be enough now for a pint on the way home. In her fashion, she turned and pulled the coins from his right hand, just as the moon came out from behind a cloud and revealed a flash of something silvery bright in his left hand. His right hand grasped her throat viciously, and she realized she could make no sound.

Poppy's windpipe was crushed in his strong fingers. Her eyes bulged with fear and pain. She saw the glint of the knife moving before her face then. It was the last thing Poppy Nellwyn saw in this world.

Chapter Two

Friday morning, August 31

The morning sun brought no warmth to the slashed, bloody, eviscerated body of the young woman lying in the alleyway off Durward Street. When Constable Burt Fenham discovered her body on his Whitechapel rounds just before he was to go off duty, he lost his breakfast of bangers and eggs at her feet, which did nothing to improve the mood of Chief Inspector Bruce Howard of Scotland Yard when he arrived some thirty minutes later in answer to the bobby's call.

As Chief Inspector Howard viewed the body at the crime scene with the constable, he removed his hat, partly as a sign of respect, but mostly to allow him, unobtrusively, to brush back unwanted tears from his eyes. Howard ran a hand through his thick white hair and murmured under his breath, "God forgive me, I'd like to get these old hands on whoever did this abomination."

He turned away from the sight. "She's no older than my own granddaughter." To a detective he had brought with him, he said wearily, "Get your photos taken, Dennis."

Chief Inspector Howard looked over the dismal surroundings, the overflowing rubbish bins against the wooden slat fence, the few windows of the brown wood lodging houses looking down upon the short alley that connected two side streets. He shook his head. At age sixty-three, Howard detested cases involving the deaths of young women, but knew he must just grit his teeth and hold on until retiring on his pension in two years.

"When you're finished there, Dennis, rope off the scene," he said, "and go over it with a fine-tooth comb. Pick up anything that looks at all out of place." He leaned against the fence and stuck a pipe between his teeth, but didn't light it. "I doubt we'll get any usable fingerprints out here," he said, more to himself than to the others.

Constable Fenham stepped over to Howard and cleared his throat. "Uh, Chief Inspector, a word with you, sir?"

Howard raised his gray eyebrows and looked up at the taller man. "Do you know something more about this, Burt? Speak up."

The bobby's forehead furrowed. "I hope you don't think I'm bloody balmy, sir. There's somethin' you should know."

"Go on."

"There was sightings, sir."

"Witnesses? Well, speak up. Someone saw the killer?"

"No, no, not witnesses. I knew I'd say it all wrong. The sightings—well, they was ghosts. Or, I should say, one ghost, some people saw more'n once." He nodded, confirming his words.

"Ghosts? Where? Out here on the streets?" Howard stuffed his pipe back in a pocket, replaced his hat, and glared at him. "I'm listening."

"On the streets, sir, yes, sir, all about these streets. Several times in the past fortnight."

"And now this killing? By a ghost? You're sure those sightings, as you call them, weren't just a flesh-and-blood man?" Howard's grim smile was humorless.

The bobby shook his head. "I never saw the—uh, man, or thing, or whatever it was, myself, sir. But the locals did."

"Who? You have names?"

"They were women, streetwalkers, you know. They saw it—or him, whichever you like best. Prowlin' the streets. They described him to me and I kept a watch out, even last night."

Howard grumbled, "All right, what did he look like? Tell me what the women saw—or thought they saw."

Fenham frowned. "Well, he wasn't tall. A bit older, had a few years on him. Dressed like a gentleman, but older clothes. Wore a top hat and a long black cape. And a three-piece suit."

The Chief Inspector scowled. "And this, ah, ghost—we'll call him that for now—did he leave any footprints, stop in at one of your pubs, buy any fish and chips?"

The bobby shook his head vigorously. "No, sir. As soon

as they saw him, he vanished, almost before their very eyes."

Howard made a growling sound. "An *invisible* ghost?"

"Yes, sir—I mean, no, sir. What I mean is, they swear they saw it. Three different women. And they say it disappeared."

Howard gestured at the body his detective was inspecting. "Constable, do you think a ghost could do that to this woman?"

Burt Fenham wiped his brow with a sleeve. "Sir, if a ghost *can* kill . . . well, I expect that's the way he'd do it."

Professor John Darnell had grown accustomed to being asked in peculiar ways and at odd times of the day and night to investigate paranormal phenomena. His original sideline, looking into reports of supernatural, psychic-world sightings, had soared as his reputation grew from solving cases like the *Titanic* mystery, the *Orient Express* phantom, and the Prime Minister's séances, and it now dominated his time more than his teaching. But he felt his mornings at the breakfast table with his wife, Penny, were inviolate. At least, he hoped they always would be.

John Darnell sat across the table from Penny as they sipped their second cups of coffee after having their fill of the kippers, toast, and eggs that Sung, their valet and cook, had provided. Darnell scowled at news in the *Times* of more thousands of British men dying in battles in France, bringing to mind the horrible scenes in the government movies of the 1916 battle of the Somme. He tossed the paper down.

"Damned hideous war." He looked up at Penny. "What say we chuck it all and bed down in the Cotswolds for a few days? I have no cases pending now."

"Wonderful! We haven't had a holiday together in months. I love our place there, and we don't use it enough." She laughed. "Imagine, just you, me, crickets, and owls."

Penny moved her chair closer to his and pressed her lips warmly on his. "It would be very relaxing. If you're serious, I can pack in half an hour."

The telephone rang in the sitting room, but neither made a move. Darnell heard Sung's shoes clop across the wooden entry floor and his subdued voice on the phone. Darnell couldn't hear the words and, in fact, wasn't trying. His attention, at the moment, was directed at the nape of Penny's neck.

Sung's head appeared around the corner of the dining room door. "A call for you, Professor. It sounds important."

He looked up. "Who is it?"

"Chief Inspector Howard."

Darnell gave Penny a puzzled look. "Nothing I know of going on with Scotland Yard. Shouldn't take a minute. Pour me some more coffee."

Penny continued to hold her husband's hand when he stood, and his fingers pulled away gently from hers as he walked toward the sitting room. Her gaze followed him, and she frowned.

Darnell sat on the arm of a chair in the sitting room, then picked up the phone base in one hand and the receiver in the other. "Darnell here, Bruce," he said. "Haven't heard from you in months. How are you?"

"Fine, fine. But I'll get right to the point, John. I'd like your help and your advice. We've got a dead body down here. It's a murder, and a horrible one at that."

"Where are you?"

"East End. I'll direct you. The thing is, the bobby says local women have seen a ghost here off and on for two weeks."

"A ghost. Well, too much gin can produce hallucinations."

"You'd better see for yourself what we've got here and, more's the point, listen to what the constable has to say. Then you can judge. Can you come?"

"Now?"

"We're waiting at the crime scene, and I want to take the body in. If you could . . ."

Darnell thought of Penny and the Cotswolds. Their trip would have to wait a day or so. Telling her the disappointing news would be the hardest part. He sighed.

"All right, Bruce. Give me some directions and half an hour. I'll be there."

Chapter Three

John Darnell stared down at the body, what was left of it. Chief Inspector Howard and Constable Fenham stood on the other side of the body, across from him.

"Horrible," Darnell said. "Just a girl." Bile rose in his throat, but he forced himself to study the body in as clinical a manner as he could. The throat was cut, the abdomen mutilated, the woman disemboweled. "Throat slashed, left to right," he said.

Howard said, "Yes, I imagine he was facing her. Then he'd be left-handed."

Darnell nodded. "Held her with his right hand, slashed her with the knife in the left, from her left to her right. Of course, if he were behind her . . ."

"It'd be the opposite," Howard said. "Right-handed."

"With this slip of a girl," Darnell said, "wouldn't you say he probably faced her, with nothing to fear?"

"Yes. I think so. Or he could have already forced her to the ground. She was a prostitute, and a young one. He was her customer, and he had her confidence."

"Those cuts—my God, they're six or eight inches long," Darnell said. He turned and spat something from his mouth before looking back. "And why in God's name would he disembowel her—gut her, like an animal?"

"One thing sure. He used a sharp knife, one with a long blade, and he knew how to use it. Whatever else, he would seem to be a psychopath."

Darnell nodded. "No one in his right mind could do this."

"You should hear what the constable learned from the women—about what they called a ghost." He walked away from the body, Darnell and Fenham following, leading them to a nearby fence.

Through cracks between broken slats, Darnell could see and hear a small crowd of people who had been drawn to the murder scene. Others hovered around both entrances of the alleyway, held back only by the presence of the detective and other constables. Darnell took a deep breath, although the air was only marginally better than near the body, and looked at Fenham. "Go ahead."

Fenham took his hat off, shifting it around in his hands. "As I was tellin' the Chief Inspector. Three women, maybe more, been seein' a ghost—what they call a ghost anyway—for two weeks down here, all about Whitechapel. Two of 'em saw him, or it, earlier last night, and came to me."

"You've not seen him, this 'ghost,' yourself?"

"No, sir. The women did. They're prostitutes, but honest ones. Said he was dressed like a gentleman, but in older clothes—you know, worn. Had a top hat and a long black cape."

"Older clothing? Nothing unusual about that around here."

"More's the thing, *old-fashioned*."

"Hmmm. Like an old ghost might wear, eh?" Darnell smiled.

Fenham looked down, sheepish.

"His face, Burt. Tell me what you know about it."

"Only what they told me. A white face—*ghost-white,* you know." He frowned. "One woman said the look of him sent shivers down her spine."

"Anything else?"

Fenham looked down again. "They said—mind you, I never saw this myself—they said he just disappeared. Into the fog."

"A disappearing ghost," Howard muttered. "Can you imagine? Wait 'til I tell the Chief Superintendent this story."

Darnell said to Howard, "Can we trace this girl's activities last night, Bruce, and talk with the three women about the ghost they saw? Can you get their addresses, any place where we can find them?"

"We'll check the local pubs. You and I can do that, John. Any loose change that prostitutes have, they'd spend there." He turned to Fenham. "Get Detective Gannet back here, Burt. We'll take the body in. The wagon's waiting. And what's the name of this one?" He nodded in the direction of the savaged body.

"I've seen her about. One of the youngest. Poppy Nellwyn."

Darnell frowned. "Poppy Nellwyn. Why does that sound familiar?" He shook his head and asked Howard, "Has the coroner seen the body?"

Howard nodded. "Yes, and he said he saw his fill of it, but he'll autopsy her when we bring her in.

"No fingerprints at the scene? No other evidence?"

"Just a few coins we found by her body. This time, they cost the poor thing her life."

The Three Hares pub sat back from the street in a dark, nondescript building between two ramshackle boardinghouses, and while it did not have a corner location, it could count on trade from nearby tenants. It was a convenient place to meet, and many couples walked out arm in arm after downing several pints at the bar or in the shadowy booths. But smells of spilled ale and greasy fish and chips, together with the faint odor of urine near the water closet in the corner, created an unpleasant mélange.

Chief Inspector Howard pinched his nose as he and Darnell entered. "God! I'm glad I haven't eaten yet."

Darnell smiled. "Why? Do you want to put in an order?"

Howard made an unintelligible noise. They walked to the bar and the Inspector motioned to the barkeep. "Over here."

The laconic red-haired man walked toward them, polishing a glass with a cloth that looked no more clean than the glass itself. "Coppers, right?"

"Right," Howard said. "Chief Inspector Howard to you. Your name?"

"Call me Rusty." He looked about the room and bent forward, saying in a low voice, "Clarence Clanahan."

"You've heard of the murder?"

"Who ain't? Bloody King George himself heard of it by now." He put the glass on a shelf and dropped the cloth on the counter. A fly lighted on it.

"Did you know her?"

"Poppy? Sure. I know 'em all. She spent every bugger spare shilling she had here. Don't know when the girl ate. Drank too much for such a young one." He looked down. "I tried to stop her drinkin' that much, I did."

"How long had she been coming in here?" Darnell asked.

The barkeep raised his eyes to Darnell's. "I been here twenty years, come November. When Poppy was a kid, her ma would bring her in with her, long before the girl, you know, took to the street. Her ma taught her to drink. And all the rest of it, too, I guess." His voice had a hard edge.

"Take last night," Howard said. "Was she in here?"

He rubbed his nose. " 'Bout midnight. Her usual time, most every night, after she got a few coins."

"Anyone with her?"

"Nah. Just her friends, you know, other women, locals."

"No man with her?"

"One thing about Poppy, she never brought her men inside."

"Did anyone follow her out when she left?" Darnell asked.

"Do I watch every flamin' body that pops in 'n' out o'here every night? Do I change their nappies for them? Make sure they're wearin' clean knickers?" He picked up a cloth and blew his nose on it. "No, nobody followed her out. I . . . well, I just happened to notice her leave. I kind of watched her more than the others, her being so young and all. Don't have any daughters of my own. And I knew her ma." He stared at Howard. "Anythin' else you want to know? I got customers."

Howard looked at Darnell, who asked, "Seen any ghosts, Rusty? Anyone with a top hat? A cape? White face?"

"Not so you'd notice. No ghosts, and no top hats. You think a ghost killed her?"

Darnell did not answer his question. To Howard, he said, "Nothing else here, then."

The Inspector nodded. "That's all for now, Clanahan."

The barkeep let his breath out slowly. He glared at the two men. "Get the bugger," he said, and turned away from them, walking toward a woman and man entwined with each other at the end of the bar.

Howard led the way to the exit. Outside, they took deep breaths, exchanged glances.

Darnell smiled. "The prostitute's best friend, Bruce. Her barkeep."

Constable Fenham rushed up to them. "Chief Inspector, I got the three women together."

"The ones who saw the ghost?"

Fenham nodded. "Yes, sir."

"Then let's see them, Bruce," Darnell said. "Now. Before the women disappear, too."

Sadie Latkins, Pearl Winfred, and Hannah Donner could have taken the parts of Shakespeare's witches, Darnell thought wryly, as he and the Inspector approached them, following the leading stride of the constable. The three women stood hunched together on the corner a few doors down from the pub. A dozen or so feet in either direction stood other women and men, watching with obvious curiosity, in a low buzz of talk, but not making any effort to join the women. The three women, in their small way, had become celebrities.

When the three men reached them, the constable said the women's names as he pointed each one out to Howard and Darnell, then stepped back to listen and observe.

Howard nodded at Darnell. "Go ahead."

"Sadie," Darnell said to the first woman, "what time did you see your ghost last night?"

She favored him with a broad, gap-toothed smile. "Coo! 'E was a proper ghost, sir. I seen 'im twice. 'Bout ten o'clock last night. Bessie was with me—but she didn't see nothin'."

"And you say he vanished?"

She nodded vigorously. "Both times. In the fog. It just swallowed 'im up. Melted right into it."

"And why do you call him a ghost? Why not just a man—maybe, shall we say, a scary man, but a man nevertheless?"

The three women exchanged glances, and Sadie spoke again. "His face, sir. A ghost face. Pasty white, y' know. And then disappearin' and all. And old-lookin' clothes. Like years ago."

Darnell asked the others, "You also saw the—ah, ghost?"

The one known as Pearl spoke first. "We was together,

Hannah and me. A week ago, at night, Walkin' about, y'know. Then we seen the man, in an alley. I never seen anythin' like it." She shuddered. "His face gimme the shivers."

"Me, too," Hannah said. "Then, he just up and fades away in the dark. But if we hadn't been together, the two of us, I don't know what 'e would've done. Maybe one of us wouldn't be here talkin' to you today. That's the whole of it."

After a few more questions verifying that descriptions of what they had seen were similar, Darnell said, "Thank you, ladies," and placed a coin in each of their hands.

"Come back anytime, ducky," Sadie said. "Your money's as good as anybody's."

As Howard, Darnell, and the constable walked away, the other locals crowded about the three women asking questions. Darnell heard one say, "Proper good job, Sadie."

"Let's go to my office, John," Howard said. "I need the reality of Scotland Yard around me to talk about this thing." He snorted. *"Ghosts!"*

Darnell had not visited Scotland Yard since the Lloyd George séance case. Across the room he saw several men, obviously reporters, held back by a uniformed officer. He recognized one of the men, Sandy MacDougall of the *Times,* a reporter he'd worked with on other cases.

"Bad news travels fast," Darnell said, and Howard grunted.

Darnell was pleased to see Sergeant Catherine O'Reilly at her desk as they passed by, toward Howard's office. He raised a hand in greeting and received a smile in return.

Inspector Howard dropped into his leather chair behind his desk, but Darnell paced slowly back and forth across the room.

"All right," Howard said, "let's have it straight, John. Ghost or no ghost?"

Darnell stopped in front of the desk. "In a generic sense, you can't prove a negative—that there *aren't* ghosts. But in specific cases I've explained so-called ghostly phenomena. No ghost, but your problem is that the public will hear of this."

"Reporters already have."

"Many people believe in the supernatural, and at the same time are afraid of it. Things seen sometimes scare less than those that are unseen and only imagined. I try to prove these things don't exist, while it seems many are trying to prove they do. These reports and the viciousness of the crime will create a minor panic, at least in Whitechapel."

Howard groaned. "What can we do?"

"You'll increase your patrols in the area, I suppose."

Howard nodded. "I'm planning to double them, in a one-mile circumference of Whitechapel."

Darnell said, "All right. I'd like to join the patrols for several hours a night for a while. If there's a reappearance of our ghost, I'll be on the spot. Maybe I'll see him myself. I'll start tomorrow night."

Howard nodded. "That would help, John. I'll advise my men you'll be observing tomorrow night. The patrols will be beefed up by then." He scowled as he looked out the window. "Now I have to go over the case with the Chief Superintendent." He grimaced. "And talk to those reporters."

Chapter Four

After making firm arrangements with Scotland Yard on Friday to begin joining police patrols in Whitechapel and Spitalfields Saturday night, Darnell returned home and told Penny the bad news—no trip to their Cotswolds country home for a while—and of his patrols in Whitechapel. "But maybe it's an isolated case," he said. "It may conclude soon. And we have tonight together."

On Saturday, he and Penny took a long walk in the afternoon, enjoyed dinner together, and he left for Whitechapel at nine p.m. At the appointed corner of Whitechapel Road, he found Constable Fenham waiting with another constable.

"Any ghosts, Burt?" Darnell asked, and held a hand out to the officer.

The constable shook his hand. "No, sir. We're in two-man teams now, every night until six a.m. The women are usually off the street by three or so, sleeping it off. This is Billy Trendle, sent over from another district to help."

"Well, Billy, glad to meet you. We'll keep each other company."

"How long will you stay, sir?" Fenham asked.

"I'll stay until three a.m., and then leave it to you."

The constable nodded. "Are you ready?"

"Lead on, Burt. One thing. If any of us sees anything at all suspicious-looking, any sign of our ghostly friend, sing out at once, so we can all take a look."

Fenham began his walk in his regular route, Darnell next to him, Billy Trendle a few steps back. Each man took in both sides of the street in their scope, peering into each alley as they passed.

Darnell asked Fenham, "How many others teams in this area?"

"Oh, within, say, two miles round, four or five other teams of two. At least one team is close enough that I could call 'em by pounding on the sidewalk with my stick." He held up his nightstick. "The main way we keep in touch if there's a problem."

To their right in an alleyway, they heard a man and woman talking. Darnell glanced at the shadowy figures in the distance, merged into one, along the brick wall. No cape. No top hat.

"No, dearie," the woman's voice came. "Money first."

Fenham said to Darnell, "We can't stop them, the street mollies. They make their living at it. As long as no one gets hurt."

"Like Poppy Nellwyn?"

"Ghosts I can't control."

As they worked their way deeper into the neighborhood, down the cobblestone side streets and courtyards, through the dirt alleys, the atmosphere seemed to seep into Darnell's pores. The smells of spilled garbage, the startled men and women interrupted in dark alleyways in their barter of sexual favors for coin, the pubs with scents of bangers and other fried meats and ale drifting out through open windows onto the street. The three men plodded on, alert to anything out of place, most watchful for any repeat visit of a top-hatted, caped man, who, ghost or mere murderer, might pop up at any corner.

From before ten p.m. until after three a.m., nothing out of the ordinary occurred, although the district itself, Darnell thought, was extraordinary. Stifling a yawn as they completed their circuit and reached the same corner where they had started, Darnell said, "I'll call it a night, men. Tomorrow, same time."

He shook their hands, stepped into his motorcar, and in thirty minutes pulled up in front of his flat. Ten minutes after that, at almost four a.m., he climbed into bed next to Penny, put his arm around her, and fell into a deep sleep.

For two more nights Darnell followed the same patrol routine with no results. Tuesday morning, September 4, he awoke late to find Penny standing before him with a tray containing a coffeepot, cream, and two cups. "Time for coffee, John. It's ten a.m."

"Ten o'clock scholar, eh? Let's have the coffee." He sat up in bed, finished a cup quickly, and poured a second. "King George doesn't get better service than this."

Penny fixed him with a deliberate stare. "Getting home at almost four a.m. . . . You do have a wife, you know. How long is this going to go on?"

"No more. I've seen all I ever want to of the Whitechapel District. More's the point, there's nothing to see—no ghosts, in any case. I'm done with it. I'll call Chief Inspector Howard today."

Penny picked the tray up and put it to one side. "That's wonderful, John. You're mine again!" She threw herself onto the bed and into his arms.

His coffee spilled as he grabbed her. Her mouth was on his and he kissed her, laughing with her, and kissed her again, more passionately. Their laughter gradually stopped as their breathing became heavier. "Yes," he said, in a husky voice, "I'm yours again. And now . . . you're mine."

That afternoon, Chief Inspector Howard lifted the knocker on Darnell's front door. Sung opened the door for him and said, "The Professor waits for you in the study. This way, please."

As they walked across the entryway, Howard said, "Your English is much improved since last year, Sung. What happened?"

The valet bowed his head a bit lower. "I have been taking classes. My son, Ho San, persuaded me to do this."

"I'm very impressed."

Sung smiled. "I found it is mostly a matter of putting in all the words, the little ones, connecting my thoughts."

"Good, good." The Inspector strode into the sitting room ahead of Sung, who stood to one side. He thrust out his gnarled hand to Darnell.

"Well, John. I see you're still in one piece." He took a seat in a nearby chair.

Darnell frowned. "I haven't been attacked by a ghost, if that's what you mean." He nodded at Sung in the doorway. "Some coffee, please, Sung?"

As Sung walked toward the kitchen, Darnell turned back

to Howard. "I've done all the patroling I need to do. Of course, you'll still keep double patrols?"

"Yes. I plan to do that for a month. So . . . you saw nothing, heard nothing?"

"Nothing. But I'm confident Burt and the other constables will be on their toes. I think they'd like to catch that ghost for you."

Inspector Howard scowled. "The judge at the inquest decreed it was 'death by person or persons unknown.' No ghosts."

Darnell lit a pipe he had been stuffing with tobacco. "Correct as far as it goes. No ghosts, but you can't discount the reports. Those women saw something, and it deserves investigation. That's what I do, of course—disproving these kinds of supposed paranormal sightings, showing their real-world source. You don't have to accept the supernatural explanation to investigate." He puffed on the pipe. "And in this case, it's not only a supernatural matter. We have a murder, too."

"But the murder's in the real world."

Darnell nodded. "Exactly." He paused. "But I haven't wasted the past three days, Bruce. There are some very interesting points about this case."

Howard interrupted abruptly. "John, I know you can't take on a case like this for no fee. I'll see that you get the Yard's special investigator payment. We'll send you a weekly check."

"Thanks, Bruce. You know I'd stay on it no matter."

"I know, but . . . you were saying?"

"All right. First, the name. Poppy Nellwyn. Remember that name? It bothered me. Any special significance to you?"

Howard shook his head. "Nothing distinguishing. Never heard it before. The locals knew her. The constable knew her, and that barkeep."

Darnell smiled. "It's Poppy Nellwyn's initials that struck me, Bruce. *P.N.* They rang a bell. You know I poke around in my old dusty volumes a lot, studying supernatural events, famous crimes, criminals. Well, I began looking for crimes like this one. I found the initials are the same as those of the first victim of Jack the Ripper. Polly Nichols."

"The Ripper? A stretch, that. He's been dead for years."

"Yes—of course, but they never caught him. The fact that the name was similar, and the initials exactly the same, got me."

The Inspector sat back, frowning. "It's been almost thirty years since 1888. Not a trace of him since."

"I'm just saying there are some odd coincidences here. The same type of crime—a grisly slashing and disembowelment—and the victims having the same initials. Maybe, Bruce, these things are just too odd to be coincidences."

"Anything else?"

Darnell nodded. "Well, of course, in addition to the nature of the crime, and the initials, the crime was committed in the Whitechapel area, where all the Ripper's killings took place."

The Chief Inspector scratched his head, frowned, and stared at Darnell. "Go on."

Sung rapped lightly on the door with one hand, balancing a tray in the other, and when Darnell nodded, he walked in and placed it on a table, then retraced his steps.

Darnell poured coffee into the two cups for Howard and himself. They sipped it silently for a moment.

Howard said, "All right. Same horrible crime, initials, and the location."

"And at least one more thing, the obvious one. The woman was a prostitute. All the Ripper's victims were of that, ah, shall we say, oldest profession."

Howard uttered something undistinguishable. "Damn it! I can't tell the Chief Superintendent or Commissioner this kind of rubbish. Murder, yes. A ghost, maybe. Jack the Ripper, never!"

Darnell laughed. "I'm only passing this on for your own use. I don't intend to call the *Times* to print my theories, believe me. And what you do with it is up to you."

"But, John, what does it mean?"

Darnell pushed long hair strands back from his forehead. "In your work, you know the parameters are wide when it comes to crime. It could be almost anything." He paused a moment. "It could be, hypothetically, some deranged person who *thinks* he's the Ripper, or wants to be. Someone who's read about him, wants to create the same kind of notoriety for himself that came to the Ripper over those several months."

"A copycat?"

Darnell raised both hands in the air. "It's the most likely explanation. It would explain the garments he wore, his odd, old-fashioned appearance, the attempts to make the women of the street think he's a ghost. And, of course, it would explain his searching out someone with the same initials, committing the crime in the same way the Ripper did, in the same area, slashing her and viciously disemboweling her."

Inspector Howard's frown deepened. "But, if it's a copycat, are you saying what I think you are?" He grimaced.

Darnell nodded. "If he's copying Jack the Ripper, he could be planning to follow his pattern." He paused. "The Ripper killed five women in all—each one more horribly than the one before. And if our killer has that plan, and if we can't stop him, we may be looking at four more murders."

Chapter Five

Chief Inspector Howard drove back to Scotland Yard in a glum mood. Even the cool breeze stirring the afternoon air did nothing for him as he breathed it in trying to restore his sense of balance. *Four more murders!* Darnell's final words echoed in his head. He thought, *God deliver me from this!*

Before the Whitechapel slashing, Bruce Howard's private thoughts in recent weeks had been of his retirement as he looked forward to spending time with his daughter and granddaughter. Not quite yet, of course. He needed his two more years. But now this new idea of Darnell's, a second Ripper at large in London, was overpowering him. It was something he couldn't handle alone. But the Chief Superintendent would laugh him out of his office with these ill-formed speculations. Ghosts? Jack the Ripper? Commissioner Cliburn would wave his hand and dismiss it all.

But Howard yearned to talk with someone about it. *If Ellie were still with me,* he thought, *I could talk with her.* She always listened, and even that helped. He wiped away moisture from his eyes, thinking of his wife, who had died four months earlier.

Reaching the Yard and walking to his office, he noticed Sergeant O'Reilly sitting at her desk, bent over papers. Their close work on the Lloyd George case had created a bond between them despite the wide difference in their official status at the Yard. He stopped over to her desk and said, "Hello, Sergeant."

O'Reilly looked up. "Good afternoon, Chief." He felt her eyes peer into his. She added, "Why so downcast?"

Howard made a decision. He said, "Come into my office. I have something to tell you."

When they entered, he closed his office door. "Sergeant," he said, motioning to a chair, "how would you like to hear one of the damnedest stories you will ever hear from these old lips?"

Her eyes widened as she sat down. "Hearing a wild story is just what I need about now. My paperwork was getting to me."

"But not a word to another soul, Sergeant, of what I tell you. I need your promise on that."

"Promise." She held up her right hand in the oath posture and smiled at him.

"By the way, how is your mother?"

O'Reilly frowned. "In the hospital for treatment. But we're hopeful."

The Chief Inspector scowled. "Bad thing to come along."

"I'm handling it all right. . . . Now, what's that story?"

Howard took a deep breath. "What would you say if I told you . . . well, Scotland Yard may have another Jack the Ripper on its hands. Not only that—some people think it's his ghost."

"My God! You mean that murder in Whitechapel?"

"You remember Professor John Darnell. He thinks it could be a copycat, imitating the Ripper. If you saw the autopsy report, you'd know why." He told her of the ghost sightings, described the murder scene and the condition of the body, and told her of Darnell describing points of similarity. "The killer—he just gutted her. There's no other way to put it."

"Ugh!" Sergeant O'Reilly shivered. "I've read the Ripper stories. Every copper has. You think we have another one?"

"I had to get it off my chest. But I also need the opinion of someone on the outside, not involved, looking in. So— is it crazy?" Howard wanted her answer, but he felt better already after telling another human being about it, getting it out of his system. He took a deep breath, and it came out as a vast sigh.

O'Reilly looked at him. "I know John Darnell as well as you do, Chief, from working with him. He wouldn't make these kinds of statements without a good basis. His points . . . they sound convincing. There are too many to be coincidences."

"And the women who claimed they saw a ghost?"

She shrugged. "I don't know. A woman could be startled into thinking that. What a horrible crime—that poor girl."

"If we've got a maniac to deal with, no woman there is safe."

"You mean . . . no prostitute?"

Howard nodded. "True. That might narrow it down." He stood. "Well, at least I've got extra patrols going. Maybe we can prevent another one with police presence. Darnell was there three nights and nothing happened." He brushed back his tangled hair. "Thanks for listening, Sergeant. But remember, mum's the word." When she left his office, he felt relieved, having told the tale. But the shadow of the murder still hung over him.

After an afternoon of little accomplishment at the office, his mind preoccupied, Howard left at dark for home. No one would be there to greet him, but he could kick off his shoes, pour a glass of whiskey, and relax until he fell asleep.

As the Inspector walked up to the door of his small house, a man stepped out from behind a shrub. He hooked one arm around Howard's neck from behind him, pulled a knife from a scabbard attached to his belt, and raised it.

Howard kicked out wildly and jammed an elbow into the man's body. The knife blade flashed as the man tried to stab it into the Inspector's back.

But Howard's kicking and arm movement made it miss its mark. It caught the Inspector on the shoulder and passed through his shirt and collar into the flesh of his shoulder and chest.

A neighbor called loudly, "What's going on there?"

Howard, dazed by the pain, whirled and struck out instinctively at the assailant. The knife hit the ground.

"Damn!" the man growled. He scooped up the knife and ran down the street and rounded the corner.

Howard collapsed. Lying there, he knew his field of view was fading and that he'd be unconscious in a moment.

As his neighbor bent over him, the Inspector spoke huskily, "Get John Darnell . . . tell John Darnell."

The last words he heard from his neighbor were, "That man was trying to kill you."

*   *   *

John Darnell approached the guard at Howard's hospital room and introduced himself. The guard nodded. "The Yard said you'd be coming, sir. Inspector spoke your name before he passed out."

Darnell entered the room and stood next to the surgeon by Howard's bed. "How soon will he come out of it, Doctor?"

"It shouldn't be too long now," Dr. Robert Fowler said. "He's a lucky man. It missed any major arteries and veins."

He shook his head at the swath of bandages on Howard's neck. "I'm worried about him. He's not a young man."

"Let's talk outside."

Dr. Fowler led the way to chairs in the hospital corridor. "The Inspector asked for you before he fell unconscious." He sat beside Darnell. "We notified his daughter as soon as we could find her address, and she's on the way here now from Weybridge. She said you need to know, and that I should fill you in on everything. Howard'll have to recuperate for at least three weeks. And it won't be safe for him to do any heavy or dangerous work—well, for quite a while."

"Is there something else? I sense there is."

The doctor frowned. "I mentioned this to his daughter, and I'll be telling her more about it when she arrives. His heart suffered some damage from both the assault and the trauma. I'm concerned about whether he should continue his line of work, a man of his age."

"Are you saying he should retire?"

"That's a decision he and his daughter must make."

Howard's daughter, Dorothy Cameron, arrived in a half hour. "I have to see him, Doctor. Is he going to be all right?"

The doctor persuaded her to sit down. As he told her about the slashing attack, she applied a handkerchief to her eyes. "He's too old to go through anything like this."

"He's going to need a lot of rest," the doctor said.

A nurse stepped out of Howard's room. "He's coming to, Doctor."

They entered the room and Darnell watched as Howard's daughter bent down and hugged him with tears in her eyes.

"You could have died, Dad. But thank God you're going

to be all right. We've got to get you well. The doctor says you'll have to take it easy."

Howard nodded. "I expected that." He held her hand. He peered across the room at Darnell. "Thanks for coming, John."

Darnell nodded. "Don't worry about anything, Bruce. Take plenty of time and get well. Doctor's orders, you know."

Howard said, "The matter we're working on, John. You'll stay on top of that?"

"Of course. I'll keep in touch with the Yard."

"They'll probably put Inspector Warren on it."

Dr. Fowler said, "That's enough conversation for now." He turned to Darnell and Howard's daughter. "He needs to rest."

After good-byes to Howard, the three left the room and stood in the hallway again.

"I'll come by often," Darnell said.

Dorothy Cameron nodded. "I'll come every day. And when he leaves here, I'll stay with him at his place until he's fully recovered. My husband will have to manage alone for a while."

Dr. Fowler frowned. "We should talk in my office for a few minutes, Mrs. Cameron. There are some things you need to know about your father's condition."

Darnell took his leave. He knew what the doctor would say and didn't want to hear the bad news twice that Howard's police career could end.

As he drove home, he thought about the attack on Howard, and the slashing in Whitechapel. Two different methods of attack, both involving knives. Could they be connected? Although Poppy's murder and the attack on Howard each involved a knife slashing, they were miles apart, in different areas. The attack on Howard did not fit in with the pattern he had expected, and it could be an isolated event. He had to operate on the theory that two different attackers were involved. And yet he wondered . . .

Reaching their flat, he decided what he should report to the man filling in for Howard, tell him what he had seen and heard at Whitechapel, what he suspected, and offer his services. He knew that was what Bruce Howard wanted him to do. What was that name Howard mentioned? Warren, yes. Inspector Warren.

*   *   *

Penny threw her arms around Darnell and held him close for a moment. "How is he, dear?"

He told her of the surgery, the daughter's visit, and his condition. "Someone will pay for this," he said.

"Come. Have a sherry. It'll calm you down."

She led him into the sitting room and filled two sherry glasses. As they sat, sipping their drinks and talking, the hall clock struck eleven.

Darnell said, "You go on up, darling. I want to sit here awhile. A few things are bothering me."

Penny kissed him lightly and rose. "Don't be too long, then."

Darnell filled his glass again and stared into it. After a moment he stood and walked over to the bookshelves on the wall. He found the thick volume on a bottom shelf and took it to the sofa with him. Darnell loosened his tie and opened the book to the title page: *Jack the Ripper's Infamous Murders.*

Chapter Six

Sergeant Catherine O'Reilly sat fidgeting at her desk at nine a.m. Minutes ago, an officer had told her of the attack on Chief Inspector Howard and she was anxious to visit him at the hospital. He'd shown confidence in her by giving her the chance to work with him on the kidnapping of the Prime Minister's daughter, and she'd grown to regard him almost as a father—or, with his white hair and manner, perhaps a grandfather. The image and relationship was one she'd not had in her life since her own father died a few years earlier.

The officer stopped by her desk again and said, "Inspector Warren wants to see you."

O'Reilly jumped up, glad for action, and hurried to Warren's office. Her heels clicked on the wood floor, a sound that still amused the almost entirely male population of Scotland Yard.

By now, after two years, she hoped they were used to it. But she still noticed smirks as she passed by their desks. *Someday,* she thought, *we'll have several female sergeants at the Yard.* She also harbored her own personal secret she would tell no one, that she aspired to one day become detective-sergeant. But the wheels of promotion ground exceedingly slow. She had no illusions, but kept the fire burning, and sometimes took the secret out and looked at it, before tucking it back into the recesses of her mind.

Inspector Warren said, "Shut the door, O'Reilly, and sit down."

He looked her up and down, and she could see the Inspector's disdain for women in that look. If anyone would speak against and try to hold back the promotion of a woman, it would be Nathaniel Warren.

"You've heard of the attack on the Chief?"

She nodded. "I want to see him."

"You'll get that chance. In fact, it fits in with what I have for you. The, ah, killing of the prostitute in Whitechapel. I assume you've heard of it?"

"The Chief Inspector told me about it. A Ripper-style killing, he said. Some kind of ghost."

"Dammit! Two things I don't want gabbed about. I don't want to hear either the word Ripper or ghost again. Is that understood?"

"Yes, sir."

"All right. The case is yours now. Can't spare anyone else. Not worth much effort, you know. Just a whore."

Just a woman, you mean, O'Reilly thought. *And I'm just another woman. All it deserves.*

She bristled. "Any murder deserves an investigation."

"And we'll give it one." Warren sniffed. "We'll give it you. Just wrap it up in two days, turn in your report, and be done with it." He began shuffling papers on his desk, his method of showing that an interview was over. "You can go by and see the Chief at the hospital, get any more details you need. Give him my regards."

She stood, knowing he expected her to leave. Regards? To his boss? He should be there himself.

As she reached the door with her hand on the knob, Warren added, "Remember. Two days. No more."

Catherine O'Reilly walked down the hospital corridor to Chief Inspector Howard's room and stopped at the open door. Inside, she saw a white-garbed nurse talking with John Darnell. The nurse nodded at Howard. "The doctor told his daughter this morning that he'd be here a few more days, then need a long recuperation at home."

Howard groaned. "Got to get back to work." He looked at the doorway as Sergeant O'Reilly entered, his face brightening. "Catherine—come in. Glad to see you."

O'Reilly nodded at the nurse, shook hands with Darnell, then impulsively bent down to the bed, hugged the Inspector, and kissed his cheek. "Never had a chance to kiss a Chief Inspector before," she said, smiling. "I couldn't resist it."

John Darnell shared the smile and the moment with them, as he took in the contrast between the demure, curly-haired blond woman and the grizzled, white-haired old man, knowing the empathy they had for each other.

"Good to see you, Sergeant," Darnell said.

"Yes. Unfortunate it's under these circumstances."

Darnell said, "A few days, Bruce. Not long now."

The Chief Inspector grimaced. "Not long here, maybe, but I don't like the sound of 'recuperation.' I'll be bored to death."

"Inspector Warren put me on the case," Sergeant O'Reilly said. "The Whitechapel killer—or should I say ghost?"

She stopped, glancing at the nurse, but the woman was not listening to their talk, writing something on a chart. The nurse left.

O'Reilly went on, "He gave me two days to finish it."

Howard shook his head. "What else did he say?"

"Just to get the details from you. He said the case didn't deserve much attention. Didn't want to acknowledge either the Ripper or ghost aspects."

Howard scowled. "That's like him. No mysteries. He likes upper-class cases he considers important. He'd rather spend a month on some society lady's missing diamonds than a 'cheap case,' as he calls it, of murder in the East End." He paused. "Sorry. Shouldn't be talking out of school."

O'Reilly laughed. "Everyone knows that about him. As you said, it's no secret he likes the spotlight. He even admits it in the staff meetings."

Darnell said, "We may be working together again, Sergeant. I've been in on this case with Bruce."

She smiled. "I know it. Whenever there are reports of ghosts or spirits, they'll find Professor Darnell." She turned to Howard. "You said it was like a Ripper case. If you can talk a bit, what else should I know about it?"

"Constable Fenham at Whitechapel is a good source of information. We still have double teams patrolling, but nothing has turned up." He sighed. "I guess I need to rest a while now. John can fill you in. He's been out there."

Darnell frowned. "I thought I was through walking the beat, but with you on the case, Sergeant, that changes that." He turned to Howard. "The Sergeant should see Whitechapel. I've decided to take her there tonight, patrol one more time."

Howard nodded, his eyes already closing. He waved a hand of dismissal. "Don't let the ghost get her, John."

That night, Darnell picked up Sergeant O'Reilly at her flat and drove to Whitechapel. It had been only two days since his last tour there, and he expected little from the new visit except to give O'Reilly the essence and feel of the case. He knew that sometimes that was more important in seeking a solution than a mere recitation of facts.

Penny had made it clear she disliked this renewal of his midnight tours. "There's a killer at large there, John," she had protested.

"This night's for Chief Howard," he'd said. "It'll be the last." But her words still reverberated in his thoughts.

Now, as they drove, O'Reilly said, "Warren put me on the case for two reasons—because I'm a woman, and because the victim was a woman. 'All it's worth,' was his opinion."

He glanced sidelong at her, and in a moment asked, "Disturbing, isn't it, that attitude? Are you still enthusiastic about police work, after two or three years of that sort of thing?"

"I know I have to accept it. I'm the first woman Sergeant. It will get better. But . . . well, there's another reason I'm on edge these days My mother's in the hospital, in serious condition. I try to see her every day, and it's depressing."

"I hope she getting recovers soon."

"She's getting good care. And this case won't interfere—don't worry about that. I can get in to see her at any hour."

As he drove on, O'Reilly staring silently out of the window, Darnell changed the subject. "Tell me about Inspector Warren."

She sighed. "He's a stuffed shirt, and that runs in the family. His father is former Metropolitan Police Commissioner Sir Charles Warren. You've heard about him?"

Darnell's mind flashed to the book he'd been reading the night before. "Commissioner Warren—he was the one on the Ripper case? His father?"

"The same. He bungled the case, some at the Yard say."

"They still talk about it down there?"

"Over tea, you know. The older coppers tell stories."

"I'll bet. Sir Charles Warren . . . I wonder if that has

anything to do with Inspector Warren's attitude on this case."

She shook her head. "He's sensitive to the word Ripper, but won't connect it. To him, it's just a slashing. A cheap case."

"No life is cheap."

They parked near the corner where Darnell had agreed to meet Constable Fenham. He was standing there under the lamppost, waiting, when they arrived.

"Burt, this is Sergeant Catherine O'Reilly, the officer I said would go around with us tonight, at least until midnight. For a look-see."

The constable took O'Reilly's outstretched hand and shook it with obvious wonder. "I've heard of you. You're the female—I mean, the famous woman sergeant, aren't you?"

"Sergeant, yes. Famous . . . ?" She smiled and shook her head. "Let's start."

The constable looked flustered. "I'll take the lead, to show you the rounds, Miss—I mean, Sergeant. But it's not Soho."

"Show us your worst, constable," O'Reilly said. "Show me your ghost, too, if you can."

The three began the circuitous walk through the district, going over a mile out from the constable's usual route to cover the entire area. They talked about the case as they walked.

Darnell described the pub that Poppy frequented. The streets looked the same this night as before—the same scenes of women and men forming one silhouette in dark alleyways, women on the corner, beckoning. He pointed out Sadie, strolling along.

"Sadie saw the ghost the night of the murder, Sergeant."

"She's seen nothing since, though?"

He shook his head. "Three women saw something—man or spirit—on separate occasions. Whoever he is, he acts real enough. He seems to go into hiding. Or vanish."

"Definitely the same man, then, this ghost they saw?"

"Yes. The descriptions matched—older man, the top hat, the cape, the old-fashioned clothes."

They came up to the The Three Hares pub. The noise of talk and the odor of ale announced it from several doors away.

"Poppy spent a lot of time and dropped a lot of her, ah, hard-earned money here. The barkeep said she drank too much."

"Can't blame her." The sergeant's nose wrinkled as they stepped through the doorway into the amalgamation of odors. The constable waited outside.

Darnell peered about. "Same barkeep. He's called Rusty. He doesn't like his real name bandied about. It seemed he was protective of the young girl. Maybe even of all the women."

"A father confessor for prostitutes? Interesting."

"Hmm—you could be right. Anything you want to ask him?"

She shook her head. "Not now." She turned toward the door.

They resumed their walk with Constable Fenham pacing along in front of them, nodding at this person, raising his nightstick to his hat to another in a sort of salute, occasionally remarking on something to Darnell and O'Reilly. The night deepened, and a light fog obscured their vision beyond a few yards ahead. They walked forward into the yellowed haze created by the streetlights.

At close to eleven, O'Reilly choked on words she was saying and pointed to an alleyway. "He's there! I saw him!"

Darnell turned and looked in the direction she pointed, a small alley between two three-story clapboard buildings. "I don't see anything—but let's go." He ran into the alley with the constable and Catherine O'Reilly close at his heels. The alley opened into an unlighted courtyard and then into another alley at the far end of it. Darnell ran through the yard and out the other alley and stopped, looking both ways on the far street. He could see no one in either direction. "Dammit! Got away."

He looked at O'Reilly with questioning eyes.

"Yes, John," she said in a firm voice. "I'm sure I saw him. Just as you described him. Top hat and cape."

Constable Fenham took his cap off and scratched his head. "Sadie says he can disappear."

The three stood looking at each other for a moment. Darnell said, "He's been watching us, stalking us. Waiting for just the right time to show himself when he could then seem to vanish."

As they walked back through the other alleyway, Darnell noticed a door in the wall they hadn't seen as they ran through the alley. He tried the handle. The door opened into a hallway lit by a single bulb at the top of a stairway. Another door led to the street on Darnell's left.

"Ducked in here, I expect. Then ducked out."

"The ghost?" Fenham asked.

Darnell gave him a grim smile. "More accurately, I think, a man who imitates a ghost. A man showing his superiority by being able to elude us."

"He took a chance," O'Reilly said, "appearing that close."

"That makes him that much more dangerous." Darnell looked at her. "I didn't see him. Tell me what do you think you saw—was it flesh and blood? Or something else?"

She shivered. "He looked ghostly enough. But even in the haze, I had the feeling he was solid flesh. Either way, popping out like that, I'm sure he'd scare any woman out of her wits."

As they walked back toward Darnell's car, Sergeant O'Reilly told Fenham to join up with his partner-constable. "Stay in teams," she said. "We'll have to keep these patrols going, now that he's been seen again. I'll advise Inspector Warren tomorrow."

Darnell returned her to her flat and talked for a moment as they sat in front of it in his car. "He only comes out at night, and he only shows himself to women—even tonight, he made sure it was you who saw him," Darnell said. "I think he's toying with us now. Wants to frighten women, feeling they will report it. Also trying to show that he can outwit the police."

"But will he kill again?"

Darnell's face was dark. "He will, if he's copying Jack the Ripper. He'll kill again within two days."

O'Reilly looked at him. "How do you know?"

"The Ripper's second victim was found in the early morning hours of September eighth. It's just past midnight now. The sixth of September."

Chapter Seven

Thursday, September 6

Penny Darnell took her husband to task at the breakfast table. "You said you were through walking the streets in Whitechapel. I heard you come in at one a.m."

"I thought you were asleep."

She frowned. "I just didn't want to talk. John, how long will this go on?"

He took a bite of crisp toast and chewed for a moment. "I promise I won't go back there unless it just can't be avoided."

"Like another slashing by that maniac?" She folded her arms and stared at him.

"He was seen last night again. By Sergeant O'Reilly."

"Yes, the blonde." Her eyes were icy. "You do spend a lot of time with her, don't you?"

Darnell laughed. "Your violet eyes are green this morning."

"Do you blame me?"

He reached over and put his arms around her. "It's you I love, you know that." He held her until he felt her body relax. "You don't want me to go back to Whitechapel."

Penny sighed. "It's just—well, that's no spook out there, John. He's obviously got a long, sharp knife he likes to kill with, and I don't want you to be attacked, the way the Chief Inspector was."

She brought the coffeepot to the table and refilled their cups. "I've been threatened by a thug with a knife, too. Remember Baldrik? How could I ever forget him? The way he scraped the back of his knife across my face." She shuddered. "I know how that feels."

He touched her hand. "That was terrible, but Baldrik

will pay for his crimes. He's awaiting execution." He drank some coffee. "But the attack on Inspector Howard was in a totally different area of London than Whitechapel. The Inspector's a man, Poppy is a woman. The pattern isn't the same at all."

"When will you know if there is a fixed pattern?"

"I've been researching the Ripper murders. I told you this might be a copycat murder. Her initials were the same as the Ripper's first victim—P.N."

"Ye-es?"

"If he's copying the Ripper, he'll kill again by the eighth. If he does, and if the initials are the same, it could mean he's planning three more killings afterward. The Ripper had five victims. One in August, three in September, one in November."

"How do you know it was five victims? Weren't there a lot of other killings in those days?"

"Yes, other murders occurred, before and after these five, but the evidence varied. They didn't look like Ripper killings. These five all clearly had the mark of the Ripper."

Penny said, "If they find the next one on the eighth, John, that's Saturday. But it could happen late tomorrow night, the seventh." She glared at him. "So I suppose you'll go to Whitechapel again tomorrow night."

"I'm afraid so. But if nothing happens then, I'll leave the rest of the ghost patrol to the police."

"John, I want to see Whitechapel, too. If you're risking your life there, I need to know what you're facing."

"Penny—"

"I insist." She set her jaw firmly and stared at him.

Darnell sighed, and nodded. An hour later they arrived in the Whitechapel area, dressed in less than elegant clothes so as not to stand out among the locals.

Darnell took Penny up and down the main streets. They walked past The Three Hares, where he let her look in for a minute, and down to the areas where the reputed ghost had been seen.

"Satisfied?" He looked at her with twinkling eyes. "Not exactly Kensington Gardens, is it?"

She sniffed. "I just want to know what you do, and what you're getting into. You're my husband, and I don't want to become a widow." She linked her arm in his. "In case you don't know it, Professor, I love you rather much."

Friday, September 7, saw the beginning of London's fall shopping, limited as it was, in the midst of the war. And as the year crept along into September, the shorter days brought less light and more nippy weather.

But Annette Camden loved fall weather. She'd get out her long coats, including the one with the genuine fur collar, and walk from the tram stop to her flat, breathing in the crisp air after working in the stuffy department store all day. She enjoyed her work at Harrods, the largest and finest store in all London, perhaps in all the world, but she looked forward to the end of her day, doing her little bit of shopping on the way home, feeding her cat, preparing her solitary dinner, reading a good book while she ate her meal.

Annette had no illusions about finding the perfect husband she read about in her romance books. A glance in any mirror reminded her of her plainness. Not unattractive, but definitely not pretty. She felt her nose looked too large for her face and her chin too small. She acknowledged that she did have the asset of a winning smile, which helped make her successful as a salesclerk in Harrods women's dresses department. Enthusiasm, energy in her work, and a good manner with customers contributed also to her becoming top salesclerk of the month more than once.

The day being Friday, she was preparing for the following day's big Saturday sales. "Got to check my stock and fix my displays," she said to her friend Lenore, as she declined a lunch invitation. "I'll catch a sandwich later."

So busy was the day, she heard nothing of the minor furor in the personnel area. An unauthorized man had been observed searching through employee time cards. His motive was unclear, and an employee called a guard. He arrived too late. The intruder had left. They put it down to something like a husband searching for his wife.

Annette Camden did notice a few men drifting through her area of the store, but there was nothing unusual about a man buying a gift for his wife in the women's section. And she had no other facts to raise any questions. Her day sped by, and at six o'clock she checked out and made her way home, not failing to pick up her morning scone at the bakery.

*   *   *

At seven p.m. that night, Professor John Darnell met Sergeant O'Reilly at Scotland Yard and the two drove in his car to Whitechapel. At the now-familiar corner, he and O'Reilly stood under the lamppost. Constable Burt Fenham and his partner, Billy Trendle, approached them from across the street.

Darnell smiled. "Ready for another stroll, Burt?"

The constable touched two fingers to his hat in the salute he often gave to superiors and officials. "Yes, sir, and Sergeant O'Reilly." He nodded at her. "But why are you back tonight? Are you expecting something to happen?"

Darnell glanced at O'Reilly, who was obviously wondering whether he'd tell Fenham what he'd told her about the dates and point out that tonight was Friday, the eighth. "You're right, I do have my suspicions, Burt. There's something special about tonight that brought me back. But— well, let's just see how the evening goes. I'd rather be wrong in what I expect tonight than be right. So lead on, Constable." Darnell clicked open his watch. Seven forty-five. Another long night lay ahead.

On the other side of London at that hour, Annette Camden had finished her quiet supper and settled down to read when all the lights suddenly went out all through her flat. She gasped. "What—?"

She stood, and was prepared to stumble about looking for a candle when a rap came at her door. She found her way to the door and opened it a crack. The hallway was also dark, and she could barely see the outline of the man in front of her from ambient street light filtering in from the window at the end of the hall. "Ye-es?"

"Repairman, mum. Fix your lights."

"Oh, yes, come in, please. Watch your step."

"Just lead me to your kitchen where the fuse box is."

She turned toward her kitchen. The man closed the door, and as they walked, he shifted his bag to his right hand and snapped the bag open with his thumb.

"The box is just—" Annette began. She never finished her sentence. Her voice was cut off and panic flooded her brain when he grabbed her.

The man's hand gripped her around her neck, stifling her

efforts to scream. In one fluid motion he pulled the knife from his bag and dropped the bag on the floor. The knife blade moved angrily, fast and deep, twice across the throat, almost severing the head from the body. Blood spurted on the kitchen floor. Light slanting in through the window revealed a gory scene as the body that was once Annette Camden fell to the floor.

She lay in a rapidly-enlarging pool of her own blood, with her unseeing eyes still wide open, but not breathing, her heart not beating. Her head lolled over to one side at an impossible angle. The man bent over her with his knife. What he did next seemed to come from practice and a crude skill, and he proceeded quickly.

He pulled her dress up above her waist and made a horizontal slash across her stomach and a vertical gash down to her pelvic area. He peeled back the skin and flesh and cut further, systematically, into the innards of her body. One by one, he cut out her intestines and other organs. He draped her intestines over her right shoulder. In just minutes, he finished his work, stood, and stepped over to the sink where he rinsed the knife and his hands. He returned the knife to the bag, stepped over the body, and found his way back to the door.

Looking out into the hallway both ways, he left Annette Camden's flat, closed the door, and took the hallway to the back stairs by which he had entered. Apart from the few words he had said to Annette Camden and a few grunts while doing his gory labors, he had uttered no sound whatsoever in the past half hour. Now, walking down the virtually deserted sidewalk toward his car parked far down the street, he softly hummed a music-hall tune.

Darnell, Constables Fenham and Trendle, and Catherine O'Reilly paced the streets of Whitechapel until three a.m., when Darnell said, "It looks like nothing will happen here tonight." They stopped under the lamppost where they had started. He shook his head. "I don't know. I guess I'm wrong on this one."

O'Reilly looked at him quizzically.

"My theory seems to be blown apart," he added. "But I'm glad it didn't happen. We don't need another murder. Maybe that killing was only an isolated case."

O'Reilly nodded. "The important thing is, a woman didn't die in Whitechapel tonight, John. That's a victory. In fact, maybe our walking the streets had something to do with that. Did you think of that? He could have seen us, and held back."

"I hope this whole bloody mess is over." Darnell said good night to Trendle and shook hands with Fenham. "Thanks, Burt. Sorry to trouble you again."

"Pleasure, sir, anytime. But I'd say we've seen the last of our ghost."

Darnell dropped off O'Reilly at the Yard and made sure she was safely away in her car, the one valuable bequest left to her by her father. He headed home, certain Penny would be glad that the killings were over, that he wouldn't have to patrol the London streets again looking for a slasher.

And yet part of John Darnell's mind would not accept his own conclusions. He had been certain there would be a killing, or at least an attempt at one, that night. He must be overlooking something.

Chapter Eight

Inspector Nathaniel Warren smoothed his long, thin moustache to pointed ends with the bit of wax he had rubbed between his fingers to liquify it. He inspected his hair, every strand of which was in place. Satisfied, he turned his attention to the tan spats he wore, covering the tops of his shiny black shoes. Yes, they were clean enough, and straight. Leaving his bachelor digs at the leisurely hour of nine a.m., he tipped his hat at a portrait of his father, retired Metropolitan Police Commissioner Sir Charles Warren, realizing his regular visit to him was due.

Twenty minutes later, after motoring to Scotland Yard in the increasingly biting cold of the early morning, he walked up to the homicide division entrance. He was accosted by reporters talking loudly in the hall outside the door, but elbowed by them through the doorway, ignoring their questions.

Two of his detectives waited for him inside the door. One said, "Inspector, there's been another murder."

Warren stopped. "In Whitechapel? Another prostitute?" The disdain was clear in his voice.

"No, sir. A saleswoman. Other side of town, not far from Vauxhall Bridge."

"Damn! Follow me." He strode to his private office and closed the door after the two men entered. "All right. The details, Blackwell." He sat at his desk and gestured toward the two straight-backed chairs facing it and fixed his gaze on the older of the two men. The two detectives took seats.

Detective Blackwell poured out the story. "I was the only one on duty here when the call came in—eight a.m.—from the local constable. A cleaning woman found the body and ran out on the street. The bobby was just turning the corner making his rounds, and she grabbed him. He called it in, and I went out there at once."

"Go on, man. Describe the victim."

Blackwell painted a bloody word picture of the body of Annette Camden, her position on the floor, the body's mutilation, and the kitchen where she had been found. "It was the worst God-awful mess I've ever seen. Just got back ten minutes ago."

"How did the press find out so soon?"

"I don't know, they just have a nose for these things. They smell 'em. That pest Sandy MacDougall of the *Times* is one of them. He's always hanging about here, sniffing around."

"Keep them out in the hall. I suppose I'll have to talk to them. Who's on duty this morning?"

"The usual crew. And the blonde."

"O'Reilly? Good. She's been scouting Whitechapel. Get her and meet me at my car in ten minutes. You'll drive. But first, get me Professor Darnell's number from O'Reilly. And get a report from the coroner when he's done with the body. Now I have to make a call."

The detectives rose and left the office before Warren finished getting his first call put through—to the Police Commissioner. The Commissioner objected to being awakened, then complained he had not yet eaten breakfast, until he finally assimilated the fact that a second slashing murder had occurred in a good district of London, not along prostitute row. He laced into Warren, saying, "For God's sake, wrap this one up quickly. One question—are both killings and the Howard attack related?"

"I don't know," Warren said. "Same modus, different areas. I'll have to call in Darnell."

There was a short silence. "Right. He's been working with Howard. And he can't be ignored after solving the Prime Minister case. Is Howard up to dealing with this yet?"

"No. He's still in hospital. I'll consult with him."

"Good. Watch your politics here. Watch your back."

Inspector Warren preened his moustache as he talked. "I do think these cases are unrelated, Commissioner. The same killer wouldn't operate in areas so vastly different."

He tugged at his moustache, one way, then the other, elaborating on his opinion.

"Maybe you're right. Keep in touch—but don't call before ten a.m. on a Saturday next time."

The noise of the Commissioner's receiver clanking down came through Warren's earpiece, and he hung up his phone.

Blackwell knocked on the door and entered, handing a note to Warren. "Darnell's number." He wheeled and left the office again, closing the door quietly behind him, and walked toward Sergeant O'Reilly, who stood waiting for him.

This new murder worried Warren, now that it had become his responsibility. A different part of town! That baffled him, but he couldn't let his concern show, not with the meddling Professor about. If he wanted to get Howard's spot as Chief Inspector, he'd have to play this exactly right.

He picked up the phone and gave the operator Darnell's number. He thought of the reporters waiting in the hall and decided to speak with them on the way out. He'd have to be alert to get any favorable publicity and notoriety, but find a way to put the blame on others if their efforts failed. He smirked. With Howard in the hospital, a female sergeant, and a college professor, that shouldn't be hard to do.

John Darnell looked down at the mutilated woman's body that lay untouched on the kitchen floor in a pool of blood. He glanced sidelong at Sergeant O'Reilly. She was bearing up well so far in facing the gruesome task of investigating this crime.

Inspector Warren stood apart, behind them, with Detective Blackwell, interrogating the constable. "And you say the woman ran right into your arms? And the time?"

"I was just comin' about the corner. She ran to me, grabbed my arm, and half dragged me back here, she did. Half past seven. I called when I found a phone." He shuddered. " 'Orrible sight."

Warren scowled. "Not much to be learned here, Blackwell. Not even much left of the body."

Darnell turned to them. "I imagine you've seen the similarity of this to the Whitechapel murder."

Warren said, "Similar, yes. The same, no. A different

neighborhood—in fact an entirely different strata here. Not a prostitute. This victim was a salesclerk at a major store, a Miss Annette Camden, I'm told—a respected, if, ah, not exactly exalted position. How would you explain her choice as a victim, if the killer is the same?"

Darnell frowned at that. "I don't, yet. I'll be working on it. But don't you see the other connections in these killings? The method, for instance?"

"Yes. But I won't jump to any conclusion. Perhaps you can come up with something more specific. I'm assigning Sergeant O'Reilly to this case." He turned to her and said, "You'll stay in touch with Blackwell and myself. Professor, see if you can uncover anything relevant. But no ghosts, eh?" He smiled at Blackwell. "Keep me informed."

O'Reilly asked, "And Chief Inspector Howard?"

"Oh, yes, of course. I understand he'll be in hospital a day or two more. Call him, or stop by." Warren pulled on his hat and turned toward the door. "Carry on."

Darnell watched Inspector Warren walk to the door in his usual, preening strut, and shook his head. "I'd say, Sergeant, the Inspector has shown a great deal of confidence in you."

Blackwell said, "I've seen enough, Sergeant. Except for the kitchen, the apartment's clean. No clues. The coroner's made his examination. Pack up the body for the morgue."

He continued to fix his gaze on O'Reilly. "I'll want a complete canvas of this building and the entire block for possible witnesses. And interview the cleaning woman again. Maybe you can get more out of her than I did. I'll be at the Yard. Keep in touch." He followed the route of the Inspector.

O'Reilly ordered the body bagged up, then stood to one side with Darnell watching the proceedings.

Darnell said, "It looks like this has been dumped in your lap, Sergeant. How do you feel about it?"

She took him into the other room, out of earshot of the medical personnel. "How do I feel? Like a lamb to slaughter. If I solve this case, Blackwell or Inspector Warren gets the credit. If I don't, I get the blame."

"Do you think the same man committed both murders?"

She ran a hand through her short, bobbed hair, and afterward it fell back into place. "I didn't see the first body, but from what you and Chief Inspector Howard said, it looks like it could be the same killer. But in this part of town, I just don't know."

"We'll have to do some digging."

"What's going on, John? You said if the Whitechapel killer copied Jack the Ripper, he'd kill again by the eighth of September. And it's the eighth. You were right."

"I don't like being right. With my theories, we wasted last night at Whitechapel. I thought the second murder, if there was one, would be in some dark alley down there. I concluded I was wrong, but didn't mind, because maybe the killings were over. Now this one, miles away. And it starts again."

"It's not exactly Jack the Ripper's pattern."

"Yes, not exactly. But that was based on my incorrect, if logical, assumption that it would be in or near Whitechapel. And I was simply wrong on that point. I need to rethink that theory. Why another area? There is one thing . . ." He paused and stared as two men carried the body out through the living room to the outside door.

The coroner, a Dr. J. J. Bentridge, stepped over to them and said, "We're done here, Sergeant. After the autopsy, we may be able to tell you more. But you saw it all with your own eyes. I don't know how much I can add to that."

Darnell asked, "You handled the Whitechapel body, Doctor. What do you think about the two of them?"

Bentridge looked about the empty room. "Either it was the same killer or one who's a perfect mimic, for God only knows what reason. But if it was someone else, then we've got two bloody maniacs on our hands." He shook his head and left.

Darnell watched as O'Reilly roped off the scene and locked the apartment door with the woman's key. They walked out to the street and stood in front of the apartment building.

"You had something else to say, I think," O'Reilly said.

Darnell nodded. "Yes. There are strong similarities in the two cases compared to the original Ripper killings—the methods, the dates, the fact that the victims are women. But in Poppy Nellwyn's case, she was a prostitute, and it was in the Ripper's area, namely, Whitechapel. That's a major difference. Another thing that tied the first Ripper case to Poppy's was a similarity of names and, especially, the fact that their initials are exactly the same for both victims. The Ripper's first victim was Polly Nichols. Now it was Poppy Nellwyn. Both sets of initials are P.N. That might have been a coincidence, but now——"

O'Reilly interrupted. "But Annette was so different from Poppy."

"Yes. And living in a different area. She was very respectable, not a prostitute. But it's no coincidence that the date was the same as that for the Ripper's second victim. Nor that the method is, of course, identically brutal and grotesque."

"So, with these differences, what ties the cases together, if it's the same killer?"

"In studying the Ripper's cases, I found that his second murder victim on September eighth was Annie Chapman."

O'Reilly thought a bit. "Wait a minute, this woman was Annette——"

"Camden. Right. The same initials as for his second victim. This time, *A.C.* The same initials couldn't be a coincidence anymore. So we have three common denominators to tie the two cases together—the method of killing, the dates, and now the common initials. It seems the killer is obsessed with these things being the same. But why these other differences—a better area, a respectable working woman? And how did he choose this area and pick this woman in particular? That's what we'll have to find out."

Chapter Nine

Detective Allan Blackwell motioned to Sergeant O'Reilly as she passed by his office with John Darnell. "Go on to my desk, John," she said. "I'll be there in a minute."

As she entered his office, Blackwell said, "Let's have your report. What have you learned?"

She stood facing him rather than taking the seat opposite his desk, hoping this wouldn't take long. "I talked to the cleaning lady. She added nothing to what we know. She cleans once a month on Saturday. This happened to be the day. She has her own key, because the, ah, victim is often away visiting her mother."

"The mother. Poor woman. We'll have to notify her. Get an address—a phone, if any."

"Got it, from her address book. In Surrey. No phone."

"Give it to me. I'll take care of that. Anything else?"

"I talked with all the tenants who were home. They heard and saw nothing."

He scowled. "As usual. No one knows. No one cares."

"Some care. One woman downstairs cried when I told her."

He glanced out through the glass door. "I see you have the Professor in tow."

She nodded. "We're talking about the two cases. Trying to get some ideas."

Blackwell smirked. "Don't get any crazy ones. He's a married man, you know."

O'Reilly blushed. "Don't be . . ." She changed the word in mid-sentence. ". . . Worried about that." She bristled, as she felt her cheeks warm. "I'll send him home, if you wish."

"No, no." Blackwell frowned. "Just a bit of humor."

She whirled and left his office mumbling, "At my expense." But as she walked to her desk, she regretted her words. She couldn't afford to be too sharp-tongued. And now that Chief Howard was out of the mainstream, she had to watch her step. Warren could make trouble for her. As she sat down at her desk opposite Darnell, she blurted out, "Politics! I hate it!" Darnell stared at her with eyebrows raised until they both laughed.

Thirty minutes later, Darnell felt comfortable with the plans he and Sergeant O'Reilly had made. "So you'll talk with the clerk in charge of the dead-file archives."

"Yes. It's Norman." She smiled. "They say he's been down there since the Norman invasion, and that's how he got his name."

"Then he ought to be able to find files from only twenty-nine years ago. Sergeant, if I'm right, we must hope to find the killer in three weeks. The Ripper's next victim was found September thirtieth."

"What do you expect to find in the old Ripper files?"

Darnell shook his head. "I don't know. Won't know until I see them. We could use a lead of some sort."

She nodded. "All right. After I see Norman, I need to go back out to the neighborhood of the Camden crime scene. I'd like to find a witness, anyone who might have seen the killer—a suspicious stranger, that is—on the street beforehand. I hope we can get a description that matches the ones you got."

"Then we'll know it's the same man." He stood. "In the other direction, I'll be revisiting Whitechapel this afternoon. I have a hunch I want to check out."

"Come back at six, then. I'll tell Norman we want to look at some old files, and make sure he'll be there tonight."

The hall clock struck one as John Darnell stepped through the front doorway, finding Penny in the entryway to meet him.

"I was hoping you'd get here in time for a late lunch," she said. "Sung is ready to serve it."

Darnell shook his head. "Ask him to put mine aside. I, ah, don't have much appetite at the moment."

Penny put a hand on his arm, then slipped it behind his

back. She gently edged him toward the sitting room. "Then a bit of sherry, John."

He nodded, and shortly they were sipping from the small, delicate glasses Sung kept near the cream-sherry bottle. Darnell told her as much as he thought he should divulge about the crime scene, leaving out the worst parts.

"That poor woman. I've probably seen her at Harrods myself. What was her name?"

"Annette Camden. Sold ladies' clothing."

Penny's eyes widened. "I did know her. I remember that name. She always said, 'I'm Miss Camden. May I help you?' " She thought a moment. "Quiet, with a wonderful smile and a nice personality. Why her?"

"Why, indeed? That's what I have to find out."

"Is there any way I can help? I knew her rather well."

"I'll think about that. If there is, I'll let you know." The hall clock struck the half hour. "There's someplace I have to go. I'll be back by four." He stood.

She rose beside him and said, "And you'll have something to eat when you come back? Promise?"

"Yes. After that, I'm due at the Yard at six."

"Not Whitechapel, with that maniac still on the loose."

"No. Not tonight. Just nice, safe, dusty old files."

But that afternoon did find Darnell in Whitechapel, in the pub called The Three Hares. Even at two o'clock in the afternoon, Darnell found that the place retained the same acrid smell. He was pleased to find Clarence Clanahan behind the bar. As he approached him, Clanahan looked up from his work and set down the glass and towel he had in his hands.

"Hello, Rusty." He looked up and down the bar. At the far end, one customer, a man bundled in a black longcoat and a floppy hat that revealed tufts of gray hair around the edges, nursed a glass of ale. Darnell leaned forward and said, "I have a few questions."

The barkeep's eyes narrowed. "What kinds of questions?"

"It's almost twenty years, you said."

"What?"

"That's how long you've worked here."

"What of it?"

"Poppy came in with her ma, you said."

"All right. Yes."

"Poppy was nineteen."

"What're you gettin' at?" Rusty Clanahan leaned against the back wall of the bar.

Darnell asked, "I'm wondering—was Poppy your daughter?"

Clanahan's eyes widened. "No." He shook his head vigorously. "I see how you could guess I was, knowing her ma and all. But you're wrong. I knew the bloke as was. It's like I said—Poppy was younger than most. I never had a daughter. Never a proper marriage, you know."

"All right. So you watched over her."

"Yes. I did that. It didn't cost me nothing. I didn't do much else for anybody. So . . . now what?"

"Just this, Rusty. The murderer killed another woman, in a different area, last night. Keep your eyes open and watch for anything unusual. Listen to streetwalkers who come in, stories they tell about what they see or hear. I want to get the man who killed Poppy and the other woman, before he strikes again."

Clanahan nodded. "If you think I can help . . . I can do that much. In fact, I'd like to get him meself. I'd wrap one of these bottles around his scalp."

"Good. So, if you see or hear anything, call me at once, or call Sergeant O'Reilly at Scotland Yard." He wrote down both numbers on a card and slid it across the bar to him.

"I'm glad to help, sir." Clanahan whispered now. "Just one thing—I heard 'e might be a ghost. Any truth in that?"

Darnell put a coin on the bar. "He's as real as that, Rusty. And just as hard."

Darnell returned to his flat, had a cold supper with Penny, and lingered with her over cups of strong coffee, talking. At the five-thirty hall clock chime, he said, "I'll be at the Yard in the basement archives for a few hours. Back by perhaps eleven."

"I'll wait up." Penny walked him to the front door and took his long coat off the rack. "Here. You'd better take this. Those archives sound cold and drafty."

At the Yard, he walked up to Sergeant O'Reilly's desk at six sharp and said, "Time for the Norman invasion?"

She nodded. "Follow me." O'Reilly led him down three flights of a back stairway to the cellar where files were kept.

"Whew!" Darnell said, seeing row after row of filing cabinets lined up from one end of the cellar to the other, the lines broken only by small passages from one aisle to the next. The musty smell of old, perhaps decaying paper permeated the room and filled his nasal cavities. He sneezed.

A thin rail of a man, five-feet-six at most, wearing a green celluloid eyeshade and a pencil tucked behind one ear, approached them, smiling. He ran fingers through his thin gray hair, as if combing it about on his practically bare scalp. "I'm Norman Pidgeon. Sergeant O'Reilly. A pleasure. And Professor Darnell, I believe. So nice to have visitors. We don't get too many down here. The current files are upstairs. These are the real relics."

Darnell had the feeling this gentleman was somewhat of a relic himself. He said, "Those are the files we need. The ones no one looks at anymore."

"Then how can I help you? You didn't specify."

O'Reilly answered. "We want to see all the files on Jack the Ripper, Norman. If you please."

He raised his eyebrows. *"The Ripper."* He breathed the words in a whisper. "Those are locked up."

"But you have the keys?"

"Yes. But they haven't been seen by anyone—except me, of course—for years. Maybe even since 1888."

"The files are closed to the public?" Darnell asked. "And to officers at the Yard?"

"The public, yes, sealed. In fact, they're called closed files. Officers? It depends on which ones. High enough, they can see anything. Not many are interested. As I said, we don't get a lot of visitors."

"You'll get them for us?" O'Reilly gave him a demure smile.

"Of course, my dear—uh, Sergeant." He turned on his heel and ambled down one of the aisles. "Just follow me. They're in the back—in the vault, we call it."

Walking through the long banks of file cabinets and seeing above the cabinets, on shelves, open racks of impersonal brown file folders, Darnell was struck by the irony that crimes involving once living, breathing people should end up in such a dead state. The files were as dead as the

THE CASE OF THE RIPPER'S REVENGE   53

criminals and victims described in them. But they might speak vital secrets to them.

Norman Pidgeon stopped at a wire-enclosed area secured by a padlocked gate. "This is it. Just take me a minute." He snapped on a light switch, which slightly increased the illumination within the enclosure.

He opened the padlock with a key from a large bunch attached by chain to his belt loop. He stepped inside, saying again, "Follow me."

In the back of that room sat a table with two straight-backed chairs against the wall. A single bulb shone above the table. At a nearby file cabinet, Pidgeon stopped and said, "I think this is the one."

After some rummaging and checking of names, he pulled out five thick brown folders and set them on the desk. "These are the files. But . . ."

"But what, Norman?" O'Reilly studied the man's face.

"I'd swear, yes, I'm sure, that one of the files is missing. It had a clasp on it, I remember that particularly. It was called the 'Private File.' " He gestured toward the stack of file folders. "Start on these. If you need anything, let me know. Of course, don't remove anything."

"Of course." O'Reilly nodded reassuringly at the custodian.

"Well, then." He retraced his steps back to the gate and turned toward the front of the cavernous room. Darnell could hear his footsteps resounding on the stone floor.

"He seemed anxious to get away," Darnell observed. "Wants to find that private file."

"I think he's concerned. He's in charge. Maybe afraid of being blamed for its disappearance."

They pulled up the two chairs to the table and each took a file. "We'll go through them individually, make notes," Darnell said, "then switch them, and later compare notes." He put two notepads and pencils on the table. "Jack the Ripper is waiting for us in these old folders."

Chapter Ten

Saturday night, September 8

Darnell took up a file. The name on the cover—*"Mary Ann (Polly) Nichols"*—struck an ominous chord of memory. It brought to mind the name Poppy Nellwyn and reminded him that the nickname of Polly was the point of reference their current killer had used. He must know much about the case, because official reports called her "Mary Ann."

Words leapt from the page—*"Mary Ann (Polly) Nichols. August 31. 42, dark-haired, petite, throat cut, abdominal mutilation, almost disemboweled."* It sounded like a description of the killing of Poppy Nellwyn, except that Poppy was much younger. *"Found in Buck's Row."* Darnell knew that was not far from where Poppy was killed. *"Last seen, 2:30 A.M., found an hour later. Weapon: A sharp 6- to 8-inch long-bladed knife."* Poppy was also killed at midnight with a long, sharp knife.

He studied the notes, sketches, and other materials in the file and made notes on a pad. He set it aside and asked O'Reilly, "How are you doing?"

She grimaced. "This Eddowes file is horrible."

"They're all gruesome." He picked up the next file—*"Annie Chapman."* He took a breath, and opened it.

"Annie Chapman, maiden name Smith. Found in the Spitalfields area, north of Whitechapel Road, not far from Buck's Row, at 6:00 A.M. on September 8. Forty-seven. Her head was almost cut off with the savagery of the knife blow. Her intestines had been taken out and thrown over her right shoulder." Again, the similarity in the method and style of murder and mutilation described in the file compared with the Annette Camden murder struck Darnell as much more than mere coincidence.

The file stated that Annie had been seen last with a man of about thirty-seven, five-foot-seven, dark-bearded and moustached. But he may have been her customer, Darnell realized—not the Ripper.

Trading files with O'Reilly, he picked up one of them. *"Elizabeth Liz Stride. Height, 5'5". Location: in Mitre Square, Berner Street, south of Whitechapel, 1:44 A.M., September 30, 1888. Found in pool of blood, clothes thrown up, throat cut with a clean-cut incision. Abdomen ripped open and intestines thrown over her right shoulder."* He felt the horror of each crime accelerating. *"A man was seen, about 28, 5'7", no beard."*

Darnell went on to the next. *"Catherine (Kate) Eddowes. Found September 30, 1888, at 2:30 A.M. Forty-six years of age, approximately. Throat cut, 6 or 7 inches across. Death was immediate. The incisions severed the victim's vocal cords down to the bone. Cuts in abdomen were oblique, great disfiguring of the face, massive mutilation. The right earlobe was cut through at an angle. The intestines were thrown over the right shoulder. A tip of the nose was cut loose, with a cut down to the upper lip and a cut across the lower lip. The left kidney is missing."* Darnell noted with irony the description of the poor woman's dress: *"A chintz skirt with three flounces; a dress bodice with a collar."* Never to wear that pitiful dress again.

The next entry interested him—the writing on the wall that was erased by then Police Commissioner Sir Charles Warren—*"The Juwes are the men that will not be blamed for nothing."*

Darnell stared at the words, the confusing language and possibly bad spelling and double negatives, realizing there could be two different interpretations—"The Jews should be *blamed*" and "The Jews should *not* be blamed." He needed to find out what the words meant, and why the Commissioner erased them. He was aware of a biblical reference to "Juwes" having to do with archaic Masonic history or legend, but doubted that was the intended meaning.

It seemed clear to him that whoever wrote the words may have done so to incriminate others. The killer could have written the words to cast blame on the Jews living in the area. If so, then reverse logic placed them in an innocent light, simply because the killer wrote the words, which in itself would make them unbelievable. Maybe there was an explanation somewhere, or even Warren's opinion, that could be revealing, at least to narrow the choices.

Darnell went on to the next entry: *"Footnote: Tuesday, October 16, 1888. A box with one half of a human kidney was received today by the police."* He muttered, "So it was a human kidney," causing O'Reilly to look up at him. He recalled a letter cited in his book that the police received from someone claiming to be the Ripper who also claimed to have consumed the other half of that kidney.

With reluctance, Darnell took up the last file. *"Marie Jeannette (Marie Jane, or Mary Jane) Kelly."* He paused. Poor Mary Kelly. How many words had been written about this unfortunate girl?

He opened the file. *"Marie Jeannette/Mary Kelly. Found at 11:30 A.M., November 9, 1888, in Miller's Court, inside common lodging room. Mutilated."* A side note said, *"(Only one of the victims found indoors.)"* He forced himself to read the horrific details of the murder and mutilation: *"Body parts cut off, thigh stripped of skin."*

The file went on to state, *"Rigor mortis had begun; death estimated to have been at 9:00 A.M. A man was seen in vicinity: short, pale, about 40, with a black moustache and a tall hat and long overcoat."* Photographs were taken of the body. He shook his head as he read that they had photographed Mary Kelly's eyes, based on the belief by many at that time that the image of the last person seen might be imprinted on her eyeballs, and that a photograph would reveal that image. But the report stated dryly: *"No photographic image was obtained."*

As he closed the Mary Kelly file, he felt as if he had virtually relived, by reviewing these files and reading these words, the abhorrence felt by the investigating police. He looked at O'Reilly.

She had also finished going through the five files and said, "Ugh." She shook her head. "There are no words that say it any better."

They stood, and Darnell checked the time. It was ten p.m. He asked, "Shall we find Norman?"

Sergeant O'Reilly stretched and tucked her notes in her bag.

Darnell heard footsteps approaching, and Custodian Pidgeon's visage appeared in the dingy light of the aisle.

"Finished?" Norman Pidgeon asked.

Darnell said, "Except for one thing, Norman—that missing file, the 'Private File,' you called it."

"Ye-es?"

"I'm sure you've seen inside it. Even though it's missing, tell us what it contained, will you?"

"It's, well, been a while." He looked at O'Reilly.

She fixed her eyes on him. "Norman—?"

He shifted from one foot to the other. "Not a word of any of this."

"Of course," Darnell said. "For our investigation only."

Norman's forehead creased. "Well, it was sort of a summary, but I felt a lot in it was just opinions. Most of it was comparing the Ripper's descriptions to people who could have been him. Questions of why the women's innards were removed." He shivered.

"It sounds like an analysis file Warren may have written."

Pidgeon nodded. "I think the Commissioner wrote it up after the last killing. He left office then."

"Did he come to any conclusion as to why the Ripper stopped killing?"

Pidgeon shook his head. "No. The Commissioner was out of the picture, resigned, just after the Mary Kelly killing. They didn't realize for a long time that there'd be no more murders. I think the Commissioner did discuss Prince Eddy."

"The Prince Eddy theory. That's far-fetched. Royalty as the Ripper?" He glanced at O'Reilly, who rolled her eyes.

Pidgeon went on, "That's all I remember just now." He looked around, as if expecting to see someone in the shadows. "I'm worried about that file. My responsibility. Someone got in here and took it."

He replaced the files, locked the cabinet, shook the drawer, and, as they reached the gate, padlocked it again. The three walked up the long aisles to the front of the room.

At the stairs, they thanked him and left the arrangements open so that they might contact him again, come back once more if need be.

"Anytime," he said. "It's nice to have the company."

"If you think of anything else, let us know," Darnell said.

Pidgeon turned to Sergeant O'Reilly. "I'll call you, Sergeant. You can count on that."

Darnell and O'Reilly walked back from the stairway to her desk and took seats. At that hour, few officers were on duty, mostly the skeleton night crew.

"I didn't hear whether you found any witnesses," Darnell said.

"Yes, the neighborhood. I walked the streets all about the flats, talked to people on the street, knocked on some doors. I found a woman who might have seen him the day before."

"The killer?"

She shook her head. "She wouldn't know that, and I wouldn't, but he was wearing a top hat, which the woman thought peculiar."

"Did you get a description?"

"Other than the hat, a dark coat—nothing on his features."

"Much as I dislike the word, it sounds like the description of whatever they saw in Whitechapel. What they called a ghost."

O'Reilly smiled. "You said it, not me."

"I have news, too. About the barkeep at The Three Hares—the pub we stopped in at that night on patrol."

"Yes?"

"He promised to help, watch for suspicious characters, and so on. He could be an asset. We'll see." Darnell rose. "Must get home. Shall we compare our notes tomorrow?"

"It's Sunday, but I think Inspector Warren may be on my back, even on a Sunday, on this one. Come in about noon."

Penny Darnell waited for her husband in the sitting room. The hall clock struck eleven just as she heard the street door open and close. "John," she called. "I'm in here."

He stepped across the room and they kissed as she rose from her chair. *"Penny kissed me when we met . . ."* he said.

"What? But it was *Jenny* in the poem."

"Penny's close enough. *'. . . jumping from the chair she sat in.'*"

"My poet. Is that what you studied tonight?"

He pulled her down next to him on the sofa. "You wouldn't believe what I read." He grimaced. "The actual police reports are worse than the accounts of the killings in my book on the Ripper."

"Then I don't want to hear them." She paused. "What will happen now? More killings?"

He pushed strands of hair back from his forehead. "I was wrong on this one—right in one way, wrong in another. I thought the victim would be in Whitechapel, another prostitute. She was neither. But the date was right, and the initials."

"So?"

"So my next guess would probably be only partially correct. The pattern is broken now. But if the killer were truly copying the Ripper, there'd be two deaths the night of the twenty-ninth."

"In Whitechapel?"

"There's the rub. There could be two killings next time, the twenty-ninth, early the thirtieth. But they could be anywhere in London."

"Whitechapel patrols can't prevent that."

"There's no way to prevent it now. And no way to warn any particular area. The police can't protect the entire city of London. And if they announce anything in the newspapers . . ."

She nodded. "Panic. I can imagine. So what do you do?"

"Go over the notes from tonight. There are many questions there. Look into the background of the Ripper murders, deeper and deeper. Search for witnesses of the current crimes. I have someone in Whitechapel who can help in that, a local keeping his eyes open. And I'll try to predict what could happen, the next time, if there is a next time."

Penny put her arm around his neck and pulled him to her. Their lips touched. "Enough of that for tonight," she said. "Just predict something about you and me, dear."

Darnell held her closely. "I predict we are going to have the rest of this evening alone together."

They rose and walked toward the stairs to the second floor of their flat.

Chapter Eleven

Sunday, September 9

After a leisurely breakfast with Penny and casual talk with Sung and his son, Ho San, Darnell drove to the hospital, where Chief Inspector Howard, recovering from his wounds, was due to be released that afternoon.

The weather was dry, brisk, and invigorating. But inside the building, the freshness of the air resolved itself into the faintly medicinal smell typical of hospital corridors. At Chief Howard's room, Darnell stopped and peered through the open door. Howard sat up in bed on top of the blankets, fully clothed, large white bandages protruding about his neck through the open collar of his shirt.

He hailed Darnell when he saw him, "John, come in."

"You're going home," Darnell said.

Howard nodded. "Waiting for Dorothy."

"Your daughter will stay with you for a while?"

"Yes. But that second slashing—I must know about it, and no one tells me anything. How did it happen? What do you think?"

Darnell took a seat next to the bed and described the scene at Annette Camden's place and the similarities and differences in circumstances in her death compared to the Whitechapel murder.

"Initials?" Howard scowled. "All you have to go on?"

"Unless you can describe your assailant, since you've thought about it. It's possible it was the same man."

"I didn't see him. Pity."

"The best we have is a general description of the killer. Not young. Top hat, dark cape or long coat. He's bold. He led us on a chase in Whitechapel. Then he singled out a saleswoman at Harrods, and God only knows why."

Howard gazed at Darnell. "I won't be coming back to the Yard, John. I know that now."

"Medical?"

"Yes. Doctor Fowler said it's the heart. Too much strain, and I could pop off just like that." Howard tried to snap his fingers but no sound came. He looked away, toward the window, and touched his eye with his knuckles.

"Some rest, Bruce. A second opinion?"

Howard shook his head. "I'll keep in touch with the office. I'm still on the rolls, and I'll keep that going as long as I can. But it's up to you, now, on this one, John. And a few other good souls down there." He lowered his voice. "Just don't rely too much on Warren. And be careful of him."

Darnell nodded. He groped for words. "We examined the Ripper files last night, O'Reilly and I."

"Bloody dangerous, that. Don't volunteer that to Warren, if he doesn't know already. His father was involved, you know."

"I know. He handled the Ripper case."

"Mishandled, more to the point. And the Inspector is as sensitive as a boil about that, and about his own reputation."

"Horrible, odd stories tied to the Ripper cases." Darnell told Howard of the photographing of Mary Kelly's eyes.

"Hah! Today we look for fingerprints. We're in the twentieth century now."

"That could be helpful, except for one thing. Our killer seems to know that, too. He might be wearing gloves."

At noon, Darnell walked into the Yard offices and to Sergeant O'Reilly's desk. He rapped on the corner. "Hello."

She looked up from papers strewn on her desk. "Just going over last night's notes. Are you ready to dig in to it?"

"Yes. Have you seen Warren?"

"No. He hasn't come in yet. Sunday, of course."

Side by side, they compared their notes, exchanged them to read the other's, discussed points of difference. Darnell dismissed the royalty theory. They both agreed Commissioner Warren's actions seemed particularly inept.

"There are questions here, and if we had answers for them,

it might explain the Ripper's motives and tell us something about our present-day killer as well. For example, what kind of man would do this? His psychology? How his mind works? Why imitate the Ripper? If we could draw his psychological portrait . . ."

O'Reilly sighed. "Let's take the real Ripper first."

He looked at his notes. "All right, let's ask questions about him. Why kill prostitutes? And why in Whitechapel?"

"Well, Whitechapel—because that's where prostitutes are. If he wanted to kill prostitutes, they were plenty there."

He nodded. "That's true. Over a thousand prostitutes at that time in the Whitechapel District alone. But why kill that category of humankind? Did he have a hatred of them? Did one of them do something to him, so he took it out on all of them?"

O'Reilly said, "You'll admit they were easy to kill, John. And he could have just hated them for what they were. Maybe with just a general—you know—a rage. A sickness. I don't know. You're the professor of psychology."

"The maniac theory? Could be, but I think it was more than that. He certainly killed the way a maniac would kill, but I think he had a motive or obsession of some kind."

"Hmm. Now my question. Why did the Ripper stop killing?"

Darnell mused for a minute. "That may be the toughest question of all. Was he simply afraid of getting caught? If so, the pure maniac idea goes out the window. A maniac wouldn't be that rational. A maniac would kill until caught. The Ripper may have been killed himself, or fled the country. But I have a new theory I've not heard expressed—that he stopped because he was prevented from killing again."

She frowned. "How do you mean that?"

"Just that he stopped killing because someone stopped him or because something happened that kept him from continuing. Some situation that was very straightforward, but not planned."

"Yes, but—well, all right."

"What do you think of some of the other bizarre theories?"

O'Reilly smiled. "Like the Prince Eddy theory? A member of the royal family killing prostitutes?"

"Yes. It's hard to give any credence to that."

"John, this is all about 1888. How about today? How do you connect the new murders with the Ripper's in 1888?"

"I think there has to be a link between the past crimes and the present ones. Some explanation of why our own killer acts so much like the Ripper, why he copies him in some respects, why he doesn't in others." He shook his head. "The connection just hasn't surfaced yet. But the more we study this copycat, the more we'll know about him."

She tossed her pencil on the desk. "So we have to watch another murder take place before we know what that connection is? Warren'll take my stripes."

As if using his name had called out the Devil, O'Reilly looked up to see Inspector Nathaniel Warren striding across the office toward her. At the desk, he stopped, and said in a curt voice, "Give me your report, Sergeant. What have you found?"

She stood up and faced him. "Sir, one woman in the neighborhood saw a suspicious-looking man on the street. A top hat, a dark coat. Not typical of the area. She didn't see the face. He seemed very strange to her."

His face reddened. "Top hat? Are you trying to tie this in to the Whitechapel murder? Are you saying it's the same man?" He looked down on the desk at the pad in front of her.

O'Reilly's eyes followed his gaze, and she gasped. She realized she had scrawled all over the pad, up, down, and across, in bold, block letters, the three words—*Jack the Ripper, Jack the Ripper, Jack the Ripper.*

Warren's face contorted as he grabbed the pad, tore the top sheet into pieces, and tossed them back on the desk. His words stumbled out, strident. "Sergeant, don't try to make this into a modern Jack the Ripper case. I won't have it. These are two separate murders. One prostitute. One unfortunate woman."

He turned to Darnell. "Are you claiming it's the ghost of the Ripper? One of your peculiar little fantasies?"

Darnell stood also, to face him. "No, Inspector. My job is to prove that ghosts *do not* exist in cases like this. And I expect to do exactly that."

Warren's frown lifted. "So we at least agree to dispense with ghosts. But within these walls, if I hear or see the words Jack the Ripper . . ." He glared at O'Reilly. "That'll be the end of one short, unremarkable career. Do I make myself clear, Sergeant?" Not waiting for a reply, he turned and strode away.

Watching as Warren entered his office and slammed the door, O'Reilly finally released the breath she was holding. "Whew!"

"He doesn't want a second Ripper case on his watch," Darnell said. "I don't blame him for that, not after the humiliating experience his father suffered in 1888."

O'Reilly nodded. "He'd be compared to him. Like father, like son, they'd say. It would bring out all the old skeletons again."

Darnell gathered up his papers, preparatory to leaving. "The problem is, skeletons from the past show up when you least expect them. And old bones rattle the loudest."

When he reached home, Darnell met Penny as she moved across the entryway toward him. He swept her into his arms. "Bring me back to reality," he said, pressing his lips on hers. "I don't know whether ghosts of the past or present are more stultifying."

"What a word. You're sounding like a professor again."

"I wouldn't mind a nice semester of just quiet teaching for a while."

"Relax, John. Sung has a nice dinner planned."

"Ask him to bring a bottle of Bordeaux and glasses to the sitting room."

The telephone rang as she turned toward the kitchen. "I'll get it," he said, and entered the sitting room. He lifted the receiver, said, "Darnell here," and was pleased to hear Chief Inspector Howard's voice, although there was tension in it.

"John. I'm glad you're home. Something you need to know."

"All right."

"Are you sitting down?"

Darnell sank into the sofa. "Yes."

"Ubel Baldrik escaped from prison ten days ago. I just heard it. They were holding the news back from me while I was in the hospital."

"Baldrik. He's a dangerous man."

"And I'm thinking Baldrik could have been the one who attacked me with that knife. Whoever it was went for a kill."

"Wasn't he due to be hanged soon for the Lloyd George case killings? What happened?"

"He was my personal project from the beginning, after you apprehended him. Having my men tie him hand and foot and carry him to the car humiliated him. My testimony at the trial on the danger he posed to society got him the death penalty. He heard me say it in court, and I'm sure he blames me more than anyone. I think, when he escaped, he came straight for me."

"I agree that's something he'd do. It's like Baldrik. But I'm wondering something else. The two murders—Poppy and Annette—could he have done them, too? To get even with the police? Because he relishes the killings? Or both?"

"There might be a connection, John. Baldrik could be our copycat. The timing of his escape would permit it, and his brutal nature and record would certainly be consistent with the violent nature of the two crimes. I'm sure you remember what they called him?"

"I'll never forget. Nor will Penny, whenever she thinks of the man who held that knife to her face and threatened to disfigure her. Yes, Bruce, I remember what they called him. *Baldrik—the Mutilator*."

Chapter Twelve

Monday, September 10

"You never answered my question, John," Penny said, in a mock accusing voice.

"Question?" He set down his coffee cup.

"Annette Camden. I asked whether I could help, and you said you'd let me know. That was Saturday. Today's Monday."

He looked at her appraisingly. "You really do want to help, don't you?"

She sniffed. "Of course I do. I knew that poor woman. She sold me many of my dresses."

"What did you have in mind?"

"Take me to Harrods. I know some people there. Just let me prowl around, as you call it, for a few hours. Drop me off, pick me up later."

Darnell said, "That sounds safe enough."

Penny laughed. "It's not like a trip to Whitechapel."

After breakfast, a bit past eleven, they left for Harrods. Darnell pulled up to the curb alongside the department store and Penny jumped out. "Then I'll see you at two o'clock, right here," she said, and walked, heels clicking, toward the entrance.

Darnell drove on to the Yard to keep an appointment he'd made with O'Reilly. He hadn't told her the subject matter of the meeting yet, feeling it was better said in person.

Penny Darnell knew all the nooks and crannies of Harrods, having strolled through the floors often, either by herself or with a friend. It took on the attributes of an outing just to see the great variety of merchandise displayed in the huge store. Of course, the women's department, where Annette Camden had worked, usually held the most interest and was her final destination. She headed straight there as she left the elevator.

She recognized several of the salespersons, women who seemed to be fixtures in the department. A gray-haired, slender woman she had seen often, a floor manager, came up to her.

"Mrs. Darnell, isn't it? May I help you?"

Penny noticed the name on her badge, Miss Percy. "Yes, but not for a dress this time. It's about Annette."

The face of the other woman darkened. "Poor girl. To die that young, so horribly. I guess she wasn't a girl, really, but at my at my age, she seemed young."

"My husband is looking into the matter with Scotland Yard. I wondered if you could tell me whatever you know about it, anything at all."

"This way, please." Miss Percy stepped away from the counter toward an unoccupied corner of the salesroom. "I don't have that much to say, but mustn't have customers overhearing. Let's see—that day, I'd invited her for lunch, I remember that. She said she was too busy with stock. Since the article appeared, she'd been even more conscientious than usual."

"Article?"

"In the *Times*. Harrods send a news release about the best salesperson for the month, and the paper runs a small article. Annette won. The article appeared the week before she died."

"Think of that last day. Did you notice any of the men who walked through, shoppers or others, anyone unusual-looking?"

She shook her head. "The police asked us all of those questions. I don't think anyone had much information that helped them."

"Anything in any other department?"

She frowned. "There was that disturbance on the second floor. The same day, I think. A man had been rummaging through time cards."

"Who saw him?"

"I don't know. I heard about it later. You could go to Personnel, ask there." She gave Penny directions to Personnel.

On the second floor, Penny found a clerk who seemed to check in employees, handle time cards and other minor employee matters. Penny introduced herself, mentioned Miss Percy, and asked, "Did you happen to see the man who was in here last Friday, the night Annette was killed? The one who caused some disturbance?"

The stocky red-haired girl nodded. "I was the one called the guard on the phone. I guess he heard me calling and left. I'd told him to clear out before, but he didn't until then."

"So you spoke with him before you made the call?"

"Across the room, from my desk. He didn't say anything, didn't turn around from the time cards he was thumbing through."

"Why would he do that, do you know? Has anything like that ever happened before?"

"I don't know. My manager thought maybe he wanted to find a friend, a wife, to see where she was working that day, to reach her."

"Do salesclerks move from one area to another?"

"Some of them do."

"May I look at the cards?"

The clerk led her to a corner where cards were set in place in a vertical rack. Penny glanced at several, seeing that they showed first and last names, floors and departments, times in and times out for each day for a week.

Seeing the names in large capitals, Penny realized the prominence of the initials. Name badges did not carry first names, only "Mr.," "Miss," or "Mrs." and the last name. The cards were a handy place where full names and therefore both initials could be obtained.

"What did the man look like?" she asked the girl.

"Not like a Harrods customer. Wore a dark jacket. Swarthy face. Looked strong—muscular, you know—from the back."

"Young? Old?"

"He wore a hat. He never turned around. I think he might have been hiding his face. He left while I was on the phone."

Penny stopped at the third-floor tea shop and ordered tea while waiting for John's return. The *Sunday Times* on the table caught her attention, a feature article by Sandy

MacDougall dominating the front page with stark head-lines: *"Second Brutal Killing and Mutilation in One Week. Scotland Yard Sifts Clues."*

Penny smiled at the word "clues." As she read the article through, twice, she doubted whether anyone actually had any real clue and hoped her trip to Harrods would help John. She sipped her tea thoughtfully. The initials. Yes. They were a clue.

John Darnell walked up to Sergeant O'Reilly's desk, a routine that was becoming familiar. "Hello, Catherine."

"John. Sit down." She nodded at the side chair next to her desk. "What's this mysterious information?"

"You haven't heard from Chief Inspector Howard?"

"Not for a couple of days."

He frowned. "I don't want to worry you unnecessarily, but I have to warn you."

" 'Mysteriouser and mysteriouser,' didn't Alice say?"

"It was 'curiouser,' actually. But it's mysterious, too. Baldrik has escaped from prison."

O'Reilly gasped. "Oh, no!"

"Chief Howard suspects it was Baldrik who attacked him. It's Baldrik's style. The knife."

O'Reilly sat silent.

"If it is Baldrik, Catherine, he may come after me. Or after you."

"So that's the message. I'm to be careful."

"Exactly. Very careful. Have someone watch your back. Ask the local constable to stop by your place sometimes and look around. Leave lights on in your flat at night."

"I don't carry a firearm."

"Talk with Warren. He could get you one."

"Hah! He'd probably be glad to get rid of me."

Darnell touched her hand. "I'm serious. You know what kind of man Baldrik is, what you went through last time with him."

"I'll never forget it—how I felt when he came into my hospital room with that horrible postmortem knife. I thought he was going to chop me up right there. But you saved me from him." She laughed, a release of built-up tension. "Another thing I won't forget is how you looked in those overalls, John."

He smiled. "Well, be careful. I've alerted my household. Penny and Sung and his son. We're taking extra precautions."

O'Reilly stared at her notepad. She had scribbled the words "Jack the Ripper" again. She scratched out the words and folded the sheet in half. "Warren could creep up behind me, look over my shoulder." She glanced about the room.

"With Baldrik out, you may wonder about the two killings—whether Baldrik could be a copycat killer?"

O'Reilly nodded. "He's got a reputation as a mutilator."

"Yes. And he's got some kind of motive—revenge on Howard, who testified against him so vigorously, perhaps on you and me, too, for putting him on death row."

"He put himself there." She thought a bit. "I wonder if he ever talked with anyone about the Ripper."

"Not to my knowledge. But from what I know, he's capable of an equal crime. He acquired that reputation. And the timing of his escape from prison would have allowed him to commit both murders."

"Does Warren know all this? The Chief Superintendent or Commissioner Cliburn must know. How will they capture Baldrik?"

"I expect to find out. I'm talking with Warren next."

She inclined her head toward Warren's office. "He's there."

Darnell stood. "All right. Remember to be careful."

Hearing the knock on his glass door, Inspector Warren looked up with annoyance from his reading. He scowled when he saw Professor Darnell at the door. Another confrontation, he thought. But he must be careful, handle the man right. He'd hate to have Lloyd George down on his head, and he knew the Professor and the Prime Minister were close.

He motioned to him, and Darnell came into the office, closing the door behind him. "Just a few minutes of your time, Inspector," he said.

Warren waved a hand toward a chair, and Darnell seated himself in it. "Proceed."

"You've heard of Ubel Baldrik's escape?"

Warren had heard it, that morning, from Howard, and

realized now why Darnell had come to him at this time. "Yes, damned nuisance! I'm assigning special search teams of two and three officers under the direction of his best detectives. We must find the man who tried to kill the Chief Inspector." As he said the words to Darnell, Warren realized the power of them. He knew what he said and did on this matter would hit the papers the next day. He'd give them that exact quote to use. He knew MacDougall was milling about the hallway with other reporters.

"There's another aspect of his escape," Darnell said.

Warren's eyes were heavy-lidded. "And that is?"

"Yesterday, Bruce told me he'd heard Baldrik had escaped about ten days ago. He could have committed both murders. Poppy Nellwyn's the night of August thirtieth, early the thirty-first, and Annette Camden's the night of September seventh or the next morning. We can't rule out the fact that he could be the Ripper copycat."

Warren spoke, tight-lipped, keeping the animosity from his voice. "I've said this before, and I'll say it every time this comes up. Jack the Ripper is not a permitted topic in these headquarters." He paused. "At least not in my office."

He'd qualified that, knowing that Commissioner Horace Cliburn might think differently about it. Or, closer to home, Chief Superintendent Martin Treadwell. He had to keep this from Treadwell. The man was an alarmist, he knew, as well as a conspiracy theorist, and Treadwell had been around as a young copper when Warren's father was Commissioner. He'd bring all the old skeletons out of the closet and rattle them.

Warren grimaced as his thoughts raced. He, Nathaniel Warren, would be the scapegoat. The second Warren to fail to capture a Ripper. Ironic, he thought, that there was no evidence, really, that there was another Ripper—copycat or otherwise.

But Darnell was going on, interrupting his dark thoughts. "I know you're sensitive to the old cases. Your father, of course, family ties, all of that. But we have to be realistic. The style of killing, and some other important factors, all point to a connection between the current murders and the Ripper case. Whether it's Baldrik, we don't know. But it's feasible."

Warren felt Darnell was holding something back. It was time to hit him with the files issue. "You've been down in our archives, I hear," Warren said, "without my permission." But watching him, he had to give Darnell credit for taking his onslaught without flinching.

"I'm working under Howard's authority," Darnell said. "He asked me into the case."

Warren took a different tack. "What did you find, then?"

Darnell's voice bit the air. "Something we didn't find. A missing file. Do you have it? The Private File?"

"Damn!" The word came out involuntarily from Warren's lips. "And if I do? As you say, the Commissioner was my father, correct? It was sensitive material, correct?" He tried to control his voice. "It has to be kept out of the wrong hands."

"I need it. There are things that could happen, things you really don't want to happen."

Warren frowned. He didn't know what Darnell referred to, but he couldn't take a chance, with Howard, Treadwell, or Cliburn ready to pounce on him. He fought an instinctive reaction and tried to remain calm. He unlocked the bottom side desk drawer and dramatically dropped a brown folder on top of his desk. "Here it is, then. Return it tonight. Personally. To my home."

Darnell picked up the file without a trace of victory in his expression or voice. "This could be valuable."

"Why? You're not investigating crimes that took place thirty years ago." Warren spat out the words, annoyed. "Just a streetwalker and a clerk, in today's world."

"Today's world is merely an extension of what has gone before. We can't leave any stone in place without looking at the grubs under it. There's too much at stake."

Warren fumed, knowing his voice betrayed his feelings, but saw no choice. The damned meddling professor must be appeased. "Tonight. My home. Eight o'clock." He stood in dismissal.

Darnell turned to leave. At the door, he inclined his head in a slight bow. "Thank you, Inspector."

Chapter Thirteen

Monday, September 10

Penny burst out with the information as she stepped into the car. "The full names were on the time cards, John, not on their name badges, which showed only last names. So Annette's full name and initials were on the cards. He could get the initials. *'A.C.'*"

Darnell smiled. "Excellent! That's a definite link. Dr. Watson couldn't have done better. But why Harrods?"

She went on. "There'd been an article in the *Times* about Annette the week before. Best salesperson of the month."

"So," Darnell said, "the killer came to Harrods looking for her because of the article. He had to see the time cards to verify her full name and the initials . . . but at the same time, of course, he obtained her address. Addresses were on the cards, right?"

"That's right. I didn't think of that at the time. But yes, they all had addresses."

When they reached home, Darnell headed for the sitting room. "Some things to go over," he said, holding up the brown file Inspector Warren had given him.

"I'll look in on Sung. You'll have to take a break for lunch soon." Penny closed the sitting room door to give him privacy.

Darnell pulled a chair up to the writing desk and spread the folder out on the desk. His brow creased as he looked at the photos of the dead bodies on the left side of the folder. He could see why the gruesome depictions of the mutilations were removed from the five main files and placed here. He lifted the top sheet and saw other photos attached to several other pages. Each set of photos was more grisly than its predecessor, with those of Mary Kelly so repulsive that he dropped the pages and averted his attention to the other side of the file.

The notes were in the now-familiar spidery, quill-pen inscriptions entered by Commissioner Sir Charles Warren. Poring over them, Darnell could see they were the Commissioner's impressions of the crime scenes and personal feelings that crossed his mind on each of those horrible nights so many years ago. Darnell felt as if he was staring into a private crystal ball of memories. Memories the old Commissioner wanted buried.

"Polly Nichols. Found Friday morning. Poor little woman. Mary Ann, but friends called her Polly. Why would a butcher disembowel such a sad, forgotten creature as this? One prostitute out of a thousand or more. Not for money. Coins were found nearby. A thought—maybe he was really a butcher, from a horse slaughter-house. Also, check man called 'Leather Apron' seen in vicinity, vicious prostitute-beater, known to demand money from them for 'protection.'" Later notes were entered: *"Cleared butchers and Leather Apron. Alibis."*

Annie Chapman. Head almost severed. Looks like he tried to fully remove it, and stopped. Intestines cut out. Just over a week later than the first killing. Friday first time, Saturday this time. Weekend murderer? Why? Leather Apron a good suspect, but also not a good lead this time. No evidence, alibi. Nothing more. Damn!"

Darnell smiled at the single word Warren had written after that entry, with a blotch of inkspot under the exclamation point showing a jamming of the quill against the sheet. "Feeling the strain," Darnell said aloud.

"Elizabeth Stride. 'Liz.' Three weeks later, but on a Sunday. Weekend again. Intestines gutted. Found 1:44 A.M. Man seen looking to be about 28, clean shaven.

"Catherine or Kate Eddowes. Found at almost same hour. But could have been killed hours apart. Distances were not great. Greater disfigurement and mutilation, face, ear lobe, intestines, nose tip. Kidney missing. Most of womb taken. The following found scrawled on wall behind body: 'The Juwes are the men that will not be blamed for nothing.' Ordered it removed at once. I know I'll be criticized, but I can't let the Jews of this area be blamed. I think the Ripper put those words there to throw us off. Nothing biblical about

it, as some say, just someone not too well educated misspelling the word 'Jews.' In any case, it was my job to take the responsibility of eliminating the suggestion. It's no clue. It's nothing."

In the handwriting of the next entry, Darnell noticed a change, a fierceness in the words: *"Half of left human kidney received in box today, October 16. The other half? Did the beast really eat it? What was the point?"*

Then: *"Marie/Mary Kelly. Jeanette middle name. Thought killings were over, nothing since September 30. Now this, November 9. The worst. Gutted. Dissected. Skinned. Like an animal. Eyeballs photographed. Idiotic practice!"*

At the end of these entries, Darnell read what appeared to be later notes or summaries.

"Summary: Disparity in descriptions of men seen at or near crime scene before or after. Chapman case: 37, 5'7", dark beard and moustache. Stride case: 28, 5'7", no beard. Another 30, 5'5", moustache. Kelly case: Short, 40, moustache, high hat, long overcoat. Summary: Killer between 28 and 40, not tall, 5'5" to 5'7", high hat, long overcoat. Uncertain aspect as to facial hair." Darnell made his own summary—about five-foot-seven, about thirty, top hat, long coat. Similar to descriptions obtained today, except for the age.

Then the final entry. *"There are those who cast suspicion on our dear Prince Albert Victor ('Eddy'), Duke of Clarence and the grandson of Queen Victoria. Only dreadful rumors. No evidence. Not to be dignified with a report or investigation. As I leave now, this horrible case ends. At least for me. And with it goes my career. I, too, am a victim of this madman."*

Darnell closed the file, sat back, and stared at it. So— that was the explanation for the mysterious words chalked on the wall. He agreed with Warren on that, and also on his curt dismissal of the suspicions against Prince Albert. But the other aspect that came through the faded writing was the depth of feelings that the Commissioner had at that time. Feelings he did not want the world ever to see.

Since Warren left just after Mary Kelly's body was found, his information abruptly stopped there, with no speculation as to what happened to the Ripper or why the killings stopped. Something Darnell would have to continue to explore.

A knock came, and Sung's head appeared as he opened the door and announced, "Lunch, Professor. Mrs. Darnell is seated."

Darnell jumped up and took a deep breath to exhale the dusty emotions of the past in the dead pages. He strode across the room and on into the dining room. After delving into the horrors of the reports, he was pleased to see Penny's smiling face and looked forward to the prospect of a strong cup of coffee.

After lunch, Darnell returned to his desk to recheck some information. Before he could begin, the door knocker reverberated in the hallway, and Sung entered the sitting room saying, "Mr. MacDougall to see you." Darnell nodded, and heard the reporter's step across the wooden floor.

"Sandy. A pleasure to see you. What brings you this way?"

Sandy MacDougall smiled. "All right. Adopt the air of innocence, like what a surprise to see me." He took Darnell's outstretched hand and gestured toward a chair. "May I?"

"Of course, of course." Darnell sat opposite him, his eyes twinkling at MacDougall's remarks. He waited for the rest of it.

MacDougall tossed his hat on a chair, and his voice took on an unaccustomed edge. "Two slashings, John. Mutilations, more's the point. Not to mention the attack on Chief Inspector Howard. What's going on?"

Darnell smoothed his hair back, wondering how much the reporter had gleaned at Scotland Yard. He reached for a pipe and filled it, watching MacDougall's face, which seemed to grow pinker with each moment.

"You've talked with the people at the Yard, I suppose."

"You know damn well I have. And you also know they told me almost nothing."

"Then why come to me?"

"Ghosts."

"The *Times* wants stories about ghosts now?" Darnell's eyes twinkled.

"I've talked with Warren." MacDougall scowled. "No help there. But something else—I've been to Whitechapel."

Darnell puffed his pipe. "And?"

"I've talked with Burt Fenham. I know what those women said they saw. He told me you patrolled out there several nights."

"True. I recommend the tour."

MacDougall sniffed. "You're the ghost-hunter. What did you see there?" He paused. "You know that I don't like to print unsubstantiated rumors about ghosts, but our public is getting alarmed. Letters, phone calls. The *Times* has a responsibility."

Darnell puffed thoughtfully. "If you're asking whether I've seen a ghost, the answer is no. Don't report that there are ghosts roaming the streets of London."

"Then what the hell is going on? My editor wants a story today. What can I print?"

Darnell pointed a finger at him. "Print the truth. You don't want to frighten your readers with unfounded rumors."

"And the truth is . . . ?"

"There were two deaths. Vicious ones. The Yard says they're unconnected. But we've seen unconnected similar cases before, even one last year. And the attack on Howard? That appears to be unrelated. The method was different. Sandy, we're only at the investigation's beginnings. I don't want to give out purely speculative thoughts. You wouldn't want to print them."

"But you've got your suspicions. I know you."

Darnell gestured with his pipe. "Wait a few weeks. Say, the first of October. This could be old history by then."

"And if it isn't? If there's another of these so-called 'unconnected' murders?"

"We'll hope there won't be. But if there is, of course we'll talk. And Inspector Warren will have much to say, too."

MacDougall rose. "You're holding back, John, for your own reasons. And I'll respect that. But only until October first—or until the next murder. Then read the *Times,* with or without your comments. I can't wait forever."

*   *   *

Darnell left his home after an early cold supper and drove to Inspector Warren's flat, rapping on the door with the knocker exactly at eight p.m. as the Inspector had instructed.

Warren himself opened the door, saying, "Butler's night off."

Darnell followed him through the hall, noticing the portrait of Commissioner Sir Charles Warren on the wall, then into the study. The Inspector immediately sat in the leather chair behind his desk. He waved a hand imperiously toward the red leather chair on the other side of the desk. "You brought the file?"

Darnell handed over the file he had been carrying quite obviously under his arm. "I'm returning it." He took a seat.

"It satisfied you?"

"As far as it goes. And I understand your feelings. Look here, Inspector, you must see similarities between the current killings and those in your file. We've got Ripper-type murders, mutilations. Two. And for good measure, Bruce's attack."

"You harped on that this morning."

"The newspapers are getting into it now. You may not be able to pretend there's no connection much longer. London could be up in arms if these things are magnified in the press."

"MacDougall."

"He's only the first. The others will follow."

Warren sat without speaking for a moment. "My father was raked over the coals for failing," he said with bitterness dripping from his words. " *'Failing miserably'* were the kinds of words they used. Letting the Ripper get away. Accused of destroying evidence. The public had lost faith in the police. People made fun of him and his bloodhounds. Superiors kept information back from him. Vigilance Committees were formed. Damn!" He paused. "Queen Victoria was involved herself, even wrote speculative letters about the crimes."

"But a lot of it was politics."

The Inspector nodded. "Yes, but the result was the same. My father, when he was at his peak as Commissioner Sir Charles Warren, saw his police career suddenly ended, his reputation destroyed, over one case. I don't want to face the same fate."

"Not facing the facts is the issue here. Eventually you'll have to admit the connection."

"The newspapers would crucify me. Another failure of the Warrens, they'd say."

"Jack the Ripper killed five women. We have two dead. If we can somehow save the others, all of them, any of them, it won't be a failure."

Warren grimaced, in a show of distaste, and stared across the desk at Darnell. "What would you have me do?"

"The killer works at night. After the first death, we thought murders might continue in Whitechapel, where the Ripper's killings took place. Then the second victim was an employee of Harrods, in a decent neighborhood. The murders were on the same dates as the first two by the Ripper. The women had the same initials as those two Ripper killings. Conclusion—someone is duplicating the first killings twenty-nine years later."

"But they're not all prostitutes, as the Ripper's were."

"Correct. That makes it harder, as does the variance in location. But in studying old and new murders, I'm convinced the next ones—two, if he keeps to the Ripper's pattern—will occur the same night, September twenty-ninth, or morning of the thirtieth." Darnell paused. "I'd urge you to send out special patrols of two constables each, as many as you can throughout London, for a few days before the end of September, say, from the twenty-seventh through the thirtieth. I'd suggest patrols go out from about eight p.m. to six a.m. Give them our best description of the current killer."

"But wouldn't that alarm the public?"

"You don't have to use the word 'Ripper' or 'copycat' killer to your men, certainly not the word 'ghost.' They know there were two gruesome murders, and you have to try to prevent further deaths. The only way is to apprehend him, or scare him off."

Warren sighed. "I can do that. We have over two weeks to prepare for the special patrols. You'll stay on the case?"

"Of course. I'll work with Sergeant O'Reilly as needed. And keep Chief Howard informed at his home."

"All right, then. I'll get the wheels in motion." He scowled. "Have to clear it with Howard and Chief Superintendent Treadwell. The Superintendent can deal with the Commissioner."

Darnell stood and took the hand Warren offered across the desk. As he shook it, he saw in the Inspector's eyes the same deep sadness evident in the portrait of the Commissioner in the hall, a worried, beleaguered look that portended disaster.

Chapter Fourteen

The man walked the streets in his other clothes, not what he considered his killing clothes, to avoid witnesses or suspicion. To the unsuspecting eye, he looked like an average Londoner—not a banker, perhaps, but one in trade, with a respectable business, a devoted wife, possibly children. The impression was one he had cultivated—taking on the countenance of an ordinary citizen. It helped him in his reconnoiters.

Inside his mind, however, swirled thoughts unlike those of any average Londoner. *Rage. Revenge.* Plans of encounters involving desperate risk to satisfy his violent urgings.

This morning, early, six a.m., he scanned the numbers on the street-corner buildings as he strolled along, newspaper under one arm, umbrella on the other, for all appearances a man going to his work. Only his work was murder.

John Darnell sat across from Penny at their breakfast table, a meal they enjoyed sharing, knowing events of the day often disrupted plans for other meals. He sipped his coffee and contemplated the case. Penny's voice broke into his thoughts.

"John."

He looked up, his ease quickly fading with her next words.

"Will there be more killings?"

He shrugged. "That's a question I wish I could answer. There's no certainty. How do you predict it? The two killings were of different kinds of people, in different parts of town."

"But if it's someone following the Ripper's pattern, even

with some differences, you mean you'll have to wait for another murder to occur?"

"Two other murders, if he's exact. Two on September twenty-ninth, in a little over two weeks. But I won't just wait, and neither will Scotland Yard. I admit it. We need a break, a new sense of direction."

They finished their breakfast and Darnell adjourned to the sitting room to pursue a thought he'd had the night before. He removed a landscape painting from a wall and replaced it with a large month-by-month calendar.

The calendar pages displayed the months of August through November 1917. He felt a need to visualize the days and dates of the murders and enter other information. He gazed at it.

The phone rang; standing next to it, he picked it up. Each time it rang lately, he felt some new atrocity might have happened. Hearing good news would be welcome.

The voice of Rusty Clanahan came, excited, over the receiver. "I think my fill-in man has seen him!"

"Seen the killer? Go ahead, man."

"I'm off work yesterday, my substitute tendin' bar. A man comes in—ugly bloke, scar, 'fish eyes,' Fitch says. He orders ale. Asks about prostitutes, to hire one. Fitch says, 'Stand out on the corner at night.' But the bloke wants addresses."

Darnell urged, "And where is Fitch now?"

"At his place, I expect. Not far. Subs around at different pubs, fills in mostly at night, sometimes all day."

Darnell glanced at a clock. "I'll be at the pub at noon."

Darnell pulled on drab street clothes, dropped his .38-special revolver in a coat pocket, and said a quick good-bye to Penny. As his car rattled toward the East End, he wondered if this could be the break he'd told Penny they needed—the first up-close, eyewitness description of the killer.

For a Tuesday noon, The Three Hares pub buzzed with activity. The smell of sausages and fish emanated from the kitchen area, and men and women filled the several booths and lined the bar.

"Lunchtime," Rusty said. "Even street girls have to eat."

Darnell brushed it aside. "Where does your substitute live?"

"I'll take you. Knew you'd want to go there." He gave a high sign to a man at the other end of the bar who stepped around behind it and approached Clanahan.

"I'll be gone for a bit. Don't drink up all the profits."

The other nodded and gave a crooked smile. He turned to a customer as Clanahan stepped from behind the bar and joined Darnell.

"Follow me," Clanahan said. "We can walk it."

The barkeep hurried down streets now familiar to Darnell, cutting through alleyways, taking the most direct, if not the most scenic route.

Darnell said, "We appreciate your help."

Clanahan scowled. "Just wonderin'. If I could've done anything to save Poppy from . . . what happened to her."

"No one could have predicted it."

"These streets are dangerous. Take her ma––Sarah, her name was. I remember she was banged up more'n once."

Darnell studied him. "I notice you like to watch over these, ah, women."

"Much as I can, being behind the bar most of the time, them out on the streets."

"Help us find Poppy's killer. That's what you can do best now."

Clanahan stopped in front of a nondescript brown-boarded, two-story structure and led the way up the inside stairs to the second floor. At the end of the hall he rapped on a door marked simply "8." After a moment, he knocked again, louder. He looked at Darnell.

Darnell frowned. "Try the door."

Clanahan gripped the handle and turned it, the door opening stiffly with a loud squeak at his touch. He stepped into the room, followed closely by Darnell. And they both stopped in mid-stride.

The body lay on the cot, one arm dangling down the left side of the thin ticking, the fingers touching the floor. The head was turned in that direction, eyes closed. Blood soaked the sheet and blanket, loosely tangled under the body.

"Migod! Stabbed in the back," Clanahan said.

Darnell stepped forward cautiously toward the bed. The

man had been stabbed several times. No knife. The killer had taken it with him. No sign of a struggle. An empty whiskey bottle and glass sat on a nearby table. Darnell felt the man had probably been drunk, or sleeping one off, when the murder took place.

"I expect he was followed home yesterday when he left The Three Hares." Darnell glared at the body. "He didn't know he'd signed his own death warrant just by answering a few questions. Later, the killer realized his exposure and silenced him."

"Dammit! Poor Fitch. What a way to die."

"Any relatives?"

"Not a soul I know of."

Darnell sighed. "Let's find a phone. I have to call Scotland Yard."

Detective Dennis Gannet, whom Darnell had met at Poppy Nellwyn's crime scene, brought Sergeant O'Reilly with him within an hour. They examined Fitch's room but found nothing revealing.

"Just a drunken bum. Some petty dispute," Gannet said.

O'Reilly shook her head. "Not with the background of what Clanahan told us. The man in the pub. It's too coincidental."

"There's no evidence," Gannet said. "But we'll keep it open. For now, just another body for potter's field, likely."

"I'd like to look into it a bit more," the Sergeant said.

Gannet nodded absently, making notes in a book. "I'll send a wagon down for him. You can see if he has any relatives. We can do that much."

Clanahan returned to the pub. Gannet left after Darnell said he'd drop O'Reilly off at the Yard later. Darnell and O'Reilly made inquiries of the few occupants of the premises, learning Fitch had no known relatives, friends, or visitors. They saw nothing of value or significance in his room after one last look, and he and O'Reilly stood outside until the morgue crew picked up the body.

"I was thinking this might be a break," Darnell said, as they walked back to his car, near the pub. "But we'll have to interpret it."

"Interpret?"

"It seems simple enough. The killer looks for prostitutes to kill, realizes he showed his face, kills the bartender."

"I hear doubt in that, John."

"The pattern of killing prostitutes was broken when An-- nette Camden, a middle-class woman, was killed in a nice neighborhood."

"But why would he come back to Whitechapel unless he planned to resume his murders down here?"

"Two possibilities. Perhaps to throw us off, to direct our attention toward Whitechapel again."

"While he plans another killing somewhere else?"

"Yes. On September twenty-ninth. But he won't succeed if he's trying to outsmart us on that." He explained the plan for doubled patrols Inspector Warren had agreed to for several days before and after the twenty-ninth.

"And the other possibility?"

"That this killing was done by someone other than the slasher. The pattern's different. The victim's a man. It's a stabbing. In fact, it's a lot like the attack on Chief Inspector Howard. In any event, the killing just doesn't fit the Ripper's pattern. I'm thinking—maybe it was Baldrik."

"Baldrik. But then we'd have two killers at large?"

"It's either that, or one person who reserves his rage and mania for when he murders and savages women, and when he goes after men he does it in a very ordinary way, just to get the job done."

"Then all we can do is wait?"

Darnell remembered Penny saying the same thing that morning. She and O'Reilly had the same concern. Other possible deaths.

As they reached his car he said, "We have to wait, yes, and for two more weeks. But meanwhile we must do all we can, study our killer, remember his pattern of seeming to copy the Ripper, and then double the patrols to try to stop him from murdering again. Whoever it is, whether it's Baldrik or some other copycat killer, he's devious and dangerous. This isn't over yet."

Chapter Fifteen

Friday, September 28

During the two weeks following his talks with Darnell, Inspector Warren showed a new diligence in gearing up for the special efforts leading up to the critical dates of September 29 and 30. Not convinced of the need for the patrols, but afraid of being accused of mishandling the cases as his father had been with the Ripper, he bent to the task. He argued the matter with Chief Superintendent Treadwell until his superior gave in and authorized the added expense.

Chief Inspector Howard, by telephone from his home, endorsed the plans and grudgingly modified his opinion of Inspector Warren upward. He also told Warren he itched to get back into the action of the case.

"Need any help, John?" Howard asked Darnell on the phone later that morning. "I could come in, help coordinate things."

"You coordinate your recuperation," Darnell said.

Howard cleared his throat. "I may go back on duty."

"What? Your doctors said—"

"Doctors be hanged! I think I know what's good for me." He paused and added, "It's two more years until my retirement day."

"But not on this case, Bruce. Not now. There's too much danger to your heart. You can't take such a burden on yet."

After more grumbling, Howard hung up, having secured a promise to be kept informed frequently by telephone.

Elsewhere in London, except for some awareness of added evening patrols, life in the city continued apace on its various levels of art and commerce, with no new gory killings, and a growing feeling that the crimes had run their course.

His Majesty's Theatre exemplified that continuation of life and business as usual. In three weeks, the theater would present a revival of *Pygmalion*, which had been first performed in London before the war, in April 1914. George Bernard Shaw felt it was time for that renewal, and he and Kathleen Eden, his personal selection to become the female star of the play and a woman he admired greatly, rehearsed the Eliza Doolittle role at the theater.

"Come, come, Kathleen," he called up to the stage from his first-row seat next to the titular director of the play. "You can get more feeling into that line. Speak it as I wrote it."

"And how is that, my dear Bernard?"

"Like this." He stood and projected his voice in a direct, unaffected, and sincere manner: *"Not bloody likely!"* He went on, combing his fingers through his bristly gray beard. "You see, it's not done with deliberateness, but with naturalness. Under that artificial layer of language which her teacher has phonetically induced, giving Eliza an aura of breeding, she is still the same little guttersnipe—excuse that expression. So saying 'bloody' is not a facade she puts on, and it's not merely part of the new small talk catching on, as others interpret it to be. It's merely her natural self coming through naturally."

Kathleen Eden smiled and gave Shaw a slight bow, a nod of the head. "All right, Bernard. Thank you. I'll remember. Natural, simple, unaffected."

"Exactly."

"Not bloody likely!" she said, and laughed. "I know, I know. Now you'll say, take it seriously. But you know I take your words seriously, Bernard. I always do, really I do."

After rehearsals ended, the night already dark but the weather pleasant enough, the two left the theater in Shaw's car. A driver performed chauffeur duties, as he had many other nights over the past few weeks. Shaw dropped Miss Eden off at her flat and the car continued on to his own flat.

Neither of them noticed the motorcar a short distance behind them that lingered, pulling to the side of the street for some moments, observing their good nights, watching the woman ascend the steps to the front door of her home.

* * *

In the St. James district of London, the flow of fashionable life, evidenced by the planning of an ornate wedding reception, occupied the thoughts and consumed the energies of Mrs. Lorraine Sheffield, a wealthy widow. News of the impending marriage of her daughter had filled many columns of space in the *Times,* not only on the society pages but, due to her prominence, occasionally even in the national news pages of the paper.

Sandy MacDougall, whose wide-ranging *Times* duties took him from political affairs to crime to Darnell's investigations of apparent paranormal mysteries, felt let down by this domestic assignment. A wedding reception was something he felt he had a right to graduate from after his years and depth of service.

"It's not just any wedding reception," his editor urged. "Even some royalty may attend. And we'll have others taking the photos, discussing what the women wear, all of that."

"My point exactly, Harold. Why do you need me on it?"

Harold Keefer stared at him. "For one thing, news has dried up. The war, of course. But for you? You're not a war reporter. Must earn your keep, Sandy. And it's important that we have a senior person there with a steady view of the big scene." He stopped, as if awaiting a further argument, then added, "Remember, the girl's marrying our publisher's son. The colonel wants you there. You should be pleased with that."

MacDougall saw he'd lost the cause. "The colonel's son. I understand now. But you know about those constable patrols. If anything else breaks, another murder. . . ?"

Harold Keefer waved a hand. "You'll go on it at once."

It all ran through MacDougall's mind as he spoke to Lorraine Sheffield that afternoon, sipping tea politely in the garden room of her home. He'd met her daughter and the daughter's fiancé, a fresh-faced young man whom he'd seen at the *Times* in the company of his publisher father. MacDougall had given them the utmost respect and courtesy, despite his residual feelings of being put upon by his boss on a matter he considered beneath his talents.

"And Mrs. Sheffield," he continued his interview, "I imagine you're overwhelmed with last-minute wedding questions and problems."

"Oh, my, yes," she said, glancing at the grandfather clock on the far wall. "So much to do, going here and there. Last night I was out until all hours. Mind you, I love it."

He did his best to carry on the talk and brought enough back to the *Times* for an article his publisher would approve.

Mrs. Sheffield met with her staff and planned her errands for that afternoon and early evening, the last-minute collection of party gifts and favors, the little things that would make her daughter's wedding perfect. She bustled about, smiling and busy.

As Friday afternoon wore on and approached dusk, the man parked on a side street near the St. James home, observing neighborhood vehicles come and go, was relatively unnoticed. He sat reading a newspaper and gave every appearance of waiting for someone. He did wait. To see if Mrs. Sheffield would again leave her house that night, as she had done often the past week.

This was not the night, of course, not *his* night, he knew that. But he must establish patterns he could use for his purposes.

When her man drove her off at between four and five p.m., the observer put his car in gear and followed. Her sojourns displayed similarities each afternoon and early evening—gift shops, a hairdresser, a bakery.

Her driver dropped her at certain spots, she pursued nearby ventures on foot, and then from a block or two away returned to the car, often by an unplanned, circuitous route. For his needs, that would be perfect. If she followed a similar pattern the next night, he would be ready. The other situation, however, would require more than a bit of luck or happenstance for things to work as well. Timing, he knew, would make the difference between success and failure in each case. And to keep to his plan, it must all be done the next night. September 29.

Chapter Sixteen

Saturday, September 29

Although John Darnell had fixed his fears on the specific night of September 29, the best additional protections he'd accomplished with Inspector Warren were the enlarged patrols of constables for the twenty-seventh through the thirtieth. Warren refused to pinpoint the twenty-ninth, to avoid raising a panic in the city through articles that would find their way into the *Times*.

The night, perhaps appropriately, offered a full moon, as had been promised by the almanac, but the moon could not be seen through the opaque fog which settled down over London that evening. Ten feet ahead, pedestrians could see others approaching, but beyond that existed merely a thick, gray murkiness. Motorists crept along on the street at a pedestrian's pace. Darnell considered the diminishment of visibility another adverse factor for the already difficult night.

The lack of focus as to locations of the possible murders was "maddening," as he put it to Chief Inspector Howard, in describing the preparations. He added, "If we knew where to station the patrols, if we could only be sure whatever happens would be in Whitechapel, maybe we could prevent the killings."

"You sound very convinced they will happen, John. What if you're wrong?"

"Bruce, I'm anxious to be wrong. But we can't dismiss out of hand the parallels of these murders to the Ripper's, even if not they're not exact." He paused. "The killer will be out on the streets of London somewhere tonight, and I will be, too. I don't know where yet, but I just can't stay home and wait."

"Then watch yourself."

*   *   *

The weather did not deter Londoners from completing their business of the day. At almost six p.m., Lorraine Sheffield's car left her home, her driver creeping along in the fog toward her destination, a dressmaker who had agreed to receive her that evening for a last fitting for her own dress, which she had neglected in the rush of other duties. When he dropped her at the shop, she told her driver, "I'll be here for at least an hour and a half, Albert. Go relax somewhere, and just be here then."

As dressmakers go, this one showed more efficiency than Mrs. Sheffield expected, and the work was done in exactly one hour.

"I'll have the dress picked up at eleven tomorrow morning," she said, and stepped out onto the sidewalk. She fully expected to see Albert and the car nearby, as he was usually early, but the thick fog prevented an easy inspection of the street. She walked a half block in one direction and, not finding her car, walked back in the other direction past the shop, expecting to see the car any moment. She shivered from the dampness of the air.

As she turned to retrace her steps to the shop, realizing she might have to wait there another half hour, a rough hand gripped her over her mouth, stifling any possibility of a scream. She felt herself being jerked into the alleyway, far enough into it that she could not be seen from the street in the fog.

In seconds, a swift, vicious, left-to-right slash of her neck, followed by another, almost severed her head. The attacker allowed the body to slump to the ground, then began his ghoulish work of mutilation. The entire matter took only a few minutes, and he exited at the other end of the alley. He turned up his blood-stained collar and buttoned it, stuffed bloody hands into his pockets and shuffled down the street, his head inclined low, but alert for any passerby.

None passed the man, and when he reached his motorcar, he stepped into it quickly. In minutes the car was taking him away from the area unseen by any eyes in the past half hour except Lorraine Sheffield's, which he'd now rendered forever sightless.

Three blocks down the street two constables walked

slowly on their appointed rounds. They gave no notice to the passing car.

John Darnell had elected to walk the streets of Whitechapel again with Burt Fenham. The pattern of the first two killings was not consistent with any further murders necessarily occurring in the East End, but the killing of the bartender Fitch, who had served an inquisitive stranger at The Three Hares, offered the only clear recent lead. His stomach told him that it was a false trail, but he had no better choice.

The night could not have been worse for such a search, with the heavy fog. The indications of where the murders would occur or whether they would in fact occur at all were equally murky. He could imagine already Inspector Warren's sly gibes the next day if the night passed uneventfully, yet he hoped nothing would happen. Better he be proved wrong than two additional grisly crimes occur. On that point, he was certain it would be two, if any at all.

Considering the obsessiveness of the first two killings, either the Ripper's pattern would be followed with two killings this night or there would be none at all, no pattern, and nothing but Darnell's own imaginings to mark the date. He continued his march through the fog, staring into alleyways, glaring at every passerby, filled with frustration and doubt, hoping that this time he truly was wrong, and that two women would not die that night.

With opening night of the *Pygmalion* revival exactly three weeks away, Kathleen Eden's attitude toward rehearsals stiffened. She must get the nuances of the words right to satisfy Shaw's temperamental perfectionism. She stayed on after he left that night to read through all her lines and hear them resound in the empty theater. She had brought her own car, the one her father bought two years ago and in which he had become totally disabled in that freak accident.

At twenty-five, her father having been her only family since her mother died giving her birth, and he now unable to provide for their needs, Kathleen had suddenly found herself responsible for both of them. She took the car in for repairs and then learned to drive it. And she began a stage career upon landing a part in a successful play the year before.

Then the letter of congratulation came from George Bernard Shaw. She knew a leading role in a Shaw play would give her a significant boost. It could make her a star. She smiled now, thinking of the many letters Shaw had since written her, enticing her to take the part. Imagine, someone like him, enticing her! But she knew of his reputation for fanciful romances confined to the pages of archly amorous letters.

At nine o'clock she wearied of the rehearsing. After completing her examination of every line, every word of her part, she felt satisfied that she could, in turn, now satisfy Shaw. She said good night to the watchman and left the theater.

Surprised at the heavy fog as she stepped outside, Kathleen turned up the collar of her light coat and fumbled in her pocket for the car keys. Her car was parked around the corner on a side street just past an alley. She never made it to her car. The top hat and dark cape would have alerted a constable to the danger, but Kathleen Eden knew nothing of that and, in fact, saw nothing of the attacker in the fog until too late.

At the end, Kathleen's mind concentrated on Eliza Doolittle. Her role was her last thought just before the man stepped out of the alleyway, pressed his hand irresistibly over her mouth, and dragged her into the fog-shrouded narrow passage.

His knife slashed her neck twice, viciously, in practiced fashion. Kathleen Eden collapsed into a heap on the ground, a savaged and already lifeless body, but one that would face further redundant perpetrations of unspeakable atrocities.

The fog continued through the night. "A real pea-souper," Burt Fenham said to Darnell. Their patrol revealed nothing out of the ordinary, and Darnell was anxious to hear other results.

Just before nine p.m., a constable ran up to the two of them, breathless, calling, "Professor, Professor."

"What is it, Constable?"

"I was callin' in, sir, to report, and they told me to find you and ask you to call Inspector Warren right away."

Constable Fenham took Darnell to the nearest pay phone box. After several anxious minutes of making connections, he reached the Inspector, who spoke in a voice carrying a mixture of defeat, regret, and horror. "They've found another victim, Professor, a woman. Same modus operandi. I'm on my way to the crime scene."

Darnell's pulse pounded. "Tell me where to meet you."

Darnell felt the murder scene reprised that of Poppy Nellwyn's outdoor alley killing, yet had the more horrific aspects of Annette Camden's death. Each one seemed worse. The woman's body lay in a pool of blood, her dress and underclothes thrown up to her shoulders. The neck was cut to the bone, almost severed. The abdomen had been ripped open and the intestines of the woman thrown over her right shoulder.

"For the love of God, Darnell," Inspector Warren groaned, "what kind of monster are we dealing with here?"

"The same kind your father dealt with in 1888. A maniac, with an obsession for mutilation."

"When this gets out, there'll be hell to pay. Do you know who she is?" Inspector Warren stared at Darnell as if holding back a horrible secret he was afraid to put into words.

"I have no idea. She's—well, rather unrecognizable, in any case."

"It's Mrs. Lorraine Sheffield, or *was* her. Her daughter is to marry the son of the publisher of the *Times*."

"I've read of that. High-society wedding."

"When MacDougall gets hold of this story, I'll be crucified."

"You did what you could. It was an impossible task to prevent this."

"They'll say I should have predicted it, warned the city."

Darnell shook off the words. "Let's talk about the crime. What do we know about it? Who discovered the body? What time? Let's get at the facts, Inspector."

Warren recounted what he had heard from the local constables and Lorraine Sheffield's driver. The driver had returned at twenty past seven and waited patiently in his car for over a half hour, thinking the work was taking longer than planned.

Finally, he entered the shop of the dressmaker. He was

shocked to learn the wife of his employer had left at seven, and it was then already after eight. He ran out of the shop and stumbled into two constables who were patrolling.

After hearing the man's explanation of his desperate worries, the three of them searched the block in the fog in both directions until one of the officers called out to the others, "I've found her."

When the others joined him in the alley and saw the remains of the woman, the constable in charge said, "You two say here, and I'll call it in to the Yard."

Warren said, "That's it. They called me. I called you, and here we are."

"This was planned," Darnell said. "I'm sure of it. It's the same killer. It all fits."

"You mean the mutilation?"

"It's the initials, man! *Liz Stride* was Jack the Ripper's third victim. And now it's Lorraine Sheffield. *L.S.*" He looked down grimly at the savaged body. "Ironically, she was killed because of her name, her initials." A thought came, and he looked at Warren and added, "And simply because the pending wedding of her daughter had been followed for weeks in the *Times*. The killer saw that her initials in the articles fit his gruesome plan, and she became his next victim."

Warren groaned. "My God. You were right all along."

"There's something else, Inspector. With this new evidence that the pattern continues, we can expect a report of another mutilation murder before morning. Copying what the Ripper did, the killer will want this the way he did it, with two killings."

After Warren and his men had examined the scene thoroughly and the body had been taken to the Yard's morgue, he and Darnell stood facing each other on the street at midnight.

"A killing in Kensington," Warren muttered, almost to himself. "What next? Where can we look? It's impossible."

"Just keep in touch with your men from the Yard. I'll be at my home if you need me. We can only hope."

"Hope? Hope what?"

"That he's unable to complete his plan. That your police presence scares him off in some other area. And that the second murder hasn't already taken place."

* * *

Thirty minutes later John Darnell, careful not to wake Penny, climbed into bed next to her. He lay awake for long minutes, staring at the ceiling, until he fell into a fitful sleep. His dreams of a wild, faceless man chasing a crying woman through the streets of London were shattered by a knocking on his bedroom door, and the urgent voice of Sung.

"Professor Darnell! Scotland Yard is on the phone."

Darnell glanced at a clock. Six a.m. Had they caught him? His mind raced as he bolted down the stairs.

"Your second victim," Warren's voice said. "We've found her. You'd better join me at the scene."

After Warren gave directions, Darnell slammed down the receiver and bounded up the stairs, quickly dressed, and said good-bye to the awakening Penny. As he drove toward the West End, he tried to block from his imagination the gory scene he expected to see. Soon enough for that. He wondered what unlucky woman had been caught up in the madness this time, and had also suffered a horrible, undeserved fate.

Reaching the scene, Darnell held back the bile in his throat with difficulty, thankful he had not had breakfast. The only redeeming feature of the deaths, this one included, was that they had been instantaneous. The two seven-inch slashes across the neck had severed the flesh to the bone, including the vocal chords and jugular. With the immediacy of the death, lack of outcry, and under cover of the fog, the killer evidently had not feared being apprehended, and his precise, grisly work seemed to have been done unhurriedly.

The body was not visible from the street where it lay, even at this hour with the fog still present, and Darnell had to walk far into the alley to see the carnage.

Again, the abdomen had been subject to severe slashing, the intestines thrown over the right shoulder. But this time there was great disfigurement of the face. The right earlobe had been cut through at an angle, the tip of the nose was detached, the skin was split from the nose to the upper lip, and a large cut had been made below the lower lip.

Darnell recalled the file description of the murder and mutilation of Kate Eddowes, also found in the early hours of September 30. The savaging was virtually identical, he realized, matching that of the Eddowes body, but he felt no surprise.

He looked into the weary and expectant eyes of Inspector Warren, who clearly wanted answers, and said, gloom in his voice, "I expect when you do your autopsy, you'll discover that the left kidney and the woman's womb have been removed."

The Inspector nodded. "Like Kate Eddowes. I know the records."

"Her initials have to be *K.E.*," Darnell said.

"They are. She's Kathleen Eden. An actress. Her purse was not disturbed, and we found identification in it."

Darnell sighed, as he and Warren walked toward the street, allowing Warren's men to do what they had to do. "Age is not one of the killer's criteria. She's quite young. Lorraine Sheffield was in her fifties."

Warren grimaced. "There's something else. You may remember this from reviewing the files." When they reached the end of the alleyway, he pointed to the wall. "The words, the same ones." Scratched on the wall with white chalk were the words: *"The Juwes are the men that will not be blamed for nothing."*

"Yes, the same. But they have no special meaning this time. Whatever message the Ripper or whoever wrote it intended in 1888, this writing is only a copy, to fulfill the killer's obsession for exactitude."

"He's a maniac, and he's killing me, too." Warren looked down at the blood-spotted felt spats over his dress shoes. "When will this madness end?"

Darnell knew Warren wanted an escape from his own destiny, which no one could give him. But one fact now stood out, and he spoke the words that might give Warren hope. "This killer can't resist carrying his insanity to the end, Inspector. But his next murder won't occur until November ninth. That allows five weeks to save an unsuspecting replica of the last Ripper victim—Mary Kelly. I'll do everything I can to help you save her."

Chapter Seventeen

They sat around the circular table—Chief Superintendent
Martin Treadwell, Inspector Warren, Chief Inspector Howard, Detectives Allan Blackwell and Dennis Gannet, Sergeant O'Reilly, and John Darnell. The Superintendent's
voice resounded off the walls of his large office.

"The Commissioner demands it. Demands that this killing stop." He glared at the others. "Does anyone here have
the smallest kernel of an idea of what can be done? Has
anyone here read the *Times* this morning?" He looked
from one to the other. "You have no appreciation of your
good fortune in not having to face Police Commissioner
Cliburn, as I must do. You'd wither at his glance, I'm sure."

Silence followed for what seemed minutes until Howard
cleared his throat. "I came in today, Chief Superintendent,
because I know this is critical. We all do."

"Your effort is admired, Chief."

"I came to make clear what Professor Darnell has been
proclaiming from the outset. This madman is copying Jack
the Ripper. Four deaths, so far. And if we do nothing about
it, he'll claim a fifth victim."

The Superintendent turned to Darnell. "I know you investigate the supernatural. That element seems to have left
this case. Real-life bloody murders now, no questions of
ghosts. But you've been studying the original Ripper case
and this one. We can't turn down help from any source."
He threw a pencil down on his desk. "I'll listen to your
views, Professor."

Darnell glanced at Inspector Warren, who nodded. He
turned to the Superintendent. "London has proved to be
at the mercy of this new killer, just as it was unable to find

Jack the Ripper in 1888. This time, the circumstances are even more difficult for Scotland Yard, since the killings have occurred in a wide strata of society and in widely separated areas of London, not just in Whitechapel."

"Nothing we don't know there." Treadwell scowled.

Darnell went on. "Right. And what we can predict must be based on the four deaths so far. This time, they weren't all in Whitechapel. That's a critical difference. But otherwise details of the murders closely mimic those of the Ripper's first four victims. They occurred on the same dates, the initials matched those of the Ripper's victims, and details of the mutilations were strikingly identical. Yesterday's postmortem of Kathleen Eden bears this out. The bizarre removal of the kidney and womb. We know there may be a wild card in this deck—Baldrik is still missing and has every potential for being our killer. It wouldn't be safe to rule him out."

Superintendent Treadwell rubbed his forehead. "Baldrik, yes. But you said something about predicting. What might that be?"

"First, in this copycat scenario, just as happened in 1888, someone will receive a letter signed Jack the Ripper."

"We've received one already, dated the twenty-fifth of September," Treadwell said.

Darnell bristled. "You've received one already? If you're holding back evidence, Superintendent, how do you expect me to help you?" He stood, stone-faced, eyes fixed upon Treadwell.

"Sit down, sit down, man. Here's the damned letter." Treadwell pulled out a single sheet and handed it to Darnell.

Darnell glanced at it. "There'll be another, dated today." In a cold voice he added, "I trust you'll share it with us?"

Treadwell smoothed back his already neat silver hair with hands trembling with nervous tremors. "You'll see it."

"There'll be others, some from crackpots. Keep them all. There were hundreds in 1888, as you know. If there is a genuine letter, we'll be able to identify it by its content. Only the killer knows the extent of his gruesome work." He paused. "And you can expect something else in the next week or two. A package."

"Oh, God!" Inspector Warren said. "The kidney!"

Darnell nodded, his face grim. "Whatever it is, preserve it for examination. We must be sure whether or not it's human, and see what it tells us."

"None of this may help us at all," Treadwell said.

"In one sense, you're right." Darnell held up the letter. "Letters and the vile package will prove the obsession of the killer, but may not help us find him. But let's look at my third prediction—that the killer will wait, now, until November ninth, the date the Ripper's fifth victim was found, before he kills again. That's gives us thirty-nine days."

"Thirty-nine days, to do what?" Treadwell challenged.

"I've jotted down things to do, if you don't mind . . ."

"Let's hear them," Warren said.

"All right. First, we need to treat these murders as individual events and investigate each one separately. The attack on Chief Inspector Howard, the bartender killing in Whitechapel—they were remarkably different from the killings of the women. Second—and this anomaly struck me last night—we have to examine why this new killer picked this odd period of time in which to do this, twenty-nine years after the original crimes. Third, we must find a way to intrigue the killer, entice him, and make him act in response to our bidding—not just wait for him to act."

"Makes sense, John," Chief Inspector Howard said. "We can't just sit on our hands."

"You'll need to use you best teams, none better to manage them than at this table. Thoroughly investigate each individual crime. The four women's murders, the bartender's murder, and the attack on Bruce. Look for connections, links among them."

Treadwell looked at Warren. "Aren't we doing all that?"

Warren said, "We can do more, with enough men."

"Detectives Blackwell and Gannet would reinvestigate the backgrounds of all the crimes and focus on Baldrik's likely movements. He could be one of our links. Sergeant O'Reilly and I will investigate the latest two murders, Sheffield and Eden."

"Our men have talked with them, but go ahead. You may stumble onto something." Treadwell looked at Warren.

Darnell went on. "Your men could look into Baldrik's

record again. What they find could help us decide whether Baldrik is involved and, in fact, whether he might even be the sole killer. Interview close members of the families and their staff and friends who may have information they don't realize is important. I want to look for something that will explain the relationship of these crimes to the first ones."

"Done," Treadwell said, with new vigor, and looked at Howard and Warren. The reliance on standard police techniques evidently gave him renewed confidence. "Anything else?"

Darnell mused aloud, in a thoughtful voice saying, "I'm also nagged by the thought that there has to be some connection in how these women were chosen to be killed. They have the same initials, yes—but many women in London have those identical initials. Why these particular women?"

Superintendent Treadwell stood. "Bruce, Nathaniel, you're in charge from the Yard's standpoint. Professor Darnell will stay in on this. Work together. Find out where a rat like Baldrik would hole up. Go door to door for witnesses. Look into garbage cans, if you have to. Bring me some news.

"You can all get busy now. I have to report to the Commissioner on this tomorrow afternoon. Believe me, you're lucky you don't have to do that. Give me something to tell him."

The Sheffield home reflected the gloom everyone there felt. A black wreath decorated the front door, and the butler's countenance was frozen and dark. He showed Darnell and O'Reilly into the sitting room, advising them that Mr. Sheffield would be down shortly to keep their appointment with him.

Darnell asked, "And is Miss Sheffield also available?"

"Yes, sir. She'll come in afterward. I've informed her."

"Thank you."

The butler left and Darnell and the Sergeant waited without speaking for several minutes. "Lovely home," O'Reilly said.

"But joyless now."

She nodded.

The door opened and a slim man, well over six feet, with thinning gray hair, entered the room. He stepped over to

Darnell as the two rose and offered his hand. He nodded at O'Reilly and said, "Please be seated again." He took a chair opposite the sofa they occupied.

Darnell began, "We're sorry—"

"Yes, I know, Professor, I know. I've already talked with the police, so please make it brief."

"We want to be sure we're not overlooking anything in our investigation to find your wife's killer."

"Then look for madmen."

Sergeant O'Reilly took up the questioning. "Do you know of anyone who had any special reason to kill her? Any enemies? Anyone following her? Any grudges against your daughter, who's about to be married? Any old suitors? Anything at all, sir?"

Darnell could see Harley Sheffield gave it due consideration out of deference to them, but the man answered shortly, "Nothing. Nothing at all. My wife is—she was—the gentlest of creatures. My daughter, Caroline, has been engaged to her young man for over a year. I'm afraid I can't help you."

"No strangers noticed in the neighborhood?" Darnell asked. "No one watching your house? You're sure?"

"Dammit, man! I'd tell you that." He lowered his eyes and brushed at them with his sleeve. "Sorry."

Sergeant O'Reilly said, "We need to speak with your daughter, too. And we'd like to interview the driver who took Mrs. Sheffield about, and your other staff."

"Of course. Whatever you need."

Ten minutes after Harley Sheffield left the room, his daughter entered. Darnell saw a gentle sophistication in the young blonde as she walked in, introduced herself, and took a seat. She waited patiently for their questions.

Sergeant O'Reilly opened the interview. "Your wedding had been planned for almost a year?"

"Yes. Bobbie—Robert and I—we were to be married today, after all the waiting and planning. But not now."

Darnell asked, "The, ah, death of your mother the night before the wedding? Is that just a coincidence? Do you see any connection between those events?"

"You mean, someone killing her to ruin the wedding? No. No one would do that. They'd have no reason. Everyone any of us knew supported the wedding."

O'Reilly asked, "No previous men friends? You had no rejected suitors who might be vengeful?"

"No. Before I met Robert, I'd been friends, close friends I'll say, with one other gentleman. But he's since married."

"And Mr. Trent? He knew of nothing?"

"I've spoken with Robert. He's totally mystified. You can speak with him, of course."

"Yes."

Darnell admired the courage and bearing of the young woman. He and O'Reilly exchanged a glance, she seeming to agree with his belief that they could learn nothing more. They concluded their questioning of the daughter. Then they spoke to Mrs. Sheffield's driver, Albert, who added nothing to what he had told the constables and Inspector Warren earlier.

"I saw nobody at the scene, guv'nor," he said. "I didn't see anybody following our car, but they might have. Somehow they found us at her dressmaker shop."

The other servants, after brief questioning, could give no help. Darnell and O'Reilly took their leave of the Sheffield home.

They drove next to the *Times* and talked with Robert Trent and his father, the publisher, Colonel Stanley Trent. They learned nothing to further their investigation but came away aware of the vitriolic anger the Colonel would vent in the *Times* and impressed with the man's dedication to helping find the killer. The younger man indicated he felt the wedding would go forward, but not until a decent interval had expired, perhaps early the following year.

"Well, that's it then," Darnell said, as he drove Sergeant O'Reilly back to Scotland Yard. "Phase one. Results, zero."

O'Reilly nodded. "Next . . . the Kathleen Eden case?"

"I'll meet you at the Yard at nine a.m. tomorrow. I'd like to see her family first."

"Yes, I would, too. It's only a father, in a wheelchair."

Darnell shook his head. "These poor families."

He dropped O'Reilly at the Yard and drove home, consumed with thoughts of the cases. After dinner, he told Penny he had work to do and closed the door of the sitting room behind him.

He poured himself a stiff amount of whiskey and took a

large swallow. He lit a pipe and sat contemplatively, staring at the calendar pages on the wall, August through November.

Struck by a thought, Darnell rummaged through bookshelves for almanacs and found one displaying what the book called "perpetual" year-by-year calendars. He flipped to 1888 and studied the year's calendar, then glanced at the large monthly calendar for 1917 he'd posted on the wall, looking for some kind of inspiration as he puffed. After some moments, he said aloud, "My God! The days and dates are the same in both years!"

He compared them again. Yes, in 1917 and 1888 the days and dates coincided exactly. "Well, I'll be damned." He checked the days and dates again—Friday, August 31, in both years; Saturday, September 8, both years; Saturday, September 29, and Sunday, September 30, both years. And the final killing, Friday, November 9, the same in both years. The killer wanted everything to be identical. Not just the dates. Even the days of the week.

He finished his drink and puffed on his pipe. What did it mean? Was it part of the obsession? A compulsion to have everything the same as the Ripper's killings? A stubborn willingness to wait until the calendars coincided? Realizing calendar day and date configurations would repeat as years advanced, Darnell again studied the yearly calendars for the entire period from 1888 to 1917 for identical patterns. He was surprised to find that calendars for the years 1894, 1900, and 1906 repeated exactly the day and date pattern of 1888, six years apart, not seven. Then he realized that leap years advanced the calendar an extra day.

But three years had the same patterns and the killer had waited, for some reason, until 1917. Why did the copycat not select 1894, 1900, or 1906 for his murders? Was he not old enough yet? Had his fury and rage not built up yet, or had some event that triggered all of this not yet occurred? Was he prevented from doing it by some external means? Or had the killer simply not thought of the diabolical day-date connection yet?

Darnell felt that when they caught the murderer they would learn why the killings occurred now, twenty-nine years later, in 1917. But he was already certain of one thing. The obsession with killing with such precision flowed from the rage of a sick and dangerous mind.

Chapter Eighteen

Darnell finished his morning coffee and prepared to leave for Scotland Yard. He had read a new *Times* article by Sandy MacDougall speculating that the killings could be committed by a copycat murderer imitating Jack the Ripper. Reading it, he suddenly realized that MacDougall had waited, as he promised, until the first of October to put out his speculative article as to the murderer. Darnell could understand his need to do it. The reporter had people badgering him, too, certainly from the top of his organization, especially now with the murder of the Sheffield woman, whose daughter was to marry the son of the publisher of the *Times,* Colonel Trent. Trent was wanting action.

The phone rang, and Darnell picked up the receiver.

"Professor Darnell?" The high-pitched, cultured voice carried a note of urgency evident even over the telephone.

"Yes. Who is it?"

"George Bernard Shaw. You may have heard of me."

"Of course." Darnell realized at once why the playwright was calling—the murder of the actress.

"Kathleen Eden was to appear in my play," Shaw said. "I'll come right to the point. I want to talk with you about her."

"Certainly. I'll bring Sergeant O'Reilly—"

"No. No police. Just you. And come now."

Darnell checked the clock. He'd have to call O'Reilly and postpone their meeting, but Shaw might help with the Eden case. "I'll do it," he said. "Tell me when and where."

"When? I said *now,* didn't I?" Shaw gave directions to his London flat in crisp syllables. "And don't be late," he added.

*   *   *

A manservant opened the door to Shaw's flat and bowed. "Mr. Shaw is expecting you, Professor. Follow me." He took Darnell back to a room looking out through glass doors and windows onto a plush green garden populated with flowering plants and ferns.

George Bernard Shaw rose from a wicker chair. "You're on time, Professor. A good sign. Sit, please."

They sat facing each other across a glass-topped table. Darnell declined Shaw's offer of tea or other refreshment.

Shaw put his fingertips together and peered over them at Darnell. "I'll get right to the point. I take quite personally this horrific killing of my star. Kathleen was an important part of my life. It's more than just the play. I'll put off the play's revival. I waited three years since the London opening for this revival, and I can wait three more if I have to. It's Kathleen. I had great plans for her. She was too remarkable a young woman to have her life cut short so viciously."

"I'm sure she was." Darnell had read of the playwright's propensity to form deep attachments with his female stars.

Staring at Darnell, Shaw struck a typical contemplative pose, fingers against his cheek, at the mouth, evoking the look of Rodin's *The Thinker*. His untrimmed gray beard jutted out in all directions. "I've read in the *Times* this morning some speculations reporters are making that there's a Jack the Ripper copycat. When the Ripper was at large in 1888, I took a strong interest in the case. I wrote letters to the *Star* under a pseudonym. Used initials—'J.C.' at first, standing for Jesus Christ. I'm afraid I was rather detached about it all then, calling the man an 'unfortunate murderer.'"

"You're not detached this time."

"No. Later, I used my own name, but I must admit one of my strongest feelings was resentment that it took killings of that vicious kind to raise any sentiment at all about the East End, which was a cesspool of poverty and crime."

"Dramatic events often precipitate reform." Darnell could relate to Shaw's experience. He'd fought hard, with others, in securing shipping reforms after his *Titanic* tragedy experience.

Shaw shook his head vigorously. "My point is, this time

it's different for me. Other things are involved. It's, well, personal." He paused, seeming to reminisce. "In '88, I thought at first Dr. Gull might have been involved in the murders."

"Why him?"

"Gull was cruel to animals. I thought he might have been cruel to women, too. I've always fought for women's rights. But I decided he was too old, and he'd suffered a stroke. I thought about all the suspects at that time. It wasn't the Sickerts, those artists. I knew them. And I'm convinced no member of royalty was involved. Prince Eddy! Hah!"

The playwright's words reminded Darnell of passages in the old Ripper files. "All right, Mr. Shaw, I understand your feelings. But how can you help us now? You want to help?"

Shaw nodded. "Absolutely. But first, a clarification. It's said you investigate paranormal events. There are rumors of a ghost of the Ripper. Do you believe in that sort of thing?"

Darnell's voice was firm. "I don't hold with spirits, sir. These crimes have moved well beyond the earlier supernatural rumors by street women in Whitechapel. They were convinced they experienced supernatural sightings. But we're looking at a flesh-and-blood maniac."

"Good! Some call me a radical, but I don't agree with that spiritualism pap, although my wife explores it, and my mother loved her Ouija board." He fixed his beady eyes under their bushy brows on Darnell. "Kathleen Eden was my next Ellen Terry. She could have starred in my plays for years. I can find a new star. But Kathleen was a sweet, intelligent woman. I can't replace her."

Darnell spoke as patiently as he could. "You said we'd come to the point. Tell me about Kathleen, that's a beginning."

Shaw sighed. "It's a matter of pluck. Her father was terribly injured in a motorcar accident. She always had a flair for acting, an instinct for it I might say, and did well in her first play last year. I wrote her, she tried out for the Eliza part, and the director and I agreed she was perfect for it."

"First her father, now her. A sad family story."

"Her father was a physician. Well recognized in recent years at the Royal Hospital. Did charity work in his earlier years. Can't practice now."

"Your plays have been, shall we say, controversial? Could resentment of your play have been a motive for killing Kathleen? To stop it?"

"Nonsense. Of course, some might be envious." He preened himself, brushing his beard with one hand. "But who could resent my play? *Pygmalion* is harmless. It's based on a Greek myth. Pygmalion was a mythical king, or sculptor. He falls in love with a statue. He prays to Aphrodite, the love goddess, and the statue comes to life as a beautiful woman, Galatea. A simple story. In my play, Henry Higgins breathes new life into Eliza by teaching her to speak proper English. It draws from the myth, but it's a bit of a Cinderella story, also, in its way."

"Sorry, I didn't see your play in 1914—rather busy just then. So, it concerned the transformation of a woman?"

"Yes, some use the word transmogrification."

Darnell drummed his fingers on the wooden chair arm. "I appreciate your interest, but I still don't know what you can do for us, Mr. Shaw."

"Perhaps I can motivate you. I want this madman brought to justice. I'll pay you a thousand pounds if you find Kathleen's killer. That's why I called you here."

"I've seen the bodies of these poor women, including Kathleen Eden's. I have my motivation. What I'm concerned with is that he'll kill again, rigidly following the Ripper's pattern. He'll take a fifth victim."

"Then you must stop him."

"I told Scotland Yard yesterday we can't just wait for this murderer to act again. We have to entice him out. I'm thinking about how to do that."

"You'd make him dance to your tune."

"Exactly. The Ripper's final victim was Mary Kelly, a prostitute, a more desperate example of womanhood than even your fictional guttersnipe, Eliza Doolittle."

Shaw snorted. "But this new murderer is killing society matrons and actresses now, not just prostitutes."

"After he killed one prostitute, he changed his approach. He looks only for women with the same initials as the Ripper's victims."

"You mean, exactly the same initials?"

"Yes. I believe now that he found them through articles in the *Times*."

"What kind of articles?"

"The second victim was a department store salesclerk. There had been a small article provided by Harrods. She was the best salesperson for the month. After that, the killer continued to read the papers, looking for reports of his crimes, no doubt, but also looking for potential victims, since that worked for him. In any case, the names of his next two targets, Lorraine Sheffield and Kathleen Eden, were prominent among the pages of the *Times*. The wedding news, in Mrs. Sheffield's case. And news of your play, for Kathleen. Initials—'L.S.' and 'K.E.' "

Shaw scowled. "Damn! Killed because of their initials. It's unbelievably cold and ironic."

"The *Times* publisher wants to do anything he can. And I have a friend there, a reporter. He wrote today's article. They may be able to help, and they have the power to reach people."

"You'll let me know what I can do?"

"I will. I'm beginning to get an idea today."

"Professor, my reward for the murderer's head stands. If you need more, just speak up, man. Whatever it takes. And come back again. I want to be involved." Shaw shook the hand of Darnell, who was impressed with the firm grip of the wiry older man, and Darnell promised to keep him informed.

As Darnell drove to Scotland Yard for his delayed meeting with Sergeant O'Reilly, he reviewed the elements of an idea as yet ill formed in his mind. It wasn't firm enough to tell the others, and would take more thought. But he was determined to find a way to make a plan work.

He thought back over his conversation with the playwright. He had at least one lead to follow up and a new idea. Their talk had given him a chance to speak his theories to a receptive audience, which stimulated his thinking. Of course, what more stimulating man was there in London than George Bernard Shaw?

Sergeant O'Reilly watched every step Darnell took as he approached her desk across the large room. "This delay has set my nerves on edge, John. Was it worth it?"

Darnell took a side chair next to her desk. "Sorry to be late, but I'm glad I saw him." He described the meeting.

"All right. We'll want to see Kathleen Eden's father today."

"I'm ahead of you on that. I've made three appointments. First, her father. Then the stage manager and watchman at the theater. And Kathleen Eden's fiancé."

Darnell's eyes widened. "She was to be married? Odd, Shaw didn't mention that."

"It was a secret. Her fiancé called me today—a Mr. Henry Broderick. He said she had kept it back not only from Shaw but most others, for some reason."

"When's the first appointment?"

"Noon. If we leave now, we can make it."

At the Eden residence, a solid brick house in a good neighborhood, they pulled up to the curb at almost noon and in moments stood at the door awaiting recognition of their knock. A white-coated, husky young man answered it. "I'm Andrew. Mr. Eden is expecting you in the study." He led them down the hall to double doors on his right, which he opened. "Please enter."

Darnell and O'Reilly walked slowly into the semi-dark room and over to a shadowy figure sitting in a wheelchair. Darnell saw that all the blinds and drapes were drawn, the only lighting in the room coming from a small lamp on a corner table. "Dr. Blayne Eden?"

The figure straightened. "Yes. But 'Kathleen's father' is the way I would put it. Please sit down."

They took seats across from him. Darnell peered at Eden's face, but with the lamp behind the man, his expression could not be discerned.

"We won't take much of your time, Dr. Eden," Sergeant O'Reilly said. "Professor Darnell and I want to ask just those questions that might help us in this case."

"To find the murderer? The beast who killed my daughter?"

"Yes. Some questions, if you please."

"Proceed. I can stand it. I have to."

"Our basic question is, do you know any reason, any at all, why Kathleen would have been singled out for this crime?"

The man's head came up and his eyes widened. "Why ask that? Wasn't it a random crime, a slashing by some insane person?"

"It would appear so, sir," O'Reilly said. "But we regard each death as an individual matter. Each victim separate."

"The *Times* said her initials were a factor."

Darnell said, "That's true. But there could be more to it."

The man seemed to give the matter thought. "Draw open those drapes," he said.

Darnell stepped over to the window and pulled the drawcords to open the drapes. Light flooded into the room through large windows.

"Kathleen liked this room this way, very light. I've sat here in the dark all morning, most of the past two days."

Darnell said, "We're terribly sorry about your daughter."

"No one can bring her back." His voice was thick and hoarse. "I know that. But it's like losing my wife again—I mean, losing the closest person to me in the world, for the second time. My wife died giving birth to Kathleen. Since then, well, I raised her. We were inseparable, until the accident. She took up acting seriously then. I saw her play last year. It was wonderful." He brushed his eyes with the sleeve of his dressing gown.

"You practiced medicine for many years." Darnell waited for the man to regain his composure.

"Many years. From the Royal Hospital until two years ago."

"Ever any problem with patients? Angry? Discontent with treatment, failure of operational technique? I have to ask it."

"You mean, someone out for revenge against me, and murdering Kathleen? No, nothing. I prided myself on that. Not that patients didn't die. They did. But it wasn't because of lack of skill. Some people just can't survive an operation because of the trauma to the body's organs."

The word "organs" struck a sharp chord in Darnell's mind regarding Kathleen Eden's attack, and he dropped that line of questioning. "I was told you did charity work. In earlier years."

"In all the years. More of it earlier, when I was getting started, but some even in my last year of practice. You have to give something back to the community, you know."

"Where did you do that work?"

"In lower-income areas. Servicing the poor. Treating injuries of sailors or longshoremen at the docks. As a clinic in the East End."

The East End! Darnell exchanged a glance with Sergeant O'Reilly. A connection. He asked his next question, knowing he knew the answer. "Whitechapel?"

Eden raised his eyebrows. "Yes, actually, among others. But that work began many years ago. Before my wife died. And ended years ago."

Darnell leaned forward, anxious. "Dr. Eden. You do know that the first woman was killed in August in Whitechapel?"

He wheeled his chair closer to Darnell. "Yes, but she was a prostitute. What are you trying to say?"

"We can't overlook the location of that first murder and the fact that you now give us, that you worked at one time in Whitechapel. It may bring a whole new perspective to this. We need to know whether your Whitechapel work connects in any way with what happened to Kathleen."

Eden frowned. "All right. I worked at a local clinic. I was a resident doctor. Other doctors helped, too. We had a nurse or two, and an orderly. Servicing the locals as best we could with the limited facilities. I began the work thirty years ago, did it off and on for twenty years, then gave it up."

"Is the clinic still there?"

Eden shook his head. "I don't know. It was there last time I was there, ten years ago. They don't tear down those old buildings. They let them fall down."

"The name of the clinic?"

"The Queen's Aide Clinic. A fancy name for an unimposing little place." His voice tightened. "Look here—I'd like to know what you're suggesting?"

"Nothing. We must follow all leads. Even the dead ends."

"I don't see what Whitechapel or that clinic has to do with my daughter. She's never set foot in either place."

"Our killer has shown no discrimination or selectivity in his choices as to types of victims. A prostitute, a salesclerk, a mother, and your daughter."

Eden seemed to wither and wheeled his chair about, showing them his back. As he wheeled away, he said, in a hoarse voice, "That's all I can take. Please go now."

They thanked him and found their way out to Darnell's car. A light mist was falling, and clouds blocked the sun's rays. "It's getting dark," Darnell said. "Looks like rain."

"Do you think it's too late to go to Whitechapel?"

"Let's find out whether the clinic still exists, and if it does, call the resident doctor, get an appointment. We'll go tomorrow. And hope this is not another dead end."

Chapter Nineteen

Darnell dropped Sergeant O'Reilly at Scotland Yard. Returning home, he found Penny waiting with a late lunch. "Wonderful!" he said, kissing her lightly. "I'm famished." They walked arm in arm into the dining room.

As soon as they took seats at the table, Sung came in with dishes on a large tray, saying, "It's still hot." He served the soup and left covered dishes containing chicken and vegetables on the table so they could serve themselves.

"Tell me everything!" Penny said. "*George Bernard Shaw.* I wish I'd been there."

Darnell nodded. "He's provocative for sure." He described his meeting with the playwright and, later, with Kathleen Eden's father. "But the remarkable thing is, I feel I really could be onto something at last. Two things that could help."

"You mean help you arrest a murderer after he kills again—or help you save a woman? That's a big difference, John. And in all London, how could you possibly find and identify her?"

"I know the killer reads the *Times,* looking for likely victims. The next woman would have the initials *M.K.,* for Mary Kelly." He paused to serve their dishes. "But I want to draw him out, not wait until November ninth for him to kill again."

"I hope you can, John. Each death becomes more horrible. And I read about what happened to Mary Kelly." She shuddered.

Inspector Nathaniel Warren sat in his study that evening after his quiet supper, a half-empty glass of scotch and water at hand, going over notes on the four cases.

Sergeant O'Reilly had reported to him on the interview of Dr. Eden and her research on the Queen's Aide Clinic. "We'll go there tomorrow," she had said. "Darnell and I."

Darnell, in fact, occupied Warren's mind just now. The man had been right about the two murders the same night of September twenty-ninth and thirtieth. Warren resented that accuracy, but knew he must use Darnell's abilities. His own career hung in the balance, and Chief Superintendent Treadwell had told him as much, privately, after the Monday meeting.

Warren also knew he'd hear from Treadwell the next day. He'd been unable to give Treadwell a good report before the Super's meeting with the Commissioner that afternoon.

He replenished his drink and took a generous sip from it. The telephone at his elbow rang jarringly, and he scooped up the receiver before it could ring again. "Warren here."

"Warren? Is it still Inspector Warren?" The gravelly voice of his father, Sir Charles, grated in his ear. "Or have you joined the ranks of unemployed ex-police?"

"Father. Are you all right? You only call when you have a problem."

"You have the problem—four murders. When I faced four murders in '88, I turned in my resignation one morning, and Mary Kelly's body was found that night. It's just like last time."

Warren's temples throbbed and his voice rose in anger. "It's not like last time, as you put it. Not at all. The crimes are different. The people are different types. It's a much harder case. And, no, I haven't resigned and, no, I haven't been discharged—although it sounds as if that wouldn't disappoint you in the least."

"Nathaniel. Calm down. Be calm, my boy."

Warren took a deep breath. "What do you want, then?"

"Want? I want to know what's going on. I want to help you if I can. I want to see you, and also this . . . this Professor Darnell I hear about."

Warren's anger subsided as he thought of his father's condition—seventy-seven, with that game leg, leaving his home seldom. Maybe he could use an outing. "Shall I send a car for you?"

"No, none of that. Bring Darnell here. And bring him tonight." He paused. "Tomorrow I might not feel up to it. I'm only in shape about every second day now."

Warren agreed, and called Darnell, who readily agreed to be picked up for the meeting. Although Warren's own visits with his father were very ordinary, he could tell from the Professor's voice he was excited about meeting the ex-Police Commissioner with firsthand knowledge of the Ripper murders.

"Seven o'clock," Warren said. "And be ready. My father's blood pressure goes up when people are late."

The light mist had turned into a continuing, drizzly rain. When Darnell saw through the sitting room window Warren's car pull up at exactly seven, he ran out to the car, collar turned up and hat turned down. "Let's go."

"It isn't far," Warren said. He turned the car around and headed back in the direction from which he had arrived. "You're probably curious why my father wants me to bring you to him."

"Yes."

Warren smiled. "I am, too. These days, at almost eighty, he's become more secretive. And he still likes to give orders. I'm one of the few people he can order about."

"I'm eager to meet him. I've read so much about Police Commissioner Sir Charles Warren, I've begun to think of him as a legend rather than a real person." Darnell paused. "What has he done all these years since he, ah, retired in 1888?"

"Retired! A euphemistic word, Professor. The Home Office gave him no choice about leaving. What has he done since? Fought in the Boer War. Unfortunately, he showed his irascibility and stubbornness there, too. But he helped with the Boy Scouts movement, a worthy cause."

He turned into side streets and wound his way through a residential neighborhood to a large, Victorian house, and parked the car at the curb. The two hurried up the walk in the rain to the front stoop, and Warren rapped on the door using the brass knocker in the shape of a lion's head. Shortly, a manservant opened the door, bowed slightly, and said, "He's expecting you."

When they entered the study and library to the right of

the door, Darnell felt a sense of stepping back thirty years in time. Photographs of Sir Charles Warren in the regalia of his official uniform adorned the walls. In one group picture he stood with a number of portly gentlemen obviously part of the Home Office at some type of ceremony being addressed by Queen Victoria. The study was steeped in events of the 1880s.

The white-haired, now paunchy man with a deeply lined face bore little resemblance to his thirty-year-old portrait except for the glinty, probing eyes. With the aid of his cane, Sir Charles Warren hobbled over to them.

"Nathaniel," he said perfunctorily, and then, "Welcome, Professor Darnell. Come, sit by the fire." He shook Darnell's hand, shifting his cane into his other hand during the process, then moved back toward the fireplace.

Sir Charles sat in what Darnell could see was the old man's regular seat, next to a side table on which rested a leather-covered album, a sherry bottle, and three glasses. Inspector Warren and he took other chairs across from the old man. "Pour the sherry, Nathaniel." He turned to Darnell, "Cigar, professor?"

"Thank you, Sir Charles, but I smoke only my pipe, usually when I'm studying a problem," Darnell said.

Inspector Warren filled three delicate glasses with sherry and handed them around. The three lifted them, almost in unison, to sip.

"These killings." Sir Charles shook his head. "They're just horrible. I can't believe they're happening. I thought I'd never see the likes of these again in my lifetime." He sipped his drink again.

Darnell waited, knowing more would come. Give him the floor; listen to the past. At some point, he knew Sir Charles would level some attack or complaint or suggestion. It was his nature.

"I failed in my job twenty-nine years ago," Sir Charles said. "Now, with four murders, things are at the same stage they were at when I left office. Professor, I hope you can give me some comfort on this. Am I to blame for these new killings by failing in the Ripper case? Why are there repeats of those grotesque killings and mutilations? How many more will die?"

Inspector Warren said, "Father, you shouldn't dwell on

these murders or get too involved. You know what your doctor said."

Sir Charles frowned at his son. "I'm merely asking the Professor for information. And my doctor's an old maid. I'm not ready to pull the grass over my head yet."

Darnell returned the former Commissioner's glinty stare. "I'll tell you what I know, sir, and what I believe. I can imagine how deeply you must feel after what you went through with the Ripper." He explained his rationale that the killer chose victims from the *Times* by their initials and dismissed the rumors about ghosts. "I've read the historical accounts of the first killings, and I know how difficult it was for you at that time. No, there's no reason for you to take blame in this. But I do have some questions, Sir Charles, if you don't mind."

"Of course, of course." He regarded Darnell intensely.

"The two murders on the same night—Liz Stride and Kate Eddowes—found not more than an hour or so apart. Do you think they were committed by the same man? I ask because we have the identical situation this time with Lorraine Sheffield and Kathleen Eden."

"I understand." Sir Charles pulled on his still bushy but now white mustache. "At that time, one man could have killed both. The method of killing was very similar, you know, the same identifying characteristics of the mutila- tions. The areas were not that far apart, maybe a half hour by foot. Yes, one man could have, then. As far as today's killings are concerned, you'll have to decide. I don't know the facts."

"The Ripper was, I take it, an opportunistic killer. He prowled the streets, found a likely victim, and killed her."

"I think that's correct. Not much planning, if that's what you mean. No thought of who they were. It just happened whenever he wanted to do it to whatever poor women were there."

Darnell nodded. "You see, that puts it in perspective for me. Our man now is, by necessity, a planner. He's obsessed with initials and days and dates. Everything has to be precise."

The old man peered at Darnell over his glasses. "And how does that relate to the Sheffield and Eden killings?"

"What you said brought home to me again the planning

aspects, the lack of opportunism of whoever is doing the killings now. He couldn't take a chance on finding the Sheffield woman outdoors at a particular time, killing her, then rushing over expecting to find Kathleen Eden also outside, conveniently awaiting her death. They might not both be available."

"And that means?" Inspector Warren asked, glancing at his father, who also gazed at Darnell.

"It means two men, to be sure the plan worked. One tracking Sheffield, finding a chance, killing her. The other tracking Eden the same way, watching for a chance when she was outdoors, exposed, able to be killed with impunity that same night."

Inspector Warren said, "One of them could be Baldrik."

Darnell nodded. "And the other, our slasher, our copycat. He thought for a moment. "The, ah, words, Sir Charles, that you erased. *The Juwes are the men that will not be blamed for nothing.'* Famous words. Their structure was peculiar. A double negative—*'not blamed for nothing.'* Possible bad spelling. What did you make of it, and why did you erase the words? They've reappeared now, with the Eden killing."

The expressive eyes of the older man showed pain. He took a deep breath, glanced at Warren, then faced Darnell. "The English, it would seem, was consistent with a man not skilled in its use. A double negative, yes. So the words *'will not be blamed for nothing'* could cancel out. They could have meant they *will* be, *should* be, blamed for *something.* Someone wanted them blamed. The spelling of the word *Juwes* troubled people. I'm convinced it had nothing to do with those old biblical stories, nothing to do with the Freemasons society, no conspiracy, as some thought. The Freemasons are a moral, God-fearing, law-abiding society. I'm a Mason. I think Juwes was just a misspelling of Jews."

"You took a lot on yourself to erase the words. They could have been considered evidence. Who did you think wrote them, and what motive did you assign to the writing?"

"I assumed the killer wrote those words. He was simply saying, *'Blame the Jews.'* " Sir Charles sat back and finished the sherry in his glass. "I couldn't let that message stand. It was too dangerous. There was too much antagonism in-

volving Jews who lived in that area at that time to allow
any more of it. One suspect was actually Jewish, but was
cleared. We could have had riots. And although I felt the
killer wrote it, even if it was only some vindictive person
who wrote the words on the wall, it would have fomented
agitation and hatred." He smiled. "Either way, I knew I
had to erase the words. And I'd do it again."

Darnell nodded. "One more thing. Did you have an opinion on who the Ripper was? I know there were many theories, several varying descriptions of him."

"Theories, yes. Everyone had one, but a Police Commissioner can't act based on a theory. There were no convincing witnesses. Some thought Sir William Gull, a doctor, had
something to do with it. He was an old man, almost as old
then as I am now. He'd experienced a stroke the year before. Two years afterward, he actually died of another
stroke. Another suspect, 'Leather Apron,' employed in the
butchering trade, had a good alibi, as it turned out. And
the theory that royalty was involved was absurd. I won't
even mention the name."

"So, in your mind, who did that leave?"

"There was a lot of speculation, but no evidence. I think
it was someone we never had on any list or suspected—
and, I might add, never caught. Some maniac, whose
twisted mind thrust him into those activities." He paused
for a deep breath. "I did what I could. I took bloodhounds
there to scout the area, hauled in known criminals. But you
can't do the impossible, although the Home Office seemed
to expect it. One thing. I don't believe it was a known
criminal or any kind of public figure. I just wish I could
have got my hands on him."

Darnell could see revived at that moment the stubborn,
fighting spirit that had put the man at odds with his superiors so long ago. Sir Charles invited Darnell to return, and
urged him and his son to keep him informed.

Inspector Warren drove Darnell back to his flat and,
as they parted, said, "I appreciate your coming tonight.
I think it may be good for my father to exercise his mind
at this stage of his life. But did you learn something to
help us?"

"What your father said crystalized my thinking. He said
he thought the Ripper could have killed Stride and Ed-

dowes himself. This time I think there were two killers. Otherwise it was too chancy; it might not come off."

"So we have to find two of them."

"They're working together, so we may find them together. Your father ruled out the classic suspects, said he felt the killings were not done by a known criminal. That leaves an ordinary maniac—if there is such a thing. And he said the message on the wall was a red herring to lead people away from the real killer, maybe by the killer to offer misdirection, maybe by someone vindictive toward Jews."

"What do you think about Baldrik as part of this?"

"He must be in the picture, even if just as a partner. Whoever is doing the killing needed a partner for one of these last two murders. And the killer this time, as your father suggested likely for the Ripper, may be an almost invisible, ordinary man with a mania. A man who may get away, just as the Ripper did, unless we take a different course of action."

"Which would be?"

"I'm thinking about that. When my idea jells, I'll tell you."

Inspector Warren scowled. "Don't wait too long."

Chapter Twenty

Queen's Aide Clinic failed to live up to its imposing name. A clapboard-sided, three-room building on a narrow street in Whitechapel only a few doors down from the local pub, it lacked identification except for the sign above its door.

The physician in charge received Darnell and Sergeant O'Reilly in a back room which obviously served both as consulting office and a place to perform minor surgery. He introduced himself as Dr. Philip Thornwall and went on, "We never get visitors from outside this area. Only the occasional doctor whose conscience bothers him and who comes down to help out. I've been on this duty twelve years now, two days weekly, and the nurses and I do our best to keep several hundred unfortunates alive. We don't have much to give them, but we do our best." He looked from one to the other. "What can I do for you?"

"The murders—" Darnell began.

"You're here about the killing," Thornwall said. "The prostitute."

"Not that, really. Actually, it's the 1888 murders."

Dr. Thornwall shook his head. "Can't help you there. As I said, I've been coming here only twelve years. Twelve years too many."

Darnell said, "Up until ten years ago, Dr. Blayne Eden assisted here."

Recognition showed in the doctor's eyes. "Oh, yes, Blayne. Our service did overlap for a year or two. He came only once a week, as I recall, and another doctor the other two days."

"Do you remember anything unusual about his service

or his patients? Anyone who might have had an enmity toward him?"

Dr. Thornwall shook his head. "It was ten years ago. But no, except I will say that any of our patients can be hard to deal with. They haven't had training in the best social skills. A man threatened to kill me just last week after I pulled his abscessed tooth."

Darnell looked about the room. "Any old records here?"

"How old?"

"1888."

The doctor smiled. "Such as they might be, they'd be at central storage at the Royal Hospital. We have patients' files for the past year or two, as long as they keep coming back. After that we figure they've moved on. Or passed on."

"I understand. And the two nurses?" He gestured toward the front room of the clinic. "Would they remember anything?"

"Daisy might. She's been helping out here forever. She told me this would be her last year, after thirty of them."

"Would you mind asking her in for a minute?"

Thornwall nodded, stepped to the door, and summoned Nurse Daisy into the back room. "Take a seat, Daisy. These officials have some questions for you."

Darnell studied the frail form of the nurse and felt she might be able to use a bit of medical help herself. He nodded at O'Reilly to question the woman.

O'Reilly smiled at the older woman. "You'll retire soon?"

"Yes, ma'am. To my daughter's farm. And about time."

"The doctor said you began working here thirty years ago."

"That's right. 1887. Exactly thirty."

"Then you remember Dr. Eden?"

"Oh, yes, ma'am. Very good doctor, professional, as they say. He doctored here, off and on, for years. Quite handsome he was, too, when he began. Like a Greek god. The locals admired him—the women did, I mean." She smiled. "I did, too. But he was married, of course."

"In the early days, those first years, Daisy," O'Reilly urged softly, "think back. Did the doctor experience any problems at the clinic? I mean, big problems, any dangerous cases, angry patients, threats, anyone who hated him?"

"Not exactly. But maybe you're thinkin' about the nurse who was killed? Pretty girl. She worked here for a while."

Darnell's eyes narrowed as the Sergeant glanced at him. He leaned forward and said, "Yes, tell us about her."

Nurse Daisy seemed to find inspiration for her memory in the ceiling She stared up at it as she told her story. "It was about a year after I started here—yes, in 1888, before the Ripper killin's began." She shuddered. "Fact is, she was slashed, too, poor girl. Killed on the street one night after leavin' the clinic late. Bloody awful—oh, excuse me, sir."

O'Reilly smiled. "And when was that?"

"As I say, before the Ripper began his killin's. Not long before, though. About, oh, July."

"The month before the first Ripper killing."

"Later, I heard they said she might have been one of them."

Darnell asked, "One of the Ripper murders?"

"Yes."

O'Reilly went on. "Do you remember anything else about the crime? Whether anyone knew why it happened, or anyone was accused of the murder? Whatever you know, Daisy, will help."

She shook her head. "Just her name, I'll never forget that. Whenever I see the flower, it reminds me of her. *Heather*, it was, ma'am. Heather Kane. Sweet little Heather."

Although Sergeant O'Reilly and Darnell asked a few other questions, nothing further could be elicited from either the nurse or the doctor. They thanked them and left the clinic.

Darnell did not realize until they stepped outside how stale the air had been inside the building. "Royal Hospital now?"

O'Reilly smiled. "You read minds, too. Yes, they might have information on that victim in the old files. The name helps a lot. I'll check the crime records at Scotland Yard later. But the clinic records, if they're at the hospital, may give more personal details."

"Two leads, then. Let's take the hospital first."

"Do you think the Ripper got her?"

Darnell said, "Maybe some dusty file will give us the answer to that."

*   *   *

The records clerk at the hospital, situated with his files in the service and storage area some would call a basement, one level below the first floor, reminded Darnell of Norman Pidgeon, file custodian at Scotland Yard. Going to gray, short, slender, eyeglassed, and quiet, yet pleased to have the rare company.

"Willard Inness, in charge of records here," he introduced himself. "And it's Sergeant O'Reilly, right? And Professor—your name, sir?"

"Darnell."

"My manager said you wanted to see some rather old files. Thirty years old?"

Sergeant O'Reilly said, "It's in connection with an ongoing investigation, and we'd appreciate your helping us with them."

"Pleased to."

"The Queen's Aide Clinic, 1887 and 1888. Files for nurses employed there."

Inness scratched his head. "That is a problem. We do keep clinic records. To be honest, we don't throw anything away down here. It's more trouble to sort and dispose of them than it is to just let everything pile up."

"Do you think you can find them?"

Inness gestured toward his desk and the two chairs next to it. "Take seats here, while I make a survey of the stacks. I'll be back as soon as I identify the area."

Darnell and O'Reilly sat at the desk. Several persons looking like medical personnel walked by carrying files either into or out of the area, using the staircase leading upstairs.

"What do you think we'll find in the files?" O'Reilly asked.

"Family references. Father, mother, husband, children. An address. There probably won't be much detail on the crime, but you'll see that at the Yard, if they have a file there on her."

She smiled. "I'll see our friend from the Norman conquest."

They talked for a few minutes as they waited. Darnell wondered how anything could be found so many years later in such a massive configuration of old files.

O'Reilly looked down the aisle. "Here he comes. It looks like he's found something."

Willard Inness approached his desk with an air of triumph. "Got them," he boasted. "Here's everything we have from 1885 to 1890 at the clinic. Pretty thin, not that much, but help yourself. You can use the table." He led them over to a table positioned under an overhead light fixture some distance down the room and deposited the files on it.

Darnell shook Inness's hand. "Great work. We'll try to make it quick. I admire your filing system."

Inness smiled broadly. "Take your time." He walked away back toward his desk.

Darnell said, "I'll take this stack, Sergeant, if you'll take that one so we can go through them faster."

"Miss Heather Kane," Sergeant O'Reilly said, looking at the files, "I hope you're in here."

The two bent over the folders, turning pages, slowly, scanning the words scrawled in ink on the forms. Darnell looked up at O'Reilly in a few minutes. "Not much here, is there? Record keeping wasn't a big issue then."

"I guess they were glad to get whatever help they could. Most of what I have here is notes on patients, not employees."

They continued to look through one folder after another. "Wait," Darnell said suddenly, "it looks like our Nurse Daisy, on this list of names of employees in 1888. Daisy Miller. Just her name, address, pay rate, date began work in 1887, last date worked. There must be another sheet of information on her."

They continued to review the files. More minutes passed, and Darnell wondered whether they'd find anything, or if they'd overlooked her records.

"Anything?" he asked, as he turned over his last folder.

"This is my last file, for 1888. Oh, just a minute." She held up a sheet of paper. "Here she is. Sparse. It says Heather Kane, age twenty-one, and—oh, it's a Mrs., not Miss. Her husband's name was Galvyn Kane. There's an address in the East End. Here, take a look."

Darnell studied it. "The last entry just says, 'Died, July 25, 1888.' No explanation. There's not much to go on."

"The Yard's files may tell us more."

He wrote down the two names and home address. "Well, so far, there's nothing mysterious here."

O'Reilly stacked the files neatly and sat staring at them. "She was so young."

"Yes." He drummed his fingers on the table.

"You expected more."

"After almost thirty years, I don't know." He sighed. "Well, we can go to this address, talk to neighbors."

"Do you think she's important, John?"

Darnell shrugged his shoulders. "It's a lead. Dr. Eden worked at the clinic when Heather Kane did. Daisy said there was talk Heather might have been a Ripper victim. In any case, she was murdered. And now Dr. Eden's daughter is murdered."

O'Reilly frowned. "A thirty-year-old connection? If the deaths had been a week or a month or a year apart, you might suspect there was some kind of vendetta against the clinic. Somebody killing its employees, or relatives of employees. But thirty years? It could be just coincidence."

"I know." Darnell stood and carried the files back to Willard Inness. "We're finished, Mr. Inness, and thank you much." He and O'Reilly said good-bye and complimented him on his record-keeping again. Inness beamed.

They soon stepped out into the street and walked to Darnell's car. He dropped her off at the Yard, with O'Reilly promising to search the old Yard files for details on Heather Kane's death and to call Darnell later.

"One more thing," Darnell said. "Check your files for murders reported on July twenty-fifth this year as well as 1888. See if any victim this year had the initials H.K. A possible repeat from 1888."

He drove home, breathing deeply of the cool air, feeling as if he had returned to the present after two trips to the dusty past. Sung served lunch and, afterward, Darnell adjourned to the sitting room to consult his book on the Ripper. He looked for references to murders in the months before August 31, 1888, when the constable found the body of Polly Nichols.

The entries in the book took a speculative tone. The author cited earlier killings, but distinguished them from the five killings traditionally attributed to the Ripper. Although the methods of killing included similarities, in that

they involved knives, they were not as vicious or as mutila-
tive as the Ripper's five. Darnell found no mention of
Heather Kane in the book. But an Emma Smith was mur-
dered on Easter Monday, April 3, 1888, and a Martha
Tabram stabbed repeatedly on August 7, which was a
Tuesday. Neither the Smith nor the Tabram killing oc-
curred on a weekend. And he knew Heather Kane died
July 25, which his wall calendar showed to be a
Wednesday.

The phone rang, and he picked it up, hearing, "Sergeant
O'Reilly here, Professor. I found the Heather Kane file."

"What's in it? Is it helpful?"

"The poor girl's throat was slashed. That's all. No other
mutilations. Not much investigation. They could not find
the husband. They left word for him at their lodgings, but
he never contacted the police. She was buried in a pauper's
grave. End of case. One interesting thing, though . . ."

"Namely?"

"She was about four months pregnant."

"Poor woman. What about the Kanes' lodgings?"

"The detective sent a constable there. It says here that
the husband couldn't be located."

"But their belongings?"

"I don't know, John. That's a dead end in this file."

"Any murders in London this year on July twenty-fifth?"

"Two murders. Two men. No women. No initials H.K."

Darnell said nothing for a moment.

"Are you there?" she asked.

"Yes. I'd like to go to the Kane address in the hospital
files, one last chance. I assume it was the same in your
files?"

"Yes."

"Then we'll go there tomorrow. I'll see you at the Yard,
say about nine."

"I can't see a connection."

"Nor I, Catherine. But remember, it's our only tie-in between one of our current victims and the murders in 1888."

Her tone changed suddenly, and her voice lowered, as if
she were afraid of being overheard. "When you come in
tomorrow, be prepared for a meeting with Inspector Warren first."

"What happened?"

"On Monday, at the big meeting here, you said a letter would come from our killer dated that day, October first."

"Yes?"

"Inspector Warren got a letter this afternoon. He told me it's also signed 'Jack the Ripper.' "

Chapter Twenty-one

Thursday, October 4

John Darnell walked into Scotland Yard, and although he saw Sergeant O'Reilly at her desk, he only raised his hand in greeting and went straight to Inspector Warren's office. He caught Warren's eye through the glass, and the Inspector beckoned him inside.

Closing the door behind him, Darnell said, "I hear you have a new letter."

Warren nodded. "I knew you'd want to see it. Here's the first one, which you saw a few days ago, and the new one I received yesterday. As you predicted, it's dated the first of October. Take a look at them."

Darnell sat and examined the two letters as they lay side by side on Warren's desk. "I'd like to study these. I have some knowledge in the area of handwriting."

"They're evidence, so they can't be taken out of the office. But use the office next to mine. It's available today. Give me your comments."

"One more thing. Could you have the actual Ripper letters brought up from the files? I'd like to compare the language and content."

"Those letters were reproduced in the press, so many people have seen them over the years. I presume you want to see if these letters show evidence that the writer tried to copy the Ripper letters."

Darnell nodded.

Warren reached into a drawer. "I've already retrieved them. These are the first three original Ripper letters. I've looked them over. You won't find much. But be careful with them—the paper's old. There's another bunch of questionable notes."

"I'll take care." Darnell took the letters and a notepad Warren supplied into the adjacent office, which was separated from Warren's by a floor-to-ceiling wall, the bottom half in wood, the top in glass. He took a seat at the desk and bent to his task. Although he seemed to feel Warren's gaze watching him, he ignored the feeling and concentrated on what he wanted to accomplish, to see how closely the new letters tracked the old.

On sheets of the notepad, Darnell copied verbatim the original Ripper letters—one dated September 25, 1888, and postmarked September 28, the second, a card, dated October 1; the third, as well as notes that discussed the delivery of the portion of a kidney, dated October 5.

Under certain letters and words on his copy of the letters he interlined his own comments and notations. Then he also copied and analyzed the two new letters, which carried almost the same dates and postmarks. One thing struck him immediately. While the superior tone of the two new letters sounded similar to that of the earlier letters, the style of writing was different.

The September 25 Ripper letter laughed at the police and their inquiries into "Leather Apron." The letter challenged, *"How can they catch me now?"* It was written in red ink, saying that was done to give it a look of actual blood—*"the proper red stuff"*—which the writer said he tried to use but couldn't because it congealed. The critical point of evidence seemed to be the promise, *"I shall clip the ladys ears off."* And it was the first letter to be signed, *"Jack the Ripper."* The letter passed through the hands of various persons at Scotland Yard and Whitehall, as well as messengers and newspaper reporters, and was printed in the *Times* October 3.

The second, shorter communication of October 1, 1888— a postcard, also in red ink—explained the double event. One he said, *"squealed a bit,"* and he couldn't finish her *"straight off,"* and there was no time to *"get ears."* The autopsy showed that Kate Eddow's right earlobe had been cut through. The time interval was such that details of the crime were known and published before the letter was posted. It was also signed, *"Jack the Ripper."*

The third letter, of October 5, threatened a *"treble event"* the next time, in language much more skilled. That event, three killings at once, of course, all knew did not occur, throwing that letter's validity into doubt, most deeming it a hoax and not written by the Ripper, although signed as such.

Another short card signed *"Jack the Ripper"* dated October 29 and sent to a vigilance committee member wrote in poor English about the kidney that had been sent by post with a card on October 16th. It was duly signed, but also questioned at the time as a possible hoax.

A number of other letters had been saved of the hundred or more received, but most appeared to be hoaxes, a popular pastime of some in England. He concentrated on the letters that looked most genuine.

Darnell studied the 1888 letters from the standpoint of content, structure, language, and handwriting, making extensive notes. Looking up, he noticed that Warren was staring at him, apparently watching him work. He nodded in acknowledgment and resumed his studies.

He took up the two 1917 letters—the first dated September 25 and the second, a postcard, dated October 1—and his verbatim copies. Each letter was written in red ink and signed *"Jack the Ripper."* The first letter heaped ridicule upon the police in braggadocious language. The second letter was short and seemed to imitate the style of some of the 1888 letters.

After another hour of studying the writing in the four letters, he bundled up his papers and glanced at Warren's office. The Inspector had left it. Darnell stepped out into the bay and saw that O'Reilly was at her desk. He walked over to her.

"My examination of these letters took longer than I thought. I want to see Warren, then we can go on to the Kane address."

"Fine. I'm caught up on reports. Here he comes." She gestured to Inspector Warren.

"You may as well come in when I speak on this." They stood together as Warren walked up to them. "I thought I'd bring Sergeant O'Reilly in and give you both my comments on the letters."

"Fine." Warren strode on to his office with the others following. Darnell could see the man was distracted, had something else on his mind. Probably his superiors raking him over hot coals.

When they were seated at a round table in Warren's office, door closed, Darnell launched into his review of the letters. "No two individuals write precisely alike. Let's take the 1888 letters first," he said. "These three, at least—I know there were many others—were not written by the same person."

Warren sniffed. "You know you're in opposition to what others said at the time, and what my father believed. But go on. Make your points. I'm listening."

"Many points. The first 1888 communication is a letter, the second a mere postcard. That shows a difference in attitude and style. The first letter consists of complete sentences, the second partial fragments. The first writer used ornate capitals for the first word of each sentence, while the writer of the card did not capitalize, and there were few complete sentences."

He went on. "Although the first used street language, the sentence structure and grammar were basically good except where obviously disguised. The writing in the first letter slanted considerably, and the ink content was light."

"Low on ink?" Warren smiled.

"The card showed no slant at all and carried more ink. Also the individual letters on the card were more separated, less connected, than those in the letter. The first letter was signed 'Yours truly,' while the second just stopped. The card seemed a poor copy of the handwriting of the first letter. And the third promised a 'treble event,' three killings the same day, which never occurred. It was invalidated, since that never happened."

"And your conclusion?"

"I think the letters were written by two different persons having a great time at the expense of Scotland Yard. Pulling the legs of the police, so to speak."

"Hoaxes."

"Exactly. Who loves a hoax more than the English?"

"And you suspect . . . ?"

"A thief or reporter wrote them, with the collusion of a constable needing a few quid on the side."

Warren scowled. "A constable. It's not impossible."

"One more thing. The writer was right-handed. The direction of the slashings on his victims shows the Ripper was left-handed."

"What about our new letters?"

"The dates are the same for the first two, and they're in red ink. But they clearly don't match the '88 communications as to style. No uneducated street humor. No exaggerated ignorance of grammar in them. They stand on their own. Serious letters from a mad, delusional mind."

"And the handwriting?"

"Look at the left slant." Darnell held out the letters toward Warren. "It shows that these are written by a left-handed person. They're both signed 'Jack the Ripper,' but he doesn't say 'Yours truly' or anything of the sort. And the size of letters and capitals, the looping, rounded strokes in place of the more angular, straight ones, the way the letters K and H are crossed, are different. There are many differences."

Warren said, "Well, if you're making the case that Jack the Ripper didn't write the new letters, I think that's quite obvious."

"No, that's not my conclusion. The point is simply that whoever wrote these new letters did not write the old hoax letters."

"You're saying our new killer did write the new letters?"

"Yes, partly to disown the other letters, which he rejects. And it's an element of his madness, a compulsion to do it."

"The first two letter dates were the same."

"Again, his compulsion. He wanted them to be the same. Listen to this year's September 25 letter . . ."

Inspector Warren,
    You police can't catch me. I have to laugh at your feeble efforts at trying. You think you know where to look. You don't. You think you know what I'm doing. You don't. But it gives me a laugh, so keep it up. I have my reasons, and, yes, I have a sharp knife and it will be working hard, punishing the guilty. Watch me.
    Jack the Ripper

Warren nodded. "To the point and short."

"Yes, and it clearly states an attitude," Darnell said. "A sense of extreme self-righteousness. The writer has a know-best attitude, a sense of being smarter than the police. It's in his psychological makeup. There are a few other clues in it as to what kind of man we're facing." He picked up the second letter. "I'll read this one, too."

Inspector Warren,
    They are happening, two more now. And more to be done. Guilty to be punished, as must be done for divine justice. Blood to be let. And you will never know, nor need to know, who I am.
    Jack the Ripper

Warren stared at Darnell. "If your analysis helps, then find him. Our men can't seem to do it, not yet."

Darnell said, "One thing is clear. He's following exactly the day and date pattern of the Ripper killings, and the initials of the victims are the same as those of the earlier victims. If we don't find him, we'll discover his next victim with initials of M.K. on the morning of November ninth."

Darnell drove toward the last address known to exist for Heather Kane, where she had lived with her husband twenty-nine years earlier. He expected to find little after all that time, but knew they had to follow the lead.

O'Reilly sat beside him, uniformed, lending official status to what they might do that day. After they were well on their way, she asked, "Does your teaching background in psychology help you understand the mental condition of the murderer? I wonder—could he have convinced himself he's actually Jack the Ripper, either the real one or a reincarnation?"

"In his mind, with his demons, of course, any delusion is possible. What we've seen so far is the outward manifestations of his madness, his rage toward women. And he's determined to repeat the crimes, copying them as closely as possible. But yes, he could believe he is the Ripper. Just as the three Whitechapel ladies may cling to their supernatural explanation—that it's the Ripper's ghost."

She smiled. "If I thought you felt they were right, I'd really worry." Then, after a moment, "John, the deaths of these four women. We hear all London is enraged by these new Ripper-type murders. But millions have died in the war—British, French, Russian, German. Thousands of men die every day, sometimes thousands in a single battle, millions in a year. Yet these four deaths cause havoc."

He nodded. "I know. The enormity of the war is so great, the immensity of millions of deaths so incomprehensible, it's hard to face, but it's at least numbing. Perhaps the human spirit rejects the magnitude of deaths as too mournful to face. It may take years for the hideousness of the war to cut through the numbness. People often only come to grips with the reality of death on a personal basis when one of their own, such as a son or a brother, is threatened with it, or dies."

"I know. My mother's illness teaches me that."

"When a few unfortunate women suffer this horrible manner of death, it brings our own humanity and mortality home more acutely. People can identify with these horrible crimes as they read about them in the *Times*. We all experience revulsion and hate for the unknown killer."

Sergeant O'Reilly frowned. "And for the women of London, there is fear, also. Any one of them could be next."

Soon they approached the neighborhood and turned into the street where Heather Kane had lived. Darnell pulled up in front of a building that bore the faded number indicated in her file. There was no evidence of current residents anywhere in the building.

"The place doesn't look occupied, or even livable," he said. Two front windows of the dilapidated two-story lodging house were covered with boards. Adjacent buildings looked little better.

"Let's try it." He walked to the door, which swung open at his touch. The interior was dark. He heard a scurrying of feet of animals along the floor as the light from the exterior slanted into the room. "Rats," he said.

He led the way into the building, along the ground floor and up a ramshackle stairway to the second floor. One step creaked. "Be careful, Sergeant. These boards aren't any too strong."

From the thickness of the dust and cobwebs, Darnell felt the building had been unused for years. What was it Dr. Eden had said? *They don't tear the buildings down. They let them fall down.*

After their inspection, revealing no evidence of anyone living there, they stepped back outside. Darnell said, "No sign of life on the entire street. We wouldn't learn anything asking questions door to door. But we passed a pub at the corner. Anyone not at some kind of job today would probably be there."

"Great," O'Reilly said with a smile. "I could use some of those delicious fried bangers they serve."

Darnell grimaced. "Don't even joke about that."

They wheeled the car about and drove back to the pub and parked. Darnell turned to O'Reilly. "Do you want to wait here?"

"Certainly not. I can take it."

They walked across the street, through the open doorway of the Fox and Crow, and up to the barkeep.

The man had already fixed his gaze on the two, and now he inclined his head toward them. He set down a glass he was polishing. "Well, Guv'nor, pleased to have you drop in." He smiled a snagtoothed grin. "Somethin' to wet your whistle, sir?"

"No, thanks." Darnell put a half crown on the bar. "We need some information."

The bartender picked up the coin and in time-honored tradition bit it with his teeth, then slipped it into a pocket. He said, "For this, I'll tell you my life story."

"No need for that. We're interested in Heather Kane and her husband. They lived here many years ago. On this street."

"How many years?"

"Say, thirty."

The bartender whistled softly. "Before my time."

"Who might know?"

He scratched his head. "Angus Wade might remember, or his friend, old Pitt." He gestured toward a table in a corner where two white-haired men sat. Their eyes, too, were fixed on Darnell and the Sergeant. The bartender went on, "If they don't know nothin' about 'em, nobody does. Them two's lived around here bloody forever."

Darnell put another coin on the bar. "Bring two more of whatever they're drinking over to them."

"That'll be ale." He turned and picked up glasses to fill as Darnell and O'Reilly walked to the table.

To the two men, Darnell said, "This is Sergeant O'Reilly of Scotland Yard. We're doing a bit of investigation. May we ask you some questions?"

The men looked up at the bartender as he approached with the large mugs of dark ale, and smiles brightened their faces.

"Coo!" one said. "Thank'ee, sir." The other nodded. They pulled their mugs closer to them, just behind the ones in front of them that were almost empty. The first man quickly drank the remains of his first glass, set it aside, and put both hands protectively around the new mug. The other did the same and said, "Ahh," wiping foam from his mouth with a sleeve.

Darnell spoke to the most likely one first, saying, "So you'll answer some questions for us?"

"Yes, sir. Question away."

"Heather Kane. Her husband, Galvyn Kane. Remember them?"

In a single movement, the heads of the two men turned to each other, and their gazes locked. The first looked back to Darnell. "Poor Heather. Me remember that? Could never forget it. Clinic nurse. They found her body not far from here."

"Did you see it?"

He shook his head vigorously. "No. I wouldn't go. but Pitt here . . ."

"You saw Heather's body, Mr. Pitt?"

Pitt scowled. "Wish I hadn't."

"She was stabbed," Darnell said.

"More like slashed," Pitt said. "Didn't see much. The constable held us back and hauled her body away quick on the cart."

"And her husband?"

Pitt looked at the other. "Sailor, wasn't he, Angus?"

"A sailor, yes. Cattle boat? Somethin' like that. He came back, they said, one night, took some things. Then vanished, he did. Never saw him much before the murder, either, come to think of it. Gone most of the time."

O'Reilly asked, "Did you know anyone else from the clinic?"

The men shook their heads in unison. "No, mum," Wade said. "There was another nurse, saw her once. And an orderly. Didn't know no names." They each took a large swallow of their ale.

Darnell looked at O'Reilly, who nodded. "Thank you, men. Enjoy your drinks."

They left the pub and soon Darnell's car was rattling down the cobblestone street and back toward Scotland Yard.

O'Reilly spoke after a bit. "He said 'slashed.' That's consistent."

"Your file on Heather Kane said the same?"

"No. It was skimpy. They might have held back on writing down the gruesome details. But Heather could have been one of the Ripper's first victims, an 'unofficial' one."

Darnell let her words stand without comment. She left the car at Scotland Yard with the remark, "I've got some reports to write. Let me know what you plan next. I'm wondering whether these leads are going nowhere, whether we're just at a dead end."

He shook his head. "We can't let it be that. Review everything we've done and heard, Sergeant. I have some ideas. I'm sure Inspector Warren is anxious for a breakthrough and he'll cooperate fully when the time comes. His career is at stake."

O'Reilly said, "Yes, and in another month, if you're right, another woman's life is, too."

Chapter Twenty-two

Friday, October 5

Sounding like giant boulders tumbling down a hill, thunder rumbled across the dark London sky. Rain came down in oversized drops, filling curbs and washing over sidewalks. In the late morning, while Penny attended to household routines, Darnell closeted himself by the fire in the sitting room, with sherry at hand. For a while, he reread sections of his volume on the Ripper murders; then he took out his notes from the Yard's files.

Sergeant O'Reilly had said she feared what she called "another dead end." And, although Darnell was attempting to fashion in his mind some semblance of a plan to end all this— a way of trying to avoid what he was sure would be the last, terrible death of another innocent woman—he could not yet see through the fog of the next few weeks. He pored over his notes and the history of Jack the Ripper's crimes.

Yes, no doubt. All official accounts set the murders by the Ripper at a count of five, even though other somewhat similar crimes—and there always were such—occurred about that time, earlier or later. They were ruled out as being too dissimilar and merely part of the frequent random killings in the area.

O'Reilly called mid-morning, saying, "Warren's fuming today. I suspect the Super's on his back. Maybe even the Police Commissioner."

"Wanting an immediate solution, I suppose."

"It's the newspapers getting to him. The *Times*—Mac-Dougall mostly—says Scotland Yard is stumbling round in the dark." She paused. "Any fresh ideas this morning?"

"No, but let's visit Chief Howard. I promised to keep him informed, and he's probably bored to tears at home."

He offered to pick her up at the Yard, and in an hour he pulled up in front at the appointed time. She ran out under an umbrella and jumped into the car. "I called the Chief," she said, "so he'll expect us."

Bruce Howard opened the door for them as they dashed up the steps to his cottage. "Come in. I've got the teakettle on." He led the way back into his small house. "About all I do anymore," he grumbled, "is drink tea and read the *Times*."

They settled into chairs in his sitting room. "My daughter decided I could manage on my own and went home two days ago. Now it's really like a morgue. I have to get back to the Yard."

O'Reilly said, "Remember your doctor's orders."

"Blast the doctor! It's my life."

Darnell nodded. "Exactly. And you've got to protect it. Pace yourself."

Howard stepped into the kitchen and returned shortly with tea and cups on a tray. "At least I can serve tea," he said. He poured the tea and sat back.

Darnell studied the Chief Inspector and was pleased to see color in the man's cheeks, even if it might just be from the pique of the moment. "I promised to fill you in with our results, such as they are." He described the visits to Shaw and Dr. Eden, and their trip to the clinic, and recapped his opinions on the letters he'd examined at the Yard.

"This is different than when the Ripper was at large," Chief Howard said, calmer, reminiscent. "After the double murders of Liz Stride and Kate Eddowes on September thirtieth, a feeling soon grew that the killings were over. But when the fifth body was found in November the city went wild again, thinking now there'd be more of them. Then they stopped. No one knew why."

"True enough," Darnell said, "but as you say, it's different now. I think one more death's predictable, based on the pattern so far, if we don't prevent it. Our murderer is copying the earlier killings, day by day, date by date, initials by initials. There'll be no variation, with his compulsion, otherwise there'd be no satisfaction for him. A man with this obsession would be crushed if his final murder were to occur on a different date. Yes, there'll be another killing the night of November eighth, or next morning. That's a month from now. It'll be a long month of frustration with much agony of waiting."

"I feel quite helpless, Chief," O'Reilly said.

Howard shook his head. "I know—but it's your *assignment,* Catherine, not your *problem.* That's Inspector Warren's. And knowing him, I imagine he's ready to blow up. He doesn't let off steam like a teapot. He stews and fumes over things until he loses his temper. When that happens, steer clear."

The telephone rang and Howard crossed the room to pick it up. They heard his end of the conversation, his expressions of surprise and disappointment. He returned with a glum face.

"Still no trace at all of Baldrik, and no more leads. I thought we'd have him in custody by now."

"Lying low," Darnell said. "I believe he was involved in at least one of the latest two murders—Sheffield's or Eden's."

"Why?"

"Simply because there were two killings that night, some distance apart, and it would have taken two men to commit them. You see, the movements of the women could not be totally predicted, and the choice of them as victims was not opportunistic—killing someone unlucky enough to be on the street, as the Ripper did. It was specifically planned to be these two women on this one night. If one man had tried to do both, he could not have been certain to find Sheffield conveniently out on the street when he wanted her, and the same for Eden. It took two men to follow these women to ensure they could both be killed that same night. Baldrik? He enjoys mutilations. He's capable of this kind of murder. He certainly could have done one of them. He has nothing to lose."

Howard nodded. "Awaiting execution."

"Yes, and I hope he can still be apprehended unless he's gone to ground like a fox, or to Italy, Greece, out of England."

Chief Howard frowned, looking at Sergeant O'Reilly. "Be cautious. He tried to kill me, I'm sure of that. And he could easily go after you." He turned to Darnell. "Have you considered that it might be Baldrik alone doing the killings?"

Darnell shook his head. "Considered and rejected. No, I don't think so. Yes, they called him the Mutilator. But the way this killer is obsessed with the names and initials of the victims, the days and the dates of the killings, all of that—it shows a more compulsive nature than Baldrik has. He kills when the fancy takes him. And there were two killers for these last two to occur the same night."

The Chief let them go after Darnell again promised to return with any news and to share his plans. As they drove in the rain back to Scotland Yard, Darnell and O'Reilly talked little, both seemingly suffering the same sense of frustration, waiting for another inevitable murder to happen on the old schedule of the Ripper.

At the Yard, as O'Reilly raised her umbrella and prepared to leave the car, Darnell said, "I just can't sit on my hands while the killer gloats. I'm developing a plan, Catherine, things you shouldn't know about yet. When I have it full in mind, I'll tell Howard and Warren, and then you."

She scowled. "You're leaving me out of it?"

"I'll tell you later. Meanwhile, do what Chief Howard cautioned. Be careful. Ubel Baldrik is at large. And he's just as dangerous as Jack the Ripper. He seems to be working with another vicious killer, and enjoying it. And he's no ghost."

After a quick lunch at home and a phone call to George Bernard Shaw, Darnell drove to the playwright's home in the still heavy rain. The dark skies matched his mood, but his mind was clear on his plan now. He'd see what Shaw thought of it.

By the fire in Shaw's study, Darnell sipped sherry the other provided. He took in the surroundings, walls of books, the oaken desk, mementoes of plays and travels Shaw kept in the room where he did his writings.

Shaw's eyes gleamed. "You have news? About Kathleen's killer?"

Darnell shook his head. "No, but I have an idea, and I need your opinion."

"Ask away, Professor."

"Your play—*Pygmalion*. When I was here, you described the change in the guttersnipe, Eliza, as a transformation.

She was schooled to fool high society into thinking she was one of them."

"Yes. By Henry Higgins."

"Could the opposite be done?"

"The opposite? Meaning, what?"

"Transform a woman of average culture into a prostitute. Only in looks and attitude, of course. Enough to deceive."

Shaw pressed the fingertips of one hand against those of the other. "Hmmm, I see. Yes, it could be done. But why?"

Darnell rose and paced back and forth for a moment. "This damned killer! I want to flush him out, make him follow *my* plan."

"I'm with you on that. Go on. Tell me how I can help."

Darnell sat across from Shaw again and leaned forward. "Here's my idea. The killer gets his victims' names from the *Times,* based on their initials. His next victim would have to have the initials M.K., for Mary Kelly, to satisfy him. He's compulsive, likes things to be just so for his gruesome work. If he saw the actual name Mary Kelly displayed in the newspaper prominently, he couldn't resist it for his last target."

"I see. And you want a woman to pose as a Mary Kelly type. You want her to be costumed as a prostitute, trained in the style of speech, so she can act as bait for him."

"An actress could do that. But only with your help."

Shaw stood, walking to the window, staring out at the rain. He turned. "No. I've lost one actress. I won't risk another."

Darnell frowned. "Not an actress, then. But let's say Scotland Yard provides a suitable woman. Will you costume her, train her how to act and speak? Make her into a Mary Kelly?"

Shaw nodded. "If the Yard sponsors it, I'll do it, if it will get Kathleen's murderer. But who would ask a woman to take that risk? What woman would do it? Her life would be at stake; she'd be taking a chance on a horrible death."

"The entire Scotland Yard force would stand ready to protect her." He paused. "I know one who'd volunteer, but I can't risk her, either. You're right about the danger. The Yard may help in that." He stood briskly. "Well, I must see my contact at the *Times.* One step at a time. I'll need his help, too, constructing a story."

"For the last act of this play," Shaw said.

"Yes. The killer's final act."

Darnell thanked Shaw and told him he would contact him as soon as the other pieces of his plan were put together. But thinking of it as he drove home, Darnell realized he needed an event before the eighth to focus the killer's attention on the bait.

At home, he called MacDougall, who readily agreed to visit him the next morning. He glanced at his calendar and saw on November 5 some words he had scrawled at some time in the past. Guy Fawkes Day. And suddenly his plan was beginning to take real form.

Chapter Twenty-three

Saturday, October 6

MacDougall arrived at ten a.m. and joined Darnell for coffee in the sitting room. He glanced at the calendars posted on the wall and looked quizzically at Darnell. "Eighteen eighty-eight?" He frowned. "Jack the Ripper, correct?" He studied the two calendars as Darnell sat quietly watching him. "My God! The days are the same as this year!"

"You've been reasonably patient, Sandy, considering that there have been two new murders since we last talked. Of course, you're critical of the Yard in your articles."

MacDougall shook his head. "Nothing personal in that. Just reflecting public opinion, that's all. We get letters, and we have to respond to them. There are a lot of bothered people out there. Angry, scared, and frustrated."

"That would describe everyone at the Yard as well."

MacDougall gestured at the calendars. "There's a story up there in those calendars. You wouldn't leave them for me to see unless you wanted to tell a story."

Darnell nodded. "I've got two stories, in fact. But they're in the strictest confidence, totally off the record. Understood?"

"I won't print anything against the public interest."

"Or endanger the Yard's investigations?"

"Agreed."

Satisfied, Darnell elaborated on the parallels between the days and dates of the Ripper murders and those occurring in the past two months. "The pattern is such that we can expect another killing on the eighth of November." He saw MacDougall's eyes widen. "Now, wait, Sandy. Don't start planning your next article. You can't panic the whole city based on my speculations. Inspector Warren would throw you in a cell and toss away the key."

"What do you expect from a reporter?"

"Your best, Sandy. That's why I'm telling you. I need your help to prevent the last killing and capture this maniac."

"I'm glad you realize he's a maniac. That's what they call him at the paper. But what help do you want?"

Darnell leaned toward the reporter. "Remember, this is in confidence. If this gets out, it could ruin everything."

"I've given my word," MacDougall grumbled. "Now talk."

"The killer selects his victims from the *Times*. He watches for names of women in the news with the same initials as the original Ripper victims. As I told you, the initials of the first four victims were the same as those of the Ripper's first four. Except for the first victim, Poppy Nellwyn—the prostitute with the bad luck of having Polly Nichols's initials—the other three were featured in articles in the *Times*."

"What are you leading up to?"

"I want to entice the killer to a woman with the initials of the fifth victim of the Ripper, namely '*M.K.*'—for Mary Kelly."

"Set a trap of some sort?"

"Right. And I'm thinking the most irresistible name for our killer is 'Mary Kelly' itself. And if she were a prostitute as well, it would complete the circle of this man's compulsion."

"You'll never find a Mary Kelly who would risk her life."

"I know, Sandy. But I'll create her." He explained how George Bernard Shaw agreed to train and costume a woman for that role. "It's a reversal of the play—passing off an ordinary woman as a Whitechapel area prostitute."

"And you want me to cover this in the *Times* in some way?" MacDougall's forehead creased. "I'd have to talk with my editor, and with Colonel Trent, the publisher."

"The Colonel's son is to marry the daughter of Lorraine Sheffield."

"I know that."

"The Colonel will want to assist in any way he can."

"But what's the plan?"

"The next killing would be on the night of November eighth. Three days earlier, November fifth, is Guy Fawkes Day. You know how wild it gets in the East End that night, with all the bonfire burnings in effigy of Fawkes. I'd like you to publicize for several days before November fifth that the name of Mary Kelly has been drawn to light the first Guy Fawkes bonfire that night in Whitechapel."

"And he'll read that. Clever."

"Yes. And the name will grab him. I don't expect him to try another killing that night, because his twisted mind is fixed definitely on the eighth. But he'll read your articles. And I'm sure he'll be in the crowd that night, watching that Guy Fawkes bonfire to single out this Mary Kelly, maybe follow her, find out what he can about her haunts down there, and get prepared."

"So she'd be bait. And you might be able to pick him out of hundreds of people in the street?" MacDougall shook his head.

"No, I agree, Sandy, that's too much to expect. But the event will get him focused on our invented Mary Kelly, so on the eighth we can grab him as he tries to take her."

"And if you miss him on the eighth?"

"We won't."

"You still haven't told me how you'll get someone to put herself in this danger."

"It will be a woman we select, who agrees, of course, to take on a disguise in order to bait and trap this killer. Someone Scotland Yard will recruit and pay."

MacDougall sat back. "I'll have to tell my editor. If you know Harold Keefer, he'll want all the details. He may call you. I'll let him talk to the colonel. They approve—or it's off."

"All right. I'm sure they'll hold it in confidence."

"November fifth is a month away. You'll call before then?"

"We'll want to begin the articles near the end of October."

"And meanwhile?"

Now Darnell frowned. "The hardest parts. Finding a woman to do it. Having Shaw train her and costume her. Making sure Shaw's theater people are sworn to confidence. Much more."

MacDougall smirked. "You'd better add a bit of prayer to all that, John. If anything goes wrong, they may be burning effigies of John Darnell next year."

*   *   *

Chief Inspector Bruce Howard arrived a few minutes late for the meeting Darnell had called to be held in Nathaniel Warren's office. He eased into a chair next to Darnell, across from Warren. "Thanks for sending a driver, Nathaniel. I haven't driven myself yet, since the hospital. The arm's still bad." He looked quizzically at Darnell. "Must be something important."

Warren scowled. "Professor Darnell hasn't seen fit to state his subject yet." He looked up as Sergeant O'Reilly opened the office door, entered quietly, and sat on the sofa against the wall.

Darnell stared at her in surprise, then looked at Warren. "I didn't expect the Sergeant. I thought it would just be you and the Chief."

"She's your, shall we say, partner? I felt she should hear anything new."

Darnell scowled. "It's just—well, perhaps you'll see why when I tell you my scheme." He smiled at Catherine O'Reilly. "How are you, Sergeant?"

She nodded, straight-faced, as reply. He remembered how she'd looked when he told her he'd inform her of the plan, as he put it, later.

Inspector Warren drummed his fingers on his desk. "All right, Professor. We're here, and we're listening."

Darnell launched into his theory that the killer watched for news of women in the *Times* with initials matching those of the Ripper's original victims, and his concern that another would be killed on the final Ripper date. "We can't sit idly by and let that happen. I've already talked with MacDougall at the *Times,* who will help me in this, and others, and I'm here to ask for your approval and your help. Indeed, they're critical."

"Go on," Warren said, frowning.

"I want to bait the killer with a woman to be publicized in the news and apparently carrying the initials he wants— '*M.K.*' In fact, I want the name actually to be Mary Kelly."

"But how?" Chief Howard's question collapsed into a coughing spell which the others endured for some moments, until he regained his voice. He looked at Darnell. "Sorry."

"Chief, it will take a volunteer, a woman the Yard has

used before as a private operative. The playwright George Bernard Shaw has agreed to train that woman to act like a prostitute."

"She'd be the bait?" Warren exchanged a glance with Howard.

"Yes. On the evening of November eighth."

"I don't like the sound of that word, 'bait,' " Howard said.

"Nor I. But I want to be clear as to the danger. This way, we can entice the killer out on our terms, at our time, and in our place. In Whitechapel. It may be our only chance to capture him and stop these killings." He told them about the plan to get a Mary Kelly into the public eye through *Times* articles focused on the Guy Fawkes Day Whitechapel bonfires.

Howard and Warren fell silent. Howard spoke first. "You know what happened to Mary Kelly, John. We young constables at that time were used to seeing the results of vicious crimes, but even we couldn't stomach it."

Warren groaned. "And I was only twelve years old then, but I'll never forget my father's reaction. Of all the slashings, the Mary Kelly murder was the one that finally tore him apart and resulted in his resignation. The Ripper practically skinned the poor woman like an animal." He glared at Darnell. "And this woman you want to play a Mary Kelly? You'd put her at risk?"

"I trust Scotland Yard can select her, and protect her."

Warren's voice grated. "Protect her, certainly. But I know of no woman who would do this. We have no operatives. Chief?"

Howard shook his head. "Perhaps a small constable in disguise could be passed off as a woman."

Warren said, "No. He'd see through that."

O'Reilly cleared her throat. "Uh, excuse me, sirs."

All eyes turned to her.

"I can do it. I'll be your Mary Kelly."

Darnell stood suddenly, knocking over his chair. He replaced it and paced back and forth. "Dammit! That's why I didn't want her here. I knew this would happen. No, absolutely not." He glared at Warren. "You don't have one undercover woman who could do this? No one who's been a plant before?"

Warren shook his head.

Darnell continued pacing, staring out through the glass-topped door at the Yard's bay. No other woman sat out there with the male officers and detectives, and he realized again the lonely position O'Reilly held as the Yard's only female Sergeant.

Howard said, "I don't know."

"There must be someone else." Darnell fixed his gaze on Warren. "Think, Inspector."

Warren shook his head. "It's not easy. One woman was killed two years ago as an operative on a special task. We've had to be very careful since."

O'Reilly walked to the desk, facing both the inspectors. "Inspector Warren, and Chief, now listen—excuse me for speaking up, but you can't find anyone to do that job. I know the area. I've been there with Professor Darnell. I know the constables, the streets, and I've, well, I've seen the women there and know something of them. I can play that part. And I'm not afraid."

"Dammit!" Darnell took his seat again and glared silently at the others, shifting his gaze from one to another.

"She's right, John," Chief Howard broke the silence in the room. "She does know this case. She's seen the other victims. She knows what's involved. But we'll have to take special measures to make sure nothing happens to her. Be damned sure of that, if I have anything to do with it."

Inspector Warren nodded. "We have no one else. But it's your call, Chief."

"You approve then, Nathaniel?"

"Yes, Chief, I do. Reluctantly, of course."

"And John?" Bruce Howard put a hand on Darnell's shoulder. "It's your plan. I think it only fair that if the Sergeant's willing to take this on, you make the final decision."

Darnell rubbed his forehead and looked askance at Sergeant O'Reilly. "I knew you'd volunteer if you knew about this plan."

She smoothed imaginary wrinkles down from her uniform skirt as she walked over to him. "John, this could be important for me. To advance at the Yard, you have to take chances and be ready for duty when the call comes."

"I know. But a woman, especially you . . . I'm sorry, but there's got to be some chivalry left, even at Scotland Yard."

"Only a woman can do this job."

Darnell looked at Howard, who nodded. He sighed. "All right. If I have to concur, I'll say yes. But I'm going to want the full force of the Yard out there to protect her." He glared at Warren. "And by God, if anything happens . . ."

Sergeant O'Reilly smiled, taking the three men into the sweeping gaze of her sparkling eyes. "Then I'm it. When do we start?"

Chapter Twenty-four

George Barnard Shaw arrived at the theater early, to be sure the stage was in order and costumes available, and awaited the others. Professor Darnell—an interesting man, he thought—had called the night before saying a woman had volunteered to take the assignment. A female Sergeant at Scotland Yard, Darnell had said.

Shaw was pleased to hear the Yard had at last weakened and placed a woman in a position of some responsibility. He was sure it was the first of many advances for women, something he had been fighting for over a period of years.

For this assignment, he hoped she had some acting ability, although the important things were the look, the clothing, and a few choice phrases and intonations. He smiled, thinking, if only his fictional Henry Higgins were here. He could turn her into a most believable streetwalker in a trice.

After making sure the stage manager had everything in readiness, Shaw pulled a straight-backed chair up to a prop table and set down his paper sack. From it, he removed several carrots and celery sticks, an apple, two slices of unbuttered whole-wheat bread, and a bottle of water. His lunch, if not fit for a king, was certainly ideal for a vegetarian and typical of Shaw's diet. As he crunched a carrot, he recalled the time the audience laughed when a moderator at a meeting introduced him as the "famous vegetarian" rather than the usual "eminent playwright."

With perfect timing, Darnell and two women of similar coloring except for their hair, one somewhat taller than the other, arrived at exactly one p.m., just as he was folding up the paper sack for use the next day. In a small procession led by the Professor, they walked down the aisle to the stage.

"Welcome, welcome," Shaw called to them, and waved them up to the stage. He wondered, why two women? He'd expected only the Sergeant. But he knew Darnell would explain it momentarily.

"Professor Darnell. Good to see you again."

"Mr. Shaw, allow me to introduce my wife, Penny. And this is Sergeant Catherine O'Reilly, who is eager to play this part."

Shaw bowed to O'Reilly, the shorter of the two. He turned to Penny. "And Mrs. Darnell? You're here to, ah, observe?"

"Yes. John tried to keep me away, but I said, if I don't go, you don't go. I'm sure seeing George Bernard Shaw direct will be an unforgettable experience."

"Thank you, dear lady. You're very kind. Although I wouldn't call it directing so much as, perhaps, educating."

Darnell said, "We're in your hands, Mr. Shaw."

"Oh, please. Call me Bernard. We'll be working with each other for quite a while to accomplish this."

Penny Darnell and Catherine O'Reilly looked at each other, smiled, then gave their full attention to the playwright.

"Now." Shaw rubbed his hands together briskly. "You, Professor, and Mrs. Darnell can sit off stage left, just out of our near sight. You can see everything there, but we'll be able to create more illusion out here, with just the Sergeant—may I call you Catherine, my dear?—and me on stage."

Darnell and Penny retreated to the wings and took seats in straight chairs facing the stage. Penny said, "This is so exciting, John."

He frowned. "It would be, if the plan wasn't so dangerous."

The stage manager approached Shaw from the opposite side of the stage. "Ready for wardrobe, sir? Shall I get some clothing for the young lady?"

Shaw nodded. "Size her up, Jarvis. I'm sure you have something back there that will work. You know what I want."

The manager walked around the sergeant, looking her up and down. "Yes, I have some things her size." He walked off the stage in the direction from which he had come.

O'Reilly said, "It feels odd to be up here on stage. I'm usually in the balcony, looking down."

"Have you seen *Pygmalion*?"

"Yes, my mother and I came to see it when it opened in London three years ago. It was excellent."

"Then you saw the transformation, or transmogrification I like to call it, of Eliza Doolittle from the type of woman she was to a society maiden."

"Yes." She laughed. "Except when she broke down into her natural speech through habit. That was hilarious. I'll never forget when she said, *'Not bloody likely.'*"

"Nor will my critics. I think they're still getting used to that kind of language being used on the stage. They referred to 'bloody' as a 'sanguinary adjective'—they wouldn't use the word or phrase in the press. Since then, it's come into more popular use in slang. They're coming around now."

"Your plays set the styles, I think."

The stage manager returned with a full, flowery skirt with a prominent patch near the bottom of it, a white petticoat, a long-sleeved checkered blouse, a worn, black vest-like garment, and an old-style bonnet with two artificial flowers sewn into its front.

"Loverly," O'Reilly said, and Shaw smiled at the reference to his play.

"Try these on, Catherine," Shaw said. "Jarvis'll show you to a dressing room."

As she followed the manager off, Shaw ambled over to the Darnells. He wanted to be sure he and Darnell had the same concept in mind. He took a chair near them and said, "We begin soon." He pulled thoughtfully on his beard. "She doesn't need acting ability, just an aptitude to mimic the speech pattern of an East End woman."

"I know a bit about what she's facing," Penny said. "I did some acting in America. High school plays and local amateur productions."

Shaw studied her face. "You definitely have the features and bearing for it." He noticed Darnell did not want to join in that exchange.

Darnell said, "Sergeant O'Reilly has observed and heard some local Whitechapel women in our investigations. I think she can pick it up. But I wish it were someone else. It's a very dangerous assignment."

Shaw frowned. "She understands the potential for danger?"

"The potential, yes. She'll be surrounded by disguised Scotland Yard detectives and constables, one within a dozen feet on either side of her. And I'll be there. We'll all be armed for the occasion. And your direction and advice should assure that our target won't see through our artifices."

Shaw considered Darnell's words. It was to be like a stage production, but played out on the grim streets of East London, not in the safe confines of a playhouse. He hoped Darnell was right about police protection. But his charge was simply to make this woman as believable in her role as possible, for her safety.

Sergeant O'Reilly returned to the stage and drew spontaneous applause from Shaw and the Darnells. Shaw walked up to her and said, "Very good, very good indeed." He walked around her, much as the stage manager had, and inspected the outfit.

"Something missing. Hmmm." He turned to Jarvis. "A small, older bag on a long string. Can you get one?"

"Yes, sir." He left the stage. While Shaw was still checking the fit and look of the garments on O'Reilly, Jarvis brought the purse to him.

Shaw said, "Fine," and hung the bag over the Sergeant's shoulder. "Now, that's perfect."

"*Coo!*" O'Reilly said.

Shaw laughed, and heard the Darnells echo it from the wings and the sounds reverberate through the playhouse. "Good, you know one useful word already. 'Coo' shows appreciation or wonder. Also, it may be handy for talking with pigeons in the Square." His eyes twinkled with humor. Keep it light, he thought, keep her in a positive spirit. "We'll teach you more of that talk."

Shaw felt the intensity of Sergeant O'Reilly's gaze as she looked into his eyes. He could see that she placed herself innocently and totally at his disposal, as if trying out for the part of an ingenue for one of his plays. He thought she was indeed that, but playing the part for much higher stakes than getting an audience's laughter.

"Yes, we'll teach you to talk," he mused, smiling at O'Reilly. "But first you'll learn how to walk. Watch me."

Shaw walked briskly across the stage in a steady pace, then back to O'Reilly. "The average person walks like that, direct. But not Whitechapel women. They're languid; they want to be enticing; sometimes they have had several tots of gin or ale at the local pub. Their walk is less purposeful and—to the men they want as, ah, customers—more inviting. Let me borrow your bag. Watch."

Shaw ambled slowly across the stage, not walking in a straight line, his hips moving undulantly from side to side with each step, drifting a bit left, then a bit right, swinging the bag gently forward and back. He alternated the direction of his gaze, moving his head from left to right slowly, to suggest that he was looking for someone. He knew the smile he wore on his own lined, wrinkled face was as unenticing as any could be, but he wanted the element complete. He strolled back to O'Reilly.

"Now, Catherine, you see what I mean?"

"Yes. You remind me just a touch of some of the women I met down there."

Shaw laughed. "Don't breathe that to a soul." He returned her bag. "Now, let me see you try it."

O'Reilly walked across the stage, imitating the style he had demonstrated, undulating, swinging the bag, looking unhurried, appearing for all the world, Shaw thought as he squinted at her critically, as if she were a true female denizen of the East End. She walked back, and Shaw clapped his hands as encouragement. "Good, good. Now, do the same once or twice more. It must become natural."

Shaw knew it would take several occasions to achieve the naturalness he wanted. O'Reilly took a half-dozen more circuits.

After some time, at Shaw's direction, she walked over to the Darnells' area and back and forth so they could observe her closely. She asked Penny, "How'm I doing?"

"You could fool me."

"All right," Shaw said. "That's good, for today. We'll do this on several more occasions over these next days and weeks until, with the cumulative effect, it's second nature to you."

"All right. Now what?"

"Now, the choice of words, the language, the intonation, the accent. Your voice must not evidence a great deal of education. Forget everything you learned about grammar in school. The East End has no reputation for advancing the proper use of English. You'll have to adopt some words and phrases you don't use in ordinary conversation. That's the essence of it. It's a matter of creating an impression. Just like on the stage."

"Gor blimey," O'Reilly said with a smile, thinking of what she heard one of the women say at The Three Hares.

"That's it. That's the kind of thing. Now, let's sit here at the table across from each other, and I'll say some words, trying to mimic a certain expression, and you can answer in kind. We'll do this a number of times, too, to get you polished—or, I should say, *unpolished.*"

Shaw took her through a litany of street slang. He knew that her use of the vernacular was critical, and that Eastenders enjoyed the fun of their own special, graphic brand of language and humor.

" 'Bloody,' of course," he said. "They use that with great fervor. Also 'flamin' and 'bugger.' Such as 'the bloody constable,' 'the flamin' barkeep,' and 'oh, bugger it.' " They may warn that someone will 'chop you about,' they may call you 'ducky,' refer to a 'dotty old hag,' and so on. I'll give you a list to practice, but I'm sure you've heard some of this."

"Yes, and it's funny," she said.

Shaw pushed on. "Dropping the 'h' is common, such as *'ow'* instead of 'how' and *'ot'* instead of 'hot,' *'ead'* rather than 'head,' *'alf'* instead of 'half' and *'ere'* and *'ave'* and *'aven't'* and so on. Drop the final 't' from words like 'expect,' making it *'expec.'* Then the word 'you' should disappear from your speech, with *'yer'* and *'ye're'* taking its place. 'God' becomes *'Gawd.'* 'What' is *'wot.'* You'll sound a little like Eliza Doolittle before her transformation. Let's try some of these."

Shaw took one word at a time, pronounced it as he wished her to learn it, and she repeated it. Each of two dozen words and phrases took a half-dozen iterations for his satisfaction.

"Don't forget the expressions on your face, twisting your lips about, raising the eyebrows, using the hands and arms, the petulant or whining tones in the voice. All of this is quite common among those seeking impact, with their more limited vocabularies, through use of their faces and bodies. They're very expressive in their way."

As the lesson carried on, Shaw was pleased at her progress and more relaxed as to her assignment. He began to feel she could indeed fool a casual stranger.

The exercise went on for well over an hour, and Shaw saw the time approaching three o'clock. He handed her a sheet. "Enough for today. Say these words and expressions on this list at home, in your privacy, of course, and come back on Thursday. We can do this at night if your duties don't permit the afternoons, and we'll do it twice a week for two hours over the next four weeks. The cumulative effect will create the best illusion and get you most comfortable in this role."

Shaw beckoned the Darnells over. "We're done for today."

O'Reilly said, "Thank you, Mr. Shaw. And the clothing?"

"Change in the dressing room, but take the clothes home with you. When you're practicing at home, it's good to have them on for the best results. Bring them with you when we meet next."

Darnell said, "You've achieved remarkable results, Bernard, in a little over two hours. I'm very encouraged."

Shaw smiled and took the Sergeant's hand. He looked into her eyes, his own twinkling. "When this is all over, dear, and if you ever tire of police work, come and see me."

Sergeant O'Reilly laughed. "Bloody good idea!"

After dropping the Sergeant at Scotland Yard, the Darnells drove home, each preoccupied with their own thoughts.

"John," Penny said, breaking the silence as they neared their neighborhood, "you know, I could have done that job. I mean, becoming Mary Kelly. I've had some acting experience."

He scowled at her. "Do you really think I'd let you take that risk? Even O'Reilly, a policewoman, is at risk, despite all our precautions. But if something goes wrong, she has her police training to fall back on, not just the acting."

Penny said nothing for some moments. Then, "I could have done more in this case. I keep thinking of Annette

Camden, how she was so attentive at the store. About her simple life, taken from her by this—this maniac!"

"You tied the *Times* articles into the initials, a critical connection. Don't worry. This plan will work. We'll get him."

Chapter Twenty-five

Saturday, October 13

The dark room, illumined by only one window looking out upon a dingy alley-like court, matched the nature of the gruesome work the man silently engaged in that night. He knew such rooms in lodging houses offered little other than a bed for sleeping, but they also gave him the anonymity of a drifter, and in this case he had fashioned his own locking device for the door to secure privacy. Until ready for his final enterprise, he determined to be unnoticed, and so must keep to himself. This package he was in the midst of preparing was the exception. His mind filled with images of how it would be received when opened.

He bent to his task, took from the glass jar the object appearing to be a piece of reddish-brown meat, and laid it in the stiff paper in the bottom of the small box. His nose wrinkled at the smell. He closed the box, wrapped it in sturdy brown paper, and bound it with stout string. With a pen dipped in a small bottle of red ink, he wrote names and an address on the paper in block printing and set the package down to survey his handiwork. He affixed postage stamps he had bought the day before. It was ready to mail, and if mailed this night would arrive by the sixteenth. He smiled grimly at that thought.

The walk to the post office, although over a mile in distance, was not unpleasant in the crisp weather and clean air, following the rain earlier that week. The garb he wore differed considerably from that which he used on other occasions, and blended him in almost invisibly with others passing by on the streets of Whitechapel. Reaching the post office and the mail receptacle in front of it, the man took one last look at the address on the parcel as he stood at the box: *"Inspector Nathaniel Warren, Scotland Yard, London."* And, in the upper left corner, sure to get their attention, his scrawled words: *"Jack the Ripper."*

Reaching his office Tuesday morning, October 16, Inspector Warren found Detective Allan Blackwell standing outside it.

"Something you'd better see on your desk," Blackwell said.

Warren ripped open the parcel wrapped in brown paper he found on his desk. "Good God!" he said, and his hand went to his mouth, covering it to stem the flow of something vile. He bent over a waste basket and emptied his mouth into it.

He motioned to Blackwell, who had been watching and now hurried in to him. Warren gestured at the box. "Where in the hell did this come from?"

"I don't know, sir, just saw the name on it. *'The Ripper.'* Whew, what a smell."

Warren nodded, still grimacing from the taste in his mouth. "The Ripper sent part of a kidney, supposedly a human one taken from Katherine Eddowes, to the newspapers in '88, and they forwarded it to the Yard. Received October sixteenth. Today's the sixteenth. And look at that name—*'Jack the Ripper.'* The killer's repeating the atrocity now."

"Repeating it, yes. But is it a kidney? And is it human?"

"I wouldn't know. We'll have to get it examined. Take this thing to the coroner. I'll keep the wrapping paper. Might learn something there."

Blackwell walked to the door, gingerly holding the closed box in one hand, away from his body. Over his shoulder he said, "I'll ask Doc Bentridge to call you when he's done."

"I want to know today, as soon as possible. Is it human, is it an animal's, what?"

Warren turned and picked up the telephone. Who should he call first—Chief Howard? The Superintendent? No, he decided. He'd wait until the coroner responded for that. He asked the operator to get him Professor Darnell and gave her the number. He drummed his fingers on the desk while he waited. From a drawer, he took a large round stick of Christmas peppermint candy, broke off a chunk, and put it in his mouth.

Darnell wondered if the days of uninterrupted breakfasts were gone forever. It seemed he could almost always count on a call on the telephone, which was becoming an increasingly annoying new convenience recently, before he could even enjoy his second cup of coffee and his reading of the *Times*.

But when he heard the news from Warren, he gulped the coffee and said a quick good-bye to Penny. Within a half hour he was in the Yard, approaching Warren's office. He rapped lightly on the door, and when Warren looked up and nodded, he walked in and closed the door.

"Let me see that wrapping paper," he said. When Warren handed it over to him, he took a seat and spread it on the outer edge of Warren's desk. "Hmmm. The printing doesn't help much. Red ink, of course, but any stationer's sells that."

He looked at the signature and writing, then took out a small magnifying glass and examined the words. He said, "Do you still have the recent letters and the Ripper letters in your desk?"

Warren said, "Yes," slid open a drawer, and extracted a sheaf of papers. He passed them to Darnell.

Darnell first took out the two letters received since August and examined the signatures and writing, comparing them under the glass to the names and address on the wrapping paper. He did the same with the letters officials had concluded were written by Jack the Ripper twenty-nine years earlier.

"Well?" Warren stared at him.

"The writing on the parcel is the same as on the letters received this year. But the writing still doesn't match the letters from '88. Of course, there's not much to work with on this paper. Just a signature and the block printing. No language idiosyncrasies to consider, no peculiarities or pet words." He sighed. "Tell me about the contents of the parcel."

"It looked like a kidney, but who knows. I'm expecting a call any moment from the coroner."

"You looked at it yourself?"

"Yes, and smelled its wonderful fragrance, and lost most of my breakfast."

Darnell gave him the wry smile he knew Warren expected. He glanced at the wrapping paper again.

The telephone rang, and the Inspector answered it abruptly, "Warren." He listened intently for two minutes, then said, "Preserve it, keep it secure," and hung up the phone. He looked at Darnell and shook his head.

"Meaning?"

"It was part of a dog's kidney. Not human."

Darnell struck the desk with his fist. "Damn! He's playing with us again. Tweaking our noses." He held up the wrapping paper toward Warren. "Did you notice this postal mark? It shows a post office in the East End."

Warren looked at it. "That one's a mile or more from Whitechapel."

"That tells us something. Was he just careless?"

"Or is it more nose-tweaking? He went there just to drop the parcel knowing we'd see the postmark?"

Darnell nodded. "We have no way of knowing how this man's mind would work on that level. Is he simple, or is he clever, or is he too clever for his own good? Is he outfoxing himself by trying to outfox us?"

"What do you mean?"

"It's like the game of trying to guess which hand a coin's in. If the person holds a coin in his left hand, the next time would it be in the right? If he holds it in the left hand twice, would the third time be in the right, or again the left, trying to outsmart the person guessing? I'm sure you've played that game."

"Yes, and lost." He smiled at Darnell. "But I'm not psychic."

"Nor am I." Darnell stood.

"So—we just wait?"

"No. We have a plan. It's moving forward. Sergeant O'Reilly has had two training sessions already."

"Do you think we'll get another letter from—whoever it is?"

"I doubt it. The third letter in 1888 didn't shed light on anything. In fact, it predicted a so-called treble event, which never happened."

Warren stood facing Darnell and ran his hand through

his hair. "We may have a treble event of our own this time. Three Scotland Yard officers pilloried—drawn and quartered, thrown to the wolves. You name it. Asked to submit resignations, just as my father was."

Darnell stopped at the door and looked back. "Three?"

"Howard, O'Reilly, and myself."

Sergeant O'Reilly looked at herself in the full-length mirror in her wardrobe door. She turned left and right, examining the outfit Jarvis had supplied. "Loverly dress, wot?" she said aloud, and smiled. She tossed her head and slithered slowly across the room, looking backward into the mirror at every second step. "Make you feel good, ducky?" She swiveled her hips and twirled her bag. She turned and walked back toward the mirror. "For drinks only? For a glass of gin? Not bloody likely. Coins. That's it, ducky."

For the past hour Catherine O'Reilly had acted her part as George Bernard Shaw showed her. Now she removed her bonnet and tossed it and the bag on the bed. She looked at herself in the mirror, saying, "Catherine Mary O'Reilly—you *like* acting!" She laughed and threw herself on the bed. She lay there, staring at the ceiling, as she unbuttoned Jarvis's slender black vest. One of the buttons came off in her hand, and she laughed again.

Chapter Twenty-six

Monday, November 5, Guy Fawkes Day

During the next three weeks, Darnell's plan moved forward. Sergeant O'Reilly met with George Bernard Shaw twice a week, Monday and Thursday afternoons, two hours each time. Penny persuaded Darnell she had to have some part in the proceedings and so she attended all the training sessions. "Just to watch," she said, "maybe give a suggestion or two. A woman's point of view."

Darnell had met with MacDougall and asked him to have Rusty Clanahan handle a lottery to draw a name to light the Whitechapel Guy Fawkes bonfire—the name predetermined to be that of Mary Kelly. Sandy wrote articles to mention Mary Kelly in the *Times*, and small pieces ran twice in the week prior to Guy Fawkes Day, and the day before, Sunday the fourth. "He's seen one of them," Darnell said to MacDougall on the phone Sunday night, "but to be sure, run a large one tomorrow, right on Guy Fawkes Day."

At breakfast Monday, Darnell read the expanded *Times* article to Penny.

> Whitechapel bonfire to be lighted tonight by local woman. Mary Kelly, selected by lot from over a hundred women, will light the Guy Fawkes Day bonfire in Whitechapel. The custom in the area results in great festivities, including fireworks and one of the largest Fawkes bonfires in the city. Eastenders are expected to throng to see the sight.

Darnell said, "We're sitting here looking at this article, and somewhere in London a certain evil man is reading it also. If he saw one article earlier, he's made his decision already. If not, he'll certainly make it when he sees this one."

Penny scowled. "A decision, yes—to kill another woman."

Darnell shook his head. "But it won't happen, Penny. Every man they can spare at the Yard will be in Whitechapel tonight."

"You've got to protect her, John. She's not Mary Kelly, that—that fictitious stageplay person. *She's Catherine Mary O'Reilly!*"

"Catherine *Mary?*"

"She told me her middle name. Mary's her mother's name also. She was telling me her mother's in hospital."

"You've gotten to know O'Reilly rather well."

"I've been at the theater eight times, John, watching her rehearse with Mr. Shaw. Yes, I know her, and oddly enough, I feel I know this Mary Kelly person, too, when she's in costume, with that special lingo, although Mary Kelly doesn't even exist."

"O'Reilly will be fine. And she'll be safe. I'll be at Whitechapel at the Guy Fawkes bonfire site tonight just as soon as it gets dark. Warren will be there, as will a large number of detectives and constables. Of course, this is only the dress rehearsal, the introduction of Mary Kelly. We don't expect any trouble. The real event is in three days."

"I'm just concerned, John."

"Yes. And so am I. Concerned, and careful."

"Add 'certain' to those qualities. Not just tonight, but the night of the eighth, too. Especially that night."

Even in Whitechapel, as she walked several blocks from the spot where she parked her car, Catherine O'Reilly found the air at dusk on Guy Fawkes Day crisp, clear, and breathable. She passed the stack of logs for the Whitechapel bonfire, said to be the largest in the area, and admired the suitably dingy yet creative effigy of Guy Fawkes.

She knew that at Darnell's request, Rusty Clanahan had taken a hand in preparing the wood stacks and the stuffed effigy which dangled from a rack over the pile of logs. Time now to stop in and see barkeep Clanahan and make herself noticed.

"Whattya say, dearie? Wanta make a bit of change?" The words came with a gust of stale whiskey and tobacco breath from a man whose hat, pulled down low on his forehead, revealed tufts of gray hair. The eyes glinted in the darkening evening.

"Naah," O'Reilly replied. "Ain't had me dinner yet, 'ave I?" She swiveled about and walked in the direction of The Three Hares pub, not rushing away, remembering to swish and sway from side to side in a languid manner as Shaw had instructed her. She released the breath she'd been holding and said, "Whew!"

Rusty Clanahan looked up from his work as she sashayed up to the bar. He put aside the glasses and towel and leaned forward toward her. "What'll it be, now . . . oh!" He lowered his voice. "It's Sergeant O'Reilly! My God!"

"Shhh. Disguise, you know. Inspector Warren told you?"

"That he did. Still, you look the part, don't you know?"

"That's what I wanted to hear. I want to look like one of the girls. Apparently," she said, smiling, "I persuaded at least one man on the street that I was one of them."

"Any problem with him? Did he follow you?" He glanced at the door and around the room.

"No. I'm glad it happened, really. It shows my play-acting is working." She looked about. "Pour me an ale, Rusty." She reached in her tattered purse and put a coin on the counter.

Clanahan drew the ale in a mug and put it in front of her. "I'm to treat you like one of them."

"Yes, definitely."

"Then take your ale to a table—that's what they'd do." He smiled. "Might get you some comp'ny, y'know."

O'Reilly sauntered over to an unoccupied table adjacent to other bare tables and near a corner, and sat quietly sipping her dark ale but not particularly enjoying it. Next time, if she had to drink, she'd order a whiskey and water, what her dad enjoyed. The thought of him gave her a moment's pause as she wondered what he'd feel if he were alive and could see her now. She sighed.

She scanned the lightly occupied room, thinking she was early, that crowds would come later. The bonfire lighting was set for six p.m., and she must meet Darnell then at the site.

"Coo! What a nice bonnet, dearie." The woman's voice sounded musical but off-key, tinny, like a bow scraped along an out-of-tune violin's strings.

The woman sat opposite her and plunked her glass down on the table, spilling a bit of the ale. " 'Scuse me, dearie," she said. She wiped it up with a sleeve. " 'Ere to watch old Guy burn?"

"To light the fire meself."

"You? You're Mary Kelly? Gor blimey, dearie!" She turned and called to two women sitting at a distant table. "Bessie, Pearl, it's Mary Kelly!" She turned to O'Reilly. "I'm Sadie. Sadie Latkins."

One of the women looked up at Sadie, then the other. They shared a glance, stood in unison, grabbed their drinks, and hurried to the table where O'Reilly sat with Sadie Latkins. The two took empty chairs at the table and stared at O'Reilly.

"Mary Kelly!" the one named Bessie said. "Famous name by now. In the papers and all." She nudged her companion. "Ever light a fire, Pearl?"

Pearl smiled, snaggletoothed. "Not with a match, I ain't. But I set many a man's heart afire, I 'ave." She cackled, the sound reverberating through the room.

Bessie said, "This 'ere's Pearl Winfred, 'n I'm Bessie Morton. If Hannah Donner was 'ere, you'd see all the queens of the city." Her laugh matched the intensity of Pearl's, but with a raspier sound. She lapsed into a cough.

Sadie asked, "When do y'do it? Light it, I mean?"

"At six. I get some coin for doin' it, so I do as I'm told."

Sadie nodded sagely. "Good idea, good idea." She squinted at O'Reilly. " 'Ave I seen you abouts before?"

O'Reilly, trying to stay in character and not think of herself as a sergeant, shook her head. "Not lately, 'ereabouts. Come back from the north. Spent the whole summer in the fields."

"Pickin'—I know, I know." Sadie took a large swallow of her ale, as if she had forgotten it was there. She wiped her mouth on her sleeve. "Done my share of that. Ain't bad."

Over the next half hour, O'Reilly sat quietly, watching and listening to the others, who contentedly drank their ale, sometimes told an off-color joke or an old story familiar to them, and laughed. She joined in the laughter. She could see the importance of the pubs and the camaraderie they enjoyed there to street women like these three, without families and with the kind of existence they led, the ignominy they would suffer later this very night just to make a few coins—just to stay alive.

Sadie's bleary eyes stared into O'Reilly's. She whispered, " 'Ad a spot o' bother 'ere, August." She exchanged glances with Bessie and Pearl. "A killin', and a bad one at that. Jus' like the Ripper. Me and Pearl, and Hannah, too, saw his ghost."

"Ghost? Of the Ripper?" O'Reilly feigned ignorance.

Pearl nodded. "Me and Hannah saw 'im in the alley. Gimme the shivers, 'e did." She shivered, as if from the memory.

"I was with Sadie," Bessie said, "when she saw 'im, but I looked too late. He was gone."

O'Reilly sensed that Bessie felt out of the limelight, wanted to be part of the adventure in some way. She asked, "Did 'e come back?" and looked at each of them.

Three heads shook. "Not 'ere—but some'ere's else."

"Wonder what time it's gettin' to be?" O'Reilly asked. "I should be goin'."

"To light the fire?" Sadie looked at her, glanced at her mug, then finished her ale in a loud gulp.

"I should do."

"Then we'll go with ye. Right, dearies?"

The others tossed down the last drops of their ale, and the four walked to the door. Sadie took O'Reilly's arm on one side and Bessie on the other. They broke into a barroom song.

O'Reilly glanced back over her shoulder at Clanahan, who nodded and winked. As they neared the stacks of wood where crowds of onlookers had already begun to gather, the women dropped O'Reilly's arms and stopped. "We'll watch from 'ere, ducky."

O'Reilly weaved her way through the people, smiling at some of them as she inched her way forward. As she approached the stacks of logs, she saw a man looking like Darnell, his height and build, but dressed oddly. Could it be him? Her eyes narrowed as she studied the man, who wore ill-fitting trousers, a dark jacket, and a sailor's cap—

a potpourri of old clothing. She walked closer to the man. Yes. It was Darnell, disguised, engaged in conversation with two other men.

One of the two men appeared to O'Reilly to have the rough bearing and dress of a natural leader, a local who would tend to take charge of such neighborhood events as this one. The other was the reporter, Sandy MacDougall. As she reached them, she saw Darnell glance at her, say a word to MacDougall, then step back from the others, fading slowly into the crowd. In that moment, O'Reilly lost sight of him.

The reporter took O'Reilly's arm and, with a gleam in his eye, brought her to the local, saying only, "Mary Kelly."

The other man tipped his cap. "Dee-lighted! I'm George Crooks." He instructed her how to hold a torch he said he'd give her. "Level to the wood, so not to scorch your outfit. Flames might go the wrong way, don't you know. You don't want to get fired up, along with Guy." He gave her a raucous laugh.

Rusty Clanahan walked up at that point and took the beefy hand of the local. In a loud voice, Rusty said the words the crowd was waiting to hear. "Let's get Guy Fawkes burnin'!" A sound of excited talk rippled through the crowd.

Mary Kelly, née Catherine O'Reilly, bent down with the lighted torch supplied by Crooks. At several spots, she applied it to the smaller pieces of wood and twigs surrounding the base of the split logs, and watched the fire catch. With several areas burning, she tossed the torch up into the pile of logs.

The fire caught well now and blazed upward with an orange brightness in the otherwise dark night. O'Reilly felt the heat on her face and stepped back a bit, noticing others who happened to be too close to the fire do the same.

The sound of crackling logs added to the overall impact of the brilliant sight, and the smell of the split wood reminded her of bonfires at her church camp, of past Guy Fawkes Day burnings, and of roaring fires in her family home's large fireplace, now cold and unused, with her father gone and her mother in the hospital. The scene was a pleasant, exciting one, and she enjoyed it, but she remained alert, remembering her mission for the night and realizing

someone might be somewhere in the crowd watching—
and waiting.

Locals admiring the fire moved about for a better view
of the blaze, as an enthusiastic throaty roar from the crowd
filled the now dark and chilling night in Whitechapel. The
bonfire created an eerie glow befitting the occasion. And
shadowy figures danced along the walls of the buildings in
the flickering orange light of the flames.

Chapter Twenty-seven

Monday night, November 5

From the shadows in the back of the crowd, the nondescript-looking man watched the proceedings with glittering eyes. Moving about as needed, he kept his gaze fixed on the figure of the woman he heard called Mary Kelly as she talked with the two men, lit the bonfire, and positioned herself to watch it. Amazing, her name being exactly the same, not just the initials. It made everything perfect. Just three more days to complete all he had started out to do. Then he'd be away. Gone forever.

He edged in a bit closer to Mary Kelly, the enticement and intrigue of seeing her up close worth the slight risk of being observed. What he wore this night, as he had during the past month or so, blended with the clothing of the men on his left and right. Older, faded work clothing. A hat, pulled down. His whiskers grown out, bristly, over the past month.

Altogether, it was an effective enough disguise on a rowdy night like this. On the eighth—now that would be a different matter. He had his special clothing set aside for that night, ready. And he'd shave the beard. It must all fit into his plan.

A dozen feet from the woman, but still well-enough concealed by other men in front of him, he gazed at her face, lit up brightly in the fire's glow. A face of innocence—odd for a woman of this type. But better, oh, so much better!

His mouth felt moist with anticipation, as if he had caught the tantalizing scents of a meal. From his pocket, he removed a flask, clicked it open, and tipped it back into his mouth. He enjoyed the feeling of the liquid burning as it flowed through his mouth and down his throat.

Yes, Mary Kelly was perfect. She'd complete his circle, tying it all together. He'd leave the police with a second complete mystery. Five murders, never to be solved. But also he'd leave his mission done, none the wiser, and him off then to far places. He took another long swig of the whiskey, tucked the flask away, and, inch by inch, edged up for a closer look at the woman he knew only as Mary Kelly. And as his fifth victim.

The fire roared and the legs of the effigy of Guy Fawkes blazed as flames licked up the trunk of the stuffed body. Fireworks lit up the sky as locals set matches to them some distance from the bonfire.

Darnell stood well back in the crowd, watching the fire and spectacular fireworks, yet focusing his attention on Sergeant O'Reilly. Keeping her in his line of vision, he knew, gave the best assurance of her safety. He was aware that constables and detectives were watching her protectively, but this was personal for him. He scanned the crowd, looking for unusual behavior, anyone who could be the killer, come to preview his crime and his victim. He felt the man must be there, that he'd seen the articles and could not resist coming. And, as far as Darnell knew, the man suspected nothing of their deception or plan.

He watched O'Reilly drift back from the throngs and join several women at its fringe. As she moved, Darnell also moved forward, but kept his distance. He glanced about to see if anyone followed her. At corners, he saw disguised detectives and constables looking like locals, eyeing the bonfire while talking among themselves. He nodded unobtrusively as he passed. If the killer was there and tried to harm O'Reilly this night, they would make sure he'd fail.

O'Reilly and the women had linked arms again, and as they moved back from the fire, and Darnell followed, he heard bits of a raucous song they sang, barely audible over the crowd noise as the women walked toward The Three Hares pub. Time, he thought, for a swig of celebratory ale. That was what they wanted. Good. He'd follow them in, take a seat in a corner, and observe. Maybe he could spot a man careless enough to enter the pub in his eagerness to see his prey up close.

*   *   *

O'Reilly felt herself dragged along by Sadie and Bessie, who had her arms locked in theirs. If Shaw could see her, would he approve? She thought he'd smile and say, *"Not bloody bad, Mary."*

Inside the pub, the others plunked her down at a table, and two hurried up to the busy bar. "Four ales, ducky," Pearl said, " 'n fill 'em up this time." She put a few coins on the bar. The ale drawn, she and Bessie took two mugs each to the table.

"Our treat, Mary," Pearl said to O'Reilly.

O'Reilly thanked them, and took an enthusiastic swig of hers in unison with the others. The four said, "Aaahh," as they finished the first large swallows, and O'Reilly was glad she remembered what Bernard Shaw impressed on her. "They like their ale, they do," he'd said. "Show that you do, too."

The pub buzzed with a dozen loud conversations, and O'Reilly smiled, keeping in the mood of the time, but alert to anything unusual within the room. In the corner of her eye, she caught a glimpse of a man she thought could be Darnell, but resisted the urge to turn toward him for a better look. The man blended into the bustle of those moving about the room.

Sadie Latkins fixed her bleary eyes on O'Reilly. "So, dearie, what now? Back to stay, in this paradise?"

O'Reilly nodded. "In and out. Some things to do, some people to see."

"King George, eh?" Pearl cackled at her own joke. "Famous lady now."

O'Reilly and the others laughed, and Bessie Morton again fell into a coughing spell in the midst of it. O'Reilly saw specks of blood on the woman's sleeve as she wiped her mouth and knew Bessie's problem instantly. Her mother had been suffering with consumption—tuberculosis, they mostly called it now—for some years. She'd seen the tell-tale blood spots on her mother's handkerchiefs, more in past months.

A disturbance seemed to break out at the bar. Rusty Clanahan gestured to his man and hurried from the pub. What had he seen? O'Reilly looked about the room for Darnell.

All the men looked alike to her in the dim light, and

many were facing other directions, sitting hunched over drinks at tables, in booths or dark corners. She could only wait. The talk and laughter of the other women brought her back to her duty. She laughed with them at a joke she had not heard.

As Rusty Clanahan walked down the street pulling on his jacket and cap, keeping the man ahead of him in view, the words of Fitch, his fill-in barkeep, only hours before he was murdered came back to him and rang in his ears. *" 'E 'ad the coldest fish eyes I ever did see, and a scar on 'is cheek, like, you know, 'alf a moon."* When Clanahan and Darnell had found Fitch dead in his lodging house, his lips could add nothing to that. But this man at the bar had those cold eyes and the same scar. If this was the killer, Clanahan knew what he'd like to do with him.

The man a block ahead of him walked unhurriedly, but looked about often to the left and right, and occasionally behind him. Clanahan kept his cap pulled low and his head down, maintaining the same shuffling yet steady pace, not gaining on him, nor losing ground. If he couldn't handle the man himself, at least he could find where he lived and tell Darnell or one of the constables on the street.

Several blocks down the street, Clanahan's quarry suddenly turned into an alleyway. Clanahan broke into a quick-step run to reach the spot before the man disappeared into some doorway. He turned into the dark alley, and partway in, he pulled up momentarily to let his eyes adjust and get his bearings.

The heavy blow came from behind him, by someone stepping out from an alcove. To Clanahan, it felt like a lead pipe, but he had no time to analyze it. He saw only a red haze in his field of vision as he groaned with the sharp pain. His world blacked out, and he slumped, in a tangle of arms and legs, to the dirt and gravel of the rough alleyway.

When Clanahan failed to return, Darnell realized the barkeep could be in trouble. He had to choose between protecting O'Reilly or going after him. She seemed to be settled in well at the table with the women and could wait an hour or so, as they had discussed, before returning to her car. He made his decision and left the pub.

Outside, he asked the constable stationed there whether he'd seen Clanahan leave, and headed in the direction the constable indicated. He hurried forward several blocks until he heard a noise and saw Clanahan stumbling toward him from an alleyway.

The man's face was bruised and bleeding, and he held a hand to the back of his neck. When he saw Darnell, he groaned.

Darnell supported him with an arm. "Sit here for a minute." He helped Clanahan sit and lean against the building. With a handkerchief, he blotted the blood from Clanahan's face.

"From behind. Back of the neck," Clanahan managed. "I was followin' the bastard."

"Just rest for a minute. Where's your home?"

"Around the corner . . . must get back."

Darnell said, "I guess a large whiskey wouldn't do you any harm just now."

"There's a cot in the pub's back room. Could lay there."

Darnell nodded.

A man dressed as a local came up to them. "Constable Figgitt," he said. "Can I help, Professor?"

"You can help get Mr. Clanahan back to his pub, you on one side, I on the other. He's had a bad blow. Can you manage now, Rusty?"

Clanahan stood, and the two walked with him slowly back to the pub and laid him on the back-room cot. As they passed, Darnell saw that O'Reilly still sat at the table, and that the women were engaged in noisy conversation.

Darnell brought a moist cloth back to the room and cleaned Clanahan's face. "I told your man you'd be in here for a while." He inspected Clanahan. "Can you tell me about it now?"

He nodded. "Same man as came in here before—my fill-in barkeep, Fitch, saw 'im—the one was killed, you know. He said the man 'ad these cold fish eyes and a queer 'alf-circle scar on 'is cheek."

Darnell tried to bring up the face of Baldrik in his mind. Did he have the scar? He certainly possessed cold, fishy eyes. The eyes of a killer.

Clanahan said, "I messed it up, didn't I? Following 'im?"

"Don't worry about it. We'll catch him." He paused and

studied the barkeep. He seemed to be handling his injury all right.

"Rusty, one question, if you can remember. When that man with the scar bought his drink at the bar, did he pick up the mug with his left or right hand?"

Clanahan took a breath and stared at the ceiling. "The left. No, wait, it was on my left, so it was his right. He was facin' me. Yes, his right. I'm sure of it now."

Darnell thanked Clanahan and cautioned him to rest. He took his place again at the table he had occupied earlier.

He pushed back the mug of ale that still sat there and looked at O'Reilly, who had now caught his eye. He lifted his cap and scratched his head, signaling it was time to leave.

O'Reilly said good night to the women, who said noisy good-byes. She walked out of the pub, and a few seconds later Darnell followed. He stayed a half block behind her until she reached her car and drove off. She was safe now.

He returned to his flat, ready with tales to tell Penny, who he knew would want to hear everything that happened. But the words Clanahan spoke—"I messed it up"—bothered him. Would the killer be so cautious now it would interfere with his capture on the eighth? As he thought about it, Darnell concluded the man would connect the fact that Clanahan pursued him with the death of the other barkeep—not with Mary Kelly. One thing sure, now. That man would not show himself at The Three Hares again. They'd have to find the killer on the streets of Whitechapel.

Chapter Twenty-eight

Monday night, November 5

Darnell arrived home in time for a late, cold supper with Penny in the sitting room. While they ate, and at her prodding, he recounted all the evening's events and adventures. They took a glass of sherry on the sofa afterward.

"Coo, ducky, ye've had a spot of bother, ain't ye?"

Darnell grimaced. "Not another one. I think I've heard enough Whitechapel talk for one night."

"I did some acting in America, John."

"So I heard. But tonight—just be Penny."

She put her arm around his shoulder and kissed him lightly. "Like this?"

"Yes. Much better." They sat staring at the fire Sung had built for them. "Reminds me of that bonfire," he said, "on about a twentieth of the scale."

"Quaint British custom—burning people."

He smiled. "Burning effigies. Straw people."

"Were you satisfied with the night?"

"Ye-es. But there is one thing, Penny. Remember Baldrik?"

She shuddered. "How could I ever forget him? That knife. His big hands."

"I know you remember him, but can you bring up his features in your memory? Do you remember any scars on his face? A half circle, crescent moon?"

Her brow wrinkled. "The two men wore masks, and then they jammed a hat down over my face. Sorry, John. I don't know."

"Hmmm. Well, no mind. But another thing—you may know this. Which hand did he use when he held the knife to your face? Can you remember? I'm sorry to bring all this up. But Baldrik may be involved in these killings."

"Which hand did he use when the men assaulted me?" She frowned, as if imagining their positions. "One held me from behind with his right hand. I think that was it. The right."

Darnell nodded. "Hard to remember, I know. And I think Baldrik had the knife in his right hand when I fought with him in the hospital. No matter—let's talk of something more pleasant."

"Like, um . . . this?" She pressed her lips on his again.

Tuesday, November 6, began with a forbidding gloom of dark clouds over the London horizon, and by late morning the downpour had begun. Darnell felt a sense of anxiety and depression stealing over him, and could not decide how much was due to the weather and how much to the fact that only forty-eight hours remained until the culmination of all his plans.

After a quick breakfast, he drove to Scotland Yard, where he knew he'd find the key players in the drama— Warren, O'Reilly, and Chief Howard—ready and anxious to prepare final arrangements for the night of November 8.

Chief Howard sat, breathing heavily, on Inspector Warren's sofa. He looked up as Darnell entered. "Did you see our man, John?"

Darnell shook his head. "No, but our barkeep friend, Rusty Clanahan, had a run-in with someone and a piece of lead pipe."

Warren drummed his fingers on his desk. "Ruined our plans, I expect."

Darnell explained why he felt the man would connect the incident to the earlier case of the fill-in bartender. "We won't be seeing him in any of the pubs. But he'll be there Thursday."

Warren's lips twisted into a wry grin. "And your actress? Did she survive her first test?"

Darnell nodded. "O'Reilly can answer for herself. Call her in."

Warren raised a hand to an assistant outside his door and in minutes had him bring Sergeant O'Reilly to his office. "Take a seat, Sergeant. And tell us about last night."

She smiled. "I felt like everyone knew I was a Sergeant in streetwalker's clothing, but apparently no one questioned my disguise. I give George Bernard Shaw credit for the rest of it."

"You'll be all right Thursday? Not too nervous? That's the big night."

"Inspector, I know you'll have men everywhere. I can handle it. Just don't let me get out of sight."

Howard asked, "How many men, Nathaniel?"

Warren ticked them off on his fingers. "Six detectives, eight constables. If he shows, he won't slip through our fingers."

"*If* he shows?" Howard looked at Darnell. "What do you think about that, John?"

"The Ripper killed five women. He'll be there. I'm sure of it. And I'm sure that if we'd done nothing, he'd kill and be gone."

"And your last-minute placements of men. You and Inspector Warren will go over them?"

"Yes. And Sergeant O'Reilly needs to know the exact spots."

"Then I'm on my way home. Have to admit I've not felt myself the past few days. Can you get that driver for me, Nathaniel?"

Warren nodded, and soon Howard left for his home. When Howard had exited the office, Warren said, "I'm afraid the Chief may be turning in his ticket soon. Retiring. Well, let's go over the positions, street corners, the men. And then I want you both to meet them all, to be sure you know who they are. Most will be in plain clothes. They know what to do." He gestured toward an assemblage of men. "We can't afford any misidentifications or slipups with a killer on those streets."

Warren spread out a map of Whitechapel on his desk and motioned Darnell and O'Reilly to his side. "Here it is, then."

After their discussion, the last Darnell felt they would have until Thursday, and upon introductions to all Warren's men, Darnell and O'Reilly moved to her desk and sat looking at each other. "I'm still concerned about you," he said, "despite all the careful precautions."

"I'll be all right."

"I'll arrive early myself and scout the area. You'll park

in your usual place and walk over. Each street along your route will be spotted with constables—these men we met."

"I'll be all right, John. I'm just the bait in the trap, remember? I'll expect the detectives to catch the rat."

"So then . . . how is your mother doing, Catherine?"

O'Reilly's eyes clouded over. "Poor dear. She's suffered so much. I don't know how much longer . . ."

The telephone on her desk rang. As she answered it, her eyebrows went up. She covered the speaker and whispered to Darnell, *"Shaw,"* and continued speaking. "Yes, in a half hour. He's here. We'll come together."

She hung up, saying, "Bernard Shaw wants to see us at his place. One last visit."

The earlier downpour had settled into a steady, unrelenting rain, blown at a sharp angle by the brisk winds. Raincoats and umbrellas brought Darnell and O'Reilly to his car, and from it to Shaw's residence, in relatively dry condition. A roaring fire in the playwright's stone fireplace welcomed them, along with Shaw's cheery greeting.

"Sit, sit," he said, "over here by the fire. Dry your toes, and I'll pour a bit of sherry."

Darnell took the glass offered, but O'Reilly declined, taking a cup of tea instead.

"Now, dear girl," Shaw said, rubbing his hands together briskly, "tell me about your acting experience last night. Tell me everything." The playwright's eyes twinkled.

O'Reilly told him about being approached by a man in the street, and Shaw said, "Magnificent!" She told him of Sadie Latkins and the other women, and the jokes, and good humor, and ale. "Ale!" Her lips twisted as she said the word. "How can they drink such stuff? I had trouble keeping it down."

"All part of acting. Of course, you're not in an artificial stage situation, and it's harder. You're in the real world, so you have to do more than pretend. You have to participate."

"I found that out."

"You must be careful not to slip out of character, you know. But it sounds as if you were very successful in your deception last night. Your dress rehearsal."

"Dress rehearsal." She frowned. "And Thursday is opening night."

Chapter Twenty-nine

Wednesday, November 7

The rain ended, but clouds still hung over London. Unable simply to remain at the flat waiting for one more day to expire, Darnell dressed in old clothes to look like a local again, pulled on a cap, and drove to Whitechapel. He parked some distance away from the pub, then casually strolled the streets, not expecting to see anything, merely seeking total familiarity with the surroundings.

He stopped in at The Three Hares and was pleased to find Clanahan behind the bar. He asked him, "Feeling better? Are you up to this?"

Clanahan nodded. "Still a big bump on the back of my head, but it's going down. I hope I can get my hands on 'im sometime."

"Let the police do that. But I'm glad you'll be about tomorrow night."

Clanahan leaned forward. "I don't think anybody suspects anything. Business as usual." He waved a hand toward the room.

Darnell agreed. At eleven a.m., the room buzzed with conversation, and the ale seemed to be flowing freely. "They're talking about that bonfire."

"Biggest one in years." Clanahan lowered his voice. "And Mary Kelly, you know. How is she?"

"She's fine. All set for tomorrow."

"One thing you may not think of, Professor, but I do, 'most every day. That poor little girl. It all started with Poppy."

"We'll avenge her. You can count on it."

*   *   *

Returning to the flat for lunch, Darnell cleaned off the grime and changed clothes. He came down the stairway to find Penny waiting to take his arm. "Lunch is served."

After a salad, hot soup, and cold beef sandwiches, they sat drinking coffee and talking at the table, when the phone rang. In a moment, Sung entered, saying, "It is Inspector Warren."

Darnell took the phone in the sitting room. "Yes, Inspector."

"The Commissioner wants to see us. My father."

"Commissioner Warren wants to see you and me?"

"Specifically you. I think I'm just invited to provide transportation. He knows about tomorrow's plans."

Darnell could readily imagine that the old man knew all their plans. The father and son were close. But who else knew?

"Transportation. So, you'll pick me up?"

"Can you be ready in thirty minutes?"

Darnell knew he had no choice. He said he'd watch for him. He gulped the last of his coffee, told Penny of his plans, and dashed upstairs to grab a leather jacket, gloves, and an umbrella. He knew Warren's car offered little protection from the elements, and the rain could begin again at any time.

Commissioner Charles Warren hobbled to the window and looked out for the fifth time. Where the hell were they? He moved to the fireplace, poked the fire, checked the sherry decanter to be sure it was filled. Only one glass stood next to it. He called out to his butler, "Two more sherry glasses, Joseph. We're having guests."

The man, who had been standing nervously in the hallway awaiting the arrival of the Commissioner's son, hurried into the dining room and returned in a few moments with two more glasses, which he placed by the decanter.

The sound of the lion's-head knocker on the front door reverberated through the hallway, and the butler headed for the door. He bowed slightly as the two men entered. "The Commissioner is expecting you in the study." He inclined his head toward the open door to the right.

Inspector Warren led the way, and Darnell followed him into the study where Commissioner Charles Warren stood, the centerpiece of the room, glaring at them with flinty eyes. "You're late," he accused them, liking to put others on the defensive, even though he knew their arrival time was prompt enough. "Joseph," he called, "you can pour that sherry now. Sit down, Professor." He glanced sidelong at Nathaniel. "You're holding up well, are you? Getting enough sleep?"

"Father, please," Inspector Warren said.

The men took the glasses of sherry the butler presented to them and sat facing the Commissioner, who claimed his own favorite chair near the fireplace. The old man brushed back his white hair and said, "Now, then." He fixed his gaze on Darnell. "This crazy plan you have, Professor." He nodded at his son. "Nathaniel's hinted at it, but I want to hear it straight from you."

"Yes, Sir Charles. I'm sure you're concerned. We all are. What would you like to know?"

The Commissioner fumed. "Everything! Play-acting? Women used to entice a killer? If this man is imitating Jack the Ripper, you need to know that he practically skinned poor Mary Kelly like an animal. Are you willing to risk that?" The man's hands trembled, but he gave no thought to it. An old man should have the right to tremble sometimes. And these events brought back sharply in his mind scenes he had been trying to forget for years. "Well?" He could see the Professor was affected by his words.

"Sir Charles, you're saying the very words that are in my heart," Darnell said. "I worry about this, believe me. But consider the alternative. What if we did nothing to attempt to bait and trap the killer? We've had four killings on the exact days and dates that Jack the Ripper used twenty-nine years ago, women with the same initials as the Ripper's first four victims. If we do nothing, whoever is doing this will no doubt kill again tomorrow night or the next morning, just as the Ripper killed Mary Kelly many years ago."

"And your plan will stop him? Are you sure of that?"

"We've enticed him with an artificial person, a new Mary Kelly. She's a policewoman. It's our one chance to catch him. We'll have detectives and constables all around her, and we'll protect her."

"If you had seen Mary Kelly, you might not be so sure."

Charles Warren rubbed his temples. "I had nightmares for months after seeing her."

"Tomorrow, Commissioner, your nightmares, and ours, will be over. This killer will not claim another victim."

Riding home silently in Inspector Warren's car a half hour later, after lengthy explanations and assurances to the former Commissioner, Darnell went over in his mind again the issues Commissioner Warren had raised. He knew the man was again feeling the pressure, just as if he were in charge of the case, and he understood that emotion. But Darnell could produce no other means, no other plan, for ending the violence. It was up to him and Scotland Yard to do their jobs and make this one work.

As the rest of the day wore on, Darnell occupied himself by speaking to Chief Howard and Sergeant O'Reilly on the phone and going through the plans, over and over. Sleep did not come easily that night, and at two a.m., John Darnell still tossed and turned in his bed, staring at the ceiling.

Chapter Thirty

Thursday night, November 8

Darkness fell early, and in Whitechapel two men sat opposite each other in an end booth of the Red Fox pub. They talked in hushed tones, one dominating the conversation, rambling, angry, sometimes incoherent, the other glum, drinking his ale, saying little. The talker went on, "Then rotting away for twenty years in that hellhole of a prison in Singapore—" He stopped and looked up at two women who had approached their table and were looking down at them.

"Hello, dearies!" one woman said. "Lookin' for a bit o' comfort, are ye?" Both women offered twisted smiles and twinkling, bloodshot eyes to go with their invitations. "Come on, let's 'ave a bit o' fun. Warm yer up on a cold night." The one speaking stopped in the midst of her prattle as one of the men looked up into her eyes.

"Get on with you," the quiet man said. "Peddle your wares on the street. Leave us gentlemen alone."

The other man said nothing now but regarded them with a malevolent stare.

The woman drew a sharp breath as they both now glared at her. "Gentlemen! Sure you are!"

She turned to her companion. "Come on, Pearl. We'll leave the *gentlemen* alone." She tried to laugh as they walked off. "Singapore! Just as glad they didn't want nothin' from us. A dark alley with them?" She shivered.

"Damned women, I hate 'em," the talkative man said. "Always hated 'em. One more night, and I'm gone. Hate London, too—the damned police, the whores, the stinkin' pubs. Give me France, Greece, Italy, even Singapore, if it ain't in jail. Different world there. A man's a man, those places."

"You got a woman there, somewhere?"

The other snarled. "Woman? No, no woman. I had a woman once. They took her from me. No one in this world like her." He stared off across the expanse of the room. Remembering his mug of ale, he scooped it up and drank half of it. He studied his companion with bleary eyes. "You got it straight, then, for tonight? Don't have to go over it again?"

"Look, I ain't stupid," the other growled his response. "I know what to do."

"And what'll you do after, when we're done with it?"

The other scowled. "I'm a dead man if I stay in England. I'm marked—and they'll get me. So I leave, too, but don't ask how or where. You go your way, and you don't ask about mine."

"Fair enough. We split. We go our own ways."

"Exactly." The man's eyes narrowed. "Now, the cash. I'll need it. You got it?"

The other looked about the room before reaching in a pocket of his long black coat. He pulled out a bulging soiled and torn envelope. "There's ten-pound notes in here, twenty of 'em. That should get you to where you want to go."

The envelope changed hands, and the man folded it and stuffed it securely in a back pocket. "Just one thing, if we get into trouble, tonight, then what?"

"Trouble? Who's to give us trouble? Nobody knows about this." He smirked. "My plan's worked so far, right? I know what I'm doing, who I'm lookin' for, and where she'll be."

"Yeah." The other stared into his mug of ale. "But I been in scrapes lately that didn't go like the careful plans of some. I don't need to tell you that."

"Your part's easy. It's only, you know—insurance. The job is mine. I want to do it myself." His eyes gleamed now, the frown marks between his thick eyebrows deepening. He brushed back strands of graying black hair, adjusted his thin black tie, and fingered a battered top hat on the table next to his drink.

"We'll just sit here a while and drink some more of this watered-down swill while we wait. Two more hours before she'll be on the street. I know the habits of the women down here. And I've been watching her. I got a room to take her to, near her usual spot, and my car's near that. By nine o'clock, ten o'clock, that's when the last of this thing begins for me. And ends for Mary Kelly."

Sadie Latkins and Pearl Winfred stepped up to the bar in The Three Hares and motioned to Rusty Clanahan. "Two ales, dearie."

Clanahan slid the brimming mugs down in front of them, they fumbled for their coins, and he picked up the money. He studied the women, giving them a wry grin. "Business slow?"

"Slow? Gawd! We was at the Red Fox . . . sorry, Rusty, we ain't no regulars there, we're not quittin' the Hares. Jus' lookin' for fresh blokes. They was fresh, yeah, they was. Flamin' crazies. Called themselves 'gentlemen,' eh, Pearl? Hah!"

Pearl laughed in response. She tasted her ale.

Sadie went on. "But Rusty, I tell you, there was something else about 'em. I don't know. They gimme the shivers, they did. One of 'em had those eyes, cold marbles, black, like his clothes. Twenty years in Singapore. Prison, 'e said. Scars on the other's face."

Clanahan looked up, startled, staring at her. "Scars? What kind?"

"I don't know. Scars. You know. From knife fights, I'm guessin'."

"But what'd they look like, the scars? Come on, Sadie!"

Pearl coughed. "One of 'em had a half-moon scar on his cheek. Made me shiver. Looked like the moon tonight."

"Damn! Do you think they're still there, those men?"

"I don't know. It's been an hour."

Clanahan frowned, and his thoughts turned inward. He tried to block out the babble of men and women warming up for the evening with chatter and drink. Some of the talk was still about the bonfire, some occasionally saying her name, Mary Kelly, talking about how she'd lit the fire. Lots of laughter, all of it inspired by the ale in front of them and the night still ahead of them.

He knew one of the two men they talked of could be the killer of Fitch. He felt it was, from Pearl's description of that distinctive scar. But what to do about it? He couldn't ruin the plans for this night, chance another mistake, as he'd almost done on the night they burned Guy Fawkes. He gingerly touched the back of his head in remembrance of his misadventure.

Clanahan had been told that constables and detectives in plain clothes would be in their positions outside, getting familiar with their spots and blending in with locals. The policewoman, as Mary Kelly, had not arrived. She was to check in with him. When she came, the trap would be baited, and Darnell and the others could do their job.

He made his decision. He'd tell Darnell, when he came, that the man with the scar was about, and was with a second man. He'd give him the location of the Red Fox. Maybe that would help. It was all he dared do. If Darnell wanted him to go to the Red Fox with him, he'd do that. He'd be glad to do that. Scowling, he took a glass from a shelf, filled it with ale, and took a long swallow.

Darnell drove toward the Whitechapel area, his mind swirling with doubts and fears. Despite the careful plans, he knew something could still go wrong. He wore the old "local" clothes again. He parked well away from the center of activity, a radius of half a mile around The Three Hares, where Sergeant O'Reilly had set a regular pattern of being seen the past few days, in her role as Mary Kelly.

As he strolled toward the pub, he reflected that although the killer had no doubt observed her, he'd made no move to approach her. The man was waiting to perform his exact replica of the Ripper's crime, sometime late this night. According to plan, Inspector Warren would have been in Whitechapel for an hour, checking on his men, watching and waiting. Sergeant O'Reilly would be last to arrive, after eight p.m., dressed, of course, in her Mary Kelly clothing. He smiled, remembering how she always added that extra touch of smearing a bit of grime and dirt on her cheeks. Shades of Eliza Doolittle indeed!

Darnell tried to look like a local, stopping at a stand to pick up a newspaper full of fish and chips. He tossed it away uneaten when he reached the pub. He saw Clanahan eye him with a high sign from the bar, and knew something had happened.

*   *   *

Sergeant Catherine O'Reilly drove as fast as she could in the dark night, rubbing unstoppable tears from her eyes with one hand. Her lips trembled as she groaned, "God! Dear God!" She pulled the car up in front of the Darnells' flat, rushed to the door, and knocked loudly.

Penny Darnell opened the door and stepped back, showing obvious surprise at the condition and appearance of Sergeant O'Reilly. "Catherine? You look very upset. Come in, please."

O'Reilly stepped into the entryway and took Penny's hand in both of hers. "I'm losing my mind, Penny. I should be at Whitechapel in a half hour, and—and, my mother's dying! I received a call tonight." The tears ran down her face.

"The hospital called you?"

"*Oh, God!* They said if I didn't get there in an hour, she could be gone. She won't last much more. I have to be with her at the end. She's all I've got." She gripped Penny's hands.

"Come into the sitting room. Tonight's the big night."

"Yes. I can't go, but I can't *not* go. There's my duty on one hand. And my mother. I don't know what to do." She collapsed into a chair and held her head in her hands. She looked up. "I thought the Professor might still be here."

"He left almost an hour ago." Penny frowned. "We're twenty minutes away from Whitechapel. There's no way to reach him. You could go there, then go on to the hospital and still be in time."

"Go there? But what'll I do?"

Penny brushed the question aside. "Is your disguise, the costume and everything, all in your car?"

"Ye-es."

"Quickly, let's bring it all in."

"But—"

"Please, Catherine, let me do the thinking on this." She took the sergeant's hand and pulled her out through the doorway to the car. They bundled up the clothing and hurried back inside with it. Back in the sitting room, Penny closed the door.

"Give me all the clothes."

"What? Oh, no!"

"Yes, I'll take your place. I know what to do, I've

watched you and Shaw enough, felt like I was studying it all myself. I know something about acting." As she talked, she stripped off her outer clothing and shoes and pulled on the Mary Kelly costume. She talked on. "You can drop me off, tell me the spots where you can be expected to be seen. I've been there with John, and I know the area."

"Professor Darnell will never speak to me again, and I can't even think what Inspector Warren will do." Sergeant O'Reilly shuddered. She watched in morbid fascination as, with each article of clothing, Penny took on more and more the appearance of the woman O'Reilly had been portraying. "You can't do this!"

"I have to do it," Penny said. "We have no choice." She stepped over to a mirror and turned about. "How do I look, dearie?" she said, in a cockney Eliza Doolittle voice. "Am I a bloody street woman, or not?"

O'Reilly said nothing. She sighed deeply, went to a potted plant sitting on a table and took a bit of dirt on her fingers. She lightly smeared some of it on Penny's face and rubbed it in, then dusted it off. "That's better. Never look too clean. You're a bit taller than me, but not enough to raise suspicion. Now tuck all that long hair of yours under the bonnet." She helped Penny push it in around the back of her neck, turned her around and studied her. "I guess you'll pass."

"Then we have to go. Come." As they hurried to the front door again, she saw Sung standing near the entrance. He stared at Sergeant O'Reilly and then at Penny. "Is it Mrs. Darnell?"

"Yes, it's me, Sung. I can't say more now. But I'll be seeing Mr. Darnell in a while. So don't worry about this."

As soon as they were seated in the car, O'Reilly turned it around and headed even faster than before toward Whitechapel. She had lost precious minutes and could only think of her mother, fighting for her life, alone, in a cold hospital bed.

O'Reilly bit her lip and drove steadily, knowing her only salvation now was to follow Penny's lead, get her there, entrust her to the police, and then go on to the hospital.

She told Penny to check in with Rusty Clanahan at The Three Hares pub. She described the women she'd met, including Sadie Latkins, Hannah, and Pearl, and specified the corner where O'Reilly had been standing each night, a block down from the pub. She explained how to identify the constables and detectives in their disguises by an agreed-upon whistling signal, and described how some would approach her, as if buying her services.

"But they'll be watching you," she said. "You don't need to seek them out. Just walk along, dressed this way, and they'll watch out for you. Dozens of eyes will be on you. Burt Fenham's the local constable. He'll be alert." She looked sidelong at Penny. "Just be careful—for God's sake, be careful! And one thing—never walk fast, it's not in character. Remember what Bernard Shaw told me—well, you heard him—be slow, languid, inviting, just trolling to meet some men, pick up some coins."

Penny nodded. She looked out at the buildings they passed. "I think we're almost there, Catherine. Just drop me off where you'd park. Point me toward The Three Hares, and I'll be going. Then hurry to your mother."

Chapter Thirty-one

Thursday night, November 8

Penny stepped out of the car onto the dark street. O'Reilly said, "Be careful, and good luck." Penny nodded and watched as the car turned around and sped quickly away. She took a deep breath and looked about her. Few people were on the street, a man or two near each corner as she walked toward the pub.

She suspected some of the men leaning against lampposts or smoking cigarettes, standing in doorways, were actually detectives or constables in their plainclothes disguises. She made no sign to them, saw no need of it, and just walked slowly toward The Three Hares. The first step, Catherine had told her, was to check in with Rusty Clanahan. Buying a mug of ale would accomplish that. She felt eyes on her, on the back of her neck, as she walked—an eerie feeling. If they were detectives' eyes, she should feel comfort, but no comfort came.

As she walked along, she recalled what her husband had said about Baldrik being involved. She shivered at the thought, at the remembrance of his knife blade he held at her cheek.

The pub appeared at last, and she strolled up to it, entered the noisy, busy room, and swaggered up to the bar. Two barkeeps kept the customers supplied. One of them said, "What'll ye have?"

"Ale, ducky. 'N' fill it up." She placed a coin on the surface and watched him draw ale into a mug.

At the far end of the bar Penny saw the other bartender, a red-haired older man, glance in her direction. He walked down and took the mug from the one who drew it from

the tap. He placed it in front of her and smiled. " 'Evenin',
Miss—oh!"

"Rusty, isn't it? I've taken her place," Penny said quickly
in a lowered voice. "You don't know me. She couldn't
come tonight—her mother's dying. I'll do what she would
have done."

"My God! You do look alike—and the clothes. But, well,
the face, up close, not quite."

"I know. I hope it isn't a problem."

"Only if someone's stood close to her, like me. Ten feet
away—you're her. I thought you was, 'til I came over
here."

"Good. I'll take a seat, drink some of this, and then go
to my spot."

"The professor was in, earlier. He's out, prowlin', I think.
You know 'im?"

Penny smiled. "Yes, I know him. The question is, will he
know me?"

She took her ale to a small unoccupied table against the
wall and sat sipping it. Without a watch, not part of her
costume, she reckoned the time now as between eight and
eight-thirty. She'd give it a while, thirty minutes as best she
could figure it, toying with the ale, then find the spot where
O'Reilly had been standing each of the past two nights and
take her position, and play her part.

She sat thinking of how O'Reilly described the pretense
of how the men—detectives and constables—would approach her, how they'd take her to a dark alleyway and
pretend to pay for her sexual favors, after which she would
resume her siren-like evening. That lay ahead for her, if
she were to do exactly as O'Reilly did. The men knew what
to do, and she could test them with the little whistle signal,
if in doubt. Of course, they'd also whisper, "Constable
Brown, miss," or the like, as O'Reilly had told her, when
they came up to her.

At what she guessed was about nine p.m., Penny pushed
her half-empty glass back and strolled out the door and to
her right, down to the corner. She took her spot, leaning
languidly against the building at the edge of the circle of
yellowed light from the lamppost. At once, a tall man
walked up and stood next to her, facing her. "Constable
Fenham, mum. You remember me, Sergeant?"

Penny lifted her head and gazed into his face. Yes, the solid, honest face she'd expect from a local constable, much as O'Reilly had said. But he wore old, faded clothes.

He looked into her face. "Oh!"

"Shhh. I'm taking Sergeant O'Reilly's place. It's all right, Burt."

"You know me? But I don't know you. You had me fooled, though. Gave me quite a start. Replacement, eh?"

"What now?"

"You're doin' her job, miss, so we walk down the street to the alley and step in there for a bit, as if, you know—"

She took his arm. "Coins, ducky," she said in a louder, cockney voice.

Fenham reached in the tattered coat pocket and put something in her hand. They walked down the street and into an alleyway.

The killer watched the tableau from his vantage point in a darkened doorway across the street, his partner next to him. "She'll be back in fifteen, twenty minutes, patting her hair back in place," he said. "That's when you do your part, and earn your keep."

"A fight is what you want? In the pub?"

"A disturbance, yes. A fight'll do it, like we said. I want you to draw in any bobby that might be walking by and take everyone's eyes off me and her. Just yell out, *'I'll kill you!'* Something like that. Grab some bloke and hold him, put him out on the floor, then beat it out the side door and on your way."

"So we watch for her."

"And when we see her coming, you head across to the pub."

Darnell stood inside the door of the Red Fox. Clanahan had told him what Sadie and Pearl said about the two men, their descriptions, the story about prison in Singapore for twenty years, how one had the scar, the other cold black eyes. He sauntered about the room, glancing into booths. Surely the man with the scar murdered Fitch. But he saw no one fitting the descriptions Clanahan had given him. Booths were occupied now, but mostly with couples or two women obviously hoping for company.

"Damn!" he said.

In a corner, he pulled his watch half out of a coat pocket, cupped in his hand. Nine-fifteen. They'd gone, the two of them. He was sure one was Baldrik, who'd escaped execution and tried to kill Chief Howard. And the other? From Singapore, after twenty years in prison? He shook his head. Time to get back to The Three Hares. He began to walk back the several blocks.

If their man was coming, whether or not one of these two, he would be making his move in the next hour or two. Darnell felt it would take place at night, but it could be a long night of watching and waiting. He thought of Sergeant O'Reilly at her station, and even though she was surrounded by police, he felt a sudden concern for her. The killer or killers were watching her, too. Darnell quickened his step. Despite the coolness of the evening, he felt perspiration bead on his forehead.

Penny Darnell, in the guise of Mary Kelly, walked slowly back to the spot where Constable Fenham had approached her. She took her position, then made as if to straighten her dress and adjust her bonnet. She stood, swinging her purse back and forth like a pendulum as she looked one way and another, watching men going back and forth, passing her by.

She would not speak to them, of course. She'd wait for the next detective or constable to come up to her and go through the charade of solicitation.

But everything changed in an instant. Loud voices erupted from the pub several doors away, and she glanced over in that direction. A number of men she felt were policemen ran from the street through the front doorway of The Three Hares into the pub. A man wearing a long black coat and odd hat shouted, *"Fight!"*

Other men ran into the pub. Long-coat turned toward her and seemed to fix his eyes on her. He walked toward Penny with a deliberate stride, swinging a black bag gently by his side in unison with each step.

Darnell heard the commotion and ran into the pub in time to see several police pile on top of two men who were fighting. One of the two pulled a knife from somewhere and lashed out with it at constables trying to overpower him. Darnell pulled his .38 revolver and sought an opening to fire. When a policeman fell away, dropping from a knife wound, he shot twice. The man with the knife fell.

Darnell ran and bent over him. "Baldrik!" he said. He saw a half-moon scar on the man's face.

"Where's your friend, Baldrik? Talk! You have nothing to lose now."

Blood oozed from the side of Baldrik's mouth. "He—he ratted on me, the bastard. I wasn't ready . . . he wanted me to be bait."

"Where is he, man?"

Baldrik tried to laugh, but it came out as a gurgle. "Where? Find her, find Mary Kelly, you'll find . . . him." His words weakened, his former guttural voice now a mere whisper.

Darnell knew he had only seconds left before he had to leave, before Baldrik would be unable to speak. "Who is he, Baldrik? You're a dead man. Tell me. I'll get him for you."

"Find woman, you'll get him . . . the docks, a ship . . ."

"Who is he? Tell me!"

Baldrik gurgled his last words. "I—I—just called him Jack."

The turmoil and noise seemed to go on uninterrupted as the man walked purposefully toward Penny Darnell. *He doesn't look like police*, she thought, and shrank back from him as he reached her.

"Never mind that, we're going for a little walk."

He grabbed her arm roughly and drew her along with him a few steps. "No!" she said. Afraid now, she swung the purse at his face and caught him in the eye with it. She had to get away! "Help!" she called, hoping a constable would hear.

"Bitch!" he snarled, tossing her purse down on the street and grabbing both of her slender wrists in his free hand. Still carrying his bag in the other, he dragged her along the street into an alleyway, across a dark court, and through an open back gate opposite the entrance. Penny knew now that this man was the killer. She screamed and struggled as they passed through the gate. Her bonnet fell off and her long auburn hair cascaded out, tumbling down about her neck.

The man paused in mid-stride at the sight as they passed under a light to look at her. "Well, a pretty head of hair we have here." He frowned, looking into her face carefully. He continued dragging her along but released her wrists and covered her mouth harshly with one hand, his arm around her back. "You bitch! You're no whore. Who are you?" But with her mouth covered, she could not answer, could not scream anymore, and he did not slow his pace. "We're almost there now. Then we'll see."

Darnell ran from the pub, down the street, and found the purse a few paces past that. His pulse raced. *He's got Catherine!* He ran on, and soon saw an alleyway and turned into it at full speed, finding himself in a dingy court. Although it was dark, he could make out a gate standing open at the far end of the court. When he reached it, he found the bonnet in the dirt at the foot of the gate. *Mary Kelly's— Sergeant O'Reilly's—bonnet.* He ran faster and shouted, "Sergeant! Sergeant! Where are you? O'Reilly!"

He heard running footfalls not far away, apparently around the corner up ahead, and suddenly heard a woman's voice call out, "John, help!" Then the sound stopped. But that voice . . . ?

He ran faster, turned the corner, and saw a man in a long coat a block away dragging a woman in the Mary Kelly costume—the Sergeant. "Stop!" he shouted and pulled out his .38. He shot in the air as he ran. The woman, struggling in the man's grasp, seemed to dig her heels into the dirt, and the man dropped her and ran off, much faster now, free of his encumbrance.

Darnell ran up to the woman. "Sergeant! Are you—oh, my God! Penny!" He scooped her up in his arms. "What are you doing here? Are you all right? Where's Catherine?"

Two policemen who had been following ran up to them.

"Get him, John," she cried. "He's getting away—I'll tell you later."

Darnell turned to the two men, one of them Inspector Warren. "I'm glad it's you, Inspector. Take care of my wife."

He ran off down the street in pursuit of the man ahead. He heard the sound of an engine starting around a corner, and a car pulling away. "Damn!"

He ran past the spot, continuing on to his own car, tore the door open, and jumped in. After two cranks of the starter the car sprang into life and he pulled away into the street. He knew where to go. *The docks,* Baldrik had said. *Ships would be leaving tonight.* Freighters. That must have been the killer's escape plan. He pushed the car's speed to the limit and in minutes reached the bottom of the boulevard approaching Tower Bridge.

He saw a car pulled in at a crazy angle at the curb, and he looked about frantically for a sign of the man. Boats were down to the left of him and to the right, but he felt he'd surprised the killer by arriving so soon, and possibly startled him into a change of plan. At last he saw him, long coat flapping in the night wind, running across Tower Bridge. Darnell ran after him, his .38 out, only a short distance behind him now.

As he watched him, he realized he was catching up, stride for stride. His quarry heard him coming and stopped suddenly at the bridge railing, dropping an open black bag on the bridge. He whirled, facing Darnell, knife in hand. Surprised, Darnell was caught off balance. The long glittering knife slashed out at him, catching Darnell in the wrist of his right hand.

Darnell dropped his revolver, but flung himself at the man, in turn knocking the knife to the floor of the bridge. When the killer stooped to reach for it, Darnell attacked him with a blistering blow to the man's jaw. As it connected, he heard a sharp crack and a yelp of pain. He struck again before the man could recover.

At the bridge entrance, another car roared up, and two detectives ran toward Darnell and the killer. When Darnell turned to see them, the killer struck him on the neck with the side of his hand, stunning him. Darnell struggled with the impact as the man climbed over the railing, stood at the edge of the bridge, and looked down at the water, crying, "You won't get me!" Before Darnell or the two detectives who had reached the spot could grab him, he jumped toward the water. But as he fell, a riverboat, not yet visible even seconds earlier, passed under the bridge from the opposite direction.

Darnell heard the resounding thud of the man's body as it struck the deck of the boat, which had passed directly under the path of the falling man. He knew it was the sound of death.

The detectives ran down to the lower level and shouted at the captain to bring the boat in to the dock. With a body landing on his boat, the captain seemed to have no reluctance in cooperating. In minutes the detectives were helping the crew secure the boat to an upriver dock. Darnell ran to the spot, carrying with him the man's black bag and knife, which he had recovered from the bridge. In the other hand he held his own retrieved revolver.

One of the detectives who had boarded the boat turned and approached Darnell. "No need for the gun," he said. "This man's gone."

Darnell and the others walked to the side of the fallen man on the deck. The boat captain stood a few feet away, staring at the body. Blood was everywhere, the man's neck and legs at bizarre angles. Yes, Darnell said to himself, he's dead. He bent down to take a close look at the man's features, but did not recognize him. The unseeing eyes of the body seemed to stare wide at the sky, and Darnell pulled the lids down to close them.

"Let's see what's in his pockets," Darnell said, and the detectives nodded. Darnell went through each pocket, discovering a quantity of money in English pounds and Italian currency.

"The *Santa Lucia* leaves tonight," the captain said, seeing the foreign bills. "Her regular trip. He was probably going to board her."

In an inside coat pocket, Darnell found the evidence he needed. His heart pounded, and he wasn't sure whether it was from the struggle or the excitement of seeing before him the faded photograph. It was of a woman, in the healthy bloom of her early twenties. She had appealing wide-set eyes, full lips, and luxuriant hair. A compelling woman. He turned over the old photograph and read the words on the back: *"To my husband, Galvyn, with love. Heather."* The woman in the photo was Heather Kane. The dead man, obviously, was *Galvyn Kane*.

Darnell stood up and stared into space for a moment. He thought back upon his trip with O'Reilly to the clinic in Whitechapel, and the stories they uncovered about that victim in July 1888, Heather Kane, the young nurse who was slashed in the street before the Ripper's serial killing began. He was putting it all together now. Quickly, he tore open the black bag again and rummaged through its contents. What else would he find?

Suddenly, with a sense of macabre completion, he found in the bottom of the bag several weathered and wrinkled old sheets of a calendar for the year 1888. They were without doubt from an original calendar from that year of the Ripper killings. Underneath that was a current calendar for 1917, which he knew was identical as to day and date with the old one. Darnell was thrilled to see that the dates were circled again and again on each calendar—August 31, September 8, September 30, and November 9. He pulled out his watch. Almost eleven p.m. Still November 8. But no final victim for November 9 to complete the man's plan.

Darnell gazed down at the body again, noticing fully now the man's pasty complexion, his once black hair streaked heavily with gray. A bitter man in his mid-fifties who'd lived for nothing for years but the equally bitter taste of revenge. *Jack the Ripper himself! The real Jack the Ripper!* Darnell knew it was him, and he had the proof in his own hands. But the Ripper had died before he could kill his second Mary Kelly—and last victim. A woman who in this bizarre turn of events could have been John Darnell's own wife, Penny.

Darnell leaned against a lamp pole and blotted the perspiration from his forehead with a handkerchief. *Penny!* What would he have done the rest of his life if he had failed?

Chapter Thirty-two

Thursday night, November 8

By midnight, everyone in Whitechapel knew of the death of the "ghost-killer," as Sadie Latkins quickly dubbed him. But none knew yet the true facts Darnell had pulled together. Inspector Warren's car roared up to the bridge with Penny by his side. When they reached Darnell, she jumped out and ran into his arms. He held her tightly, as if never to let her go.

Warren came up to them at last and cleared his throat. "So this is our copycat killer, John?"

Darnell gestured at the dead man. "No, Inspector. That's not a copycat. It's the man your father searched for, almost thirty years ago, the man responsible for the murders of five poor women in 1888 and four when he came back this year for his revenge."

"You mean . . ."

"Yes. He's the real Jack the Ripper. No copycat. And not Baldrik, either, who helped him do some of his killings. The real Jack himself. And I've got the proof of it, for all the world to see."

"Are you sure, John? I can't believe it, after all these years." Warren stood open-mouthed, staring down at the body, as did the other officers. All Warren seemed to be able to say was, "The Ripper . . . Jack the Ripper."

Penny clung to Darnell. "Is it really all over now, John? Is it really him and he's really dead at last? No double ending? No one else lying in wait for us somewhere?"

"No, darling. Because of your bravery—foolhardy bravery, I might say—we got him. I shudder to think . . ."

"What now, John?" Inspector Warren said.

"It's late, I know, but we should go to Scotland Yard.

I'll tell you all about it there. Show you the proof. Tell you how all the pieces fall together." He gestured at the body. "Have your men take that thing to your morgue."

"And Mrs. Darnell?"

"I'll bring her along with me. She's entitled to hear the story after what she's been through here tonight. She was the star, in more ways than one."

Warren nodded. "Chief Howard's waiting at the Yard. Said he had to come down, couldn't sleep at home on this night."

Darnell looked at Penny. "And Sergeant O'Reilly? What happened to her?"

As Darnell listened with wonder, Penny explained about O'Reilly's mother being in desperate condition in the hospital, how she had donned the costume and had O'Reilly drop her off in Whitechapel. "But I don't know where she is. Does anyone know?" She looked at Warren, who shook his head.

"Then let's go to the Yard," Darnell said. "She'll come there." He put the photo in a pocket, took in one hand the black bag containing the knife the Ripper had dropped, the calendars, and two other long knives, and took Penny's arm in his other hand. They walked to his car. He held open the door for her and at last was able to smile as he said, "Step in . . . *Mary Kelly.*"

Inspector Warren's office buzzed with loud conversations among Chief Howard, Warren, Constable Burt Fenham, Penny, and John Darnell. They stopped suddenly when Sergeant O'Reilly came up to the door and stood facing them. The silence continued for a moment until she said, sobbing, "She's gone. I'm sorry. I—I don't know what to say. But I had her last half hour with her."

Penny jumped up and ran to her. She put her arms around her and soothed her as Catherine O'Reilly cried on her shoulder. But after a minute, O'Reilly abruptly said, "I have to stop crying. Thank you, Penny." Still, her unending tears continued to roll quietly down her cheeks. Penny blotted them with a handkerchief Darnell handed her and led O'Reilly to a sofa. She sat next to her while O'Reilly tried to compose herself.

Darnell stood, facing the others, saying, "I'll tell you

what I know, now." The others looked at him with attention. "I can't tell you how relieved I am to say it's all over. The Jack the Ripper case is ended—both the original one from 1888 and our new one this year. Because the same man was the murderer in each series of killings. The true Jack the Ripper."

The conversation boomed up again, all also applauding Darnell's words. Howard said, "Thank God!"

Darnell held up a hand. "That applause belongs to Penny. She risked her life tonight." He smiled at her, then went on. "Some of what I'm going to tell you," he said, "Sergeant O'Reilly will recall. We discovered some of this together. Some of it may make sense as you hear it. Some of it may be challenged by those who weren't there tonight or weren't there in 1888. But I'm convinced this night puts an end to all the crimes of Jack the Ripper."

He took a breath. "It began, of course, twenty-nine years ago, but not with the death of Polly Nichols, the Ripper's first victim, on Friday, August thirty-first, 1888. Let's back up to the night of July twenty-fifth, a month earlier. A doctor in a Whitechapel clinic kept his unfortunate nurse working late at night, after regular hours, at the office. A fair supposition is that he may have been interested in her as a woman, not just as a nurse. She was a beautiful young woman, and her husband was away at sea. How far he went with his ideas, we don't know, maybe not far, and we'll never know. But something upset her. Anxious to get away, she ran from the clinic office into the dark streets.

"A man on the deserted street of that neighborhood at that late hour accosted her and slashed her with a long knife. That woman was Heather Kane, and she was four months pregnant. She was assaulted and slain while her husband, Galvyn Kane, in his regular occupation as a sailor, was away on his ship.

"When Kane returned and learned of the circumstances of the death of his wife, you can imagine that he went simply berserk. His madness simmered down into a seething rage. No doubt he went to the clinic, learning what he could about what happened just before his wife was murdered. In his rage, he planned vengeance on the doctor, an eye for an eye, by killing the doctor's wife."

"I think he must have gone crazy with grief," Penny said.

"And insanely dangerous," Warren said. "But why didn't he kill the doctor's wife at the time, if he blamed the doctor for her death? Why kill prostitutes instead?"

Darnell nodded. "Good point. The answer is that the doctor's wife had died in childbirth. And the doctor himself dropped out of sight soon after that, leaving the clinic. So the Ripper—we'll call him that now—in his frustration and fury, began killing surrogate victims, women on the street in Whitechapel, common prostitutes, as substitutes. To vent his rage. His twisted mind saw it as avenging his wife."

Warren persisted. "And why prostitutes?"

"The women were readily available and defenseless. He saw them perhaps as another cause of Heather's death. The way men treated common prostitutes on the street, taking what they wanted, slaughtering them. But he didn't reckon with the furor the killings soon caused in London. He wasn't rational. So finally, after five murders, some of his rage was spent. I can imagine he began looking for the doctor again, wanting to find him and avenge himself on the doctor's family in some way. I think he found the doctor and learned about his wife and young daughter."

Warren pressed, "But why did he stop killing then?"

"As a sailor, he'd be in port often on the weekends. He'd come in Thursday or Friday, ship out Sunday night or Monday morning. I think some of you know the Ripper's killings were always on the weekend. Polly Nichols's body was found about four a.m. Friday morning, Annie Chapman's at six a.m. on a Saturday, Liz Stride at about two a.m. Sunday, Kate Eddowes on a Sunday about two a.m., and Mary Kelly on a Friday at almost noon. The killings fit his schedule, I'm sure, of shipping in and out of London."

Warren frowned. "And why did he stop?"

"For one of two reasons. He may have felt the pressure from the police searches too intensive and became so afraid of being caught that he left the country. Or—as they did with sailors at that time who were drunk or not coming aboard on time—some of his shipmates may have just hauled him aboard ship one night and sailed away, on a longer trip that time. A trip, with his twenty years in prison in Singapore, that was to last twenty-nine years."

Sergeant O'Reilly was peering at him closely now, obviously listening, seeming to forget her own troubles for the moment. "What a horrible man he must have been," she said. "What a horrible life he must have led—losing his wife, murdering women, with all that hate inside him."

Darnell nodded and went on. "So, twenty-nine years later he returns, with vengeance still in mind." He turned to Howard. "The man who attacked you, Bruce, had to be Baldrik. The attack was his idea, for his own revenge, and the style of attack was typical. Baldrik always had a knife with him. He died in Whitechapel tonight, finally paying the price for his previous murders but saving the cost of execution. After he escaped prison, Kane had probably met and hired him in some Whitechapel pub to help with his plan."

Warren said, "So Baldrik killed that barkeep, Fitch."

"That seems clear, based on Clanahan's identification by his scar and method of killing—simply stabbed. Baldrik knew Fitch could have identified him and probably Kane. On the double-murder night in September, Baldrik killed Lorraine Sheffield, following Kane's instructions on mutilation details, while Kane revenged himself on Kathleen Eden, daughter of the man he blamed for his wife's death. Dr. Blayne Eden worked with Heather Kane at the Whitechapel clinic in 1888."

Inspector Warren said, "Then why didn't he stop killing after Kathleen Eden's death, if that was what he wanted? Why did he take the bait of the fictitious Mary Kelly and risk everything to kill her, too?"

"He definitely wanted to kill the doctor's daughter," Darnell said. "But he also wanted other things—he wanted to go unpunished; he wanted to repeat exactly the obsessive pattern of killing he had established in 1888 to bring back the thrill of that. Remember, he chose the same days of the week, the same dates in the 1917 calendar as in 1888, the same initials of the women, the same grisly methods of killing and mutilation. He had to go on and kill an 'M.K.' on November 8 this year, to fulfill his compulsion. As it turned out, it was another 'Mary Kelly,' or so he thought. It was his psychological makeup, his obsessiveness, that drove him to it, and his slyness, too."

Warren said, "As a policeman, I think I can guess at a practical reason he had to go on with the final killing. It would complete a show of an obsessive rage, which would throw off any normal investigation of the Kathleen Eden murder. His one exposure to police procedure was his connection to Dr. Eden."

Darnell nodded. "That's exactly right, Nathaniel. He had a devious, criminal mind now, after years of scheming in a dingy prison. He hid his Kathleen Eden murder among the others, so his reason for killing her could never be traced back in any way to Dr. Eden, or the clinic, or Heather Kane. He concealed his primary crime within the other four."

Howard caught Darnell's attention. "How do you know he was in prison all those years, John?"

"We found that out from Sadie Latkins. She and Pearl approached Baldrik and Kane in the Red Fox pub. She heard one man tell the other about his twenty years in a Singapore prison. She told Clanahan about it and gave him the descriptions of the men, and he told me. So he was in prison for twenty years, and when he got out, he found enough money somehow to get back here—stole it, no doubt—and begin his second killing spree that had festered in his soul, that he'd dreamed about for thousands of long nights in the dank cells of what he called his 'hellhole' prison. He'd figured out the matching of calendar days and dates, all of that, and fixed his plan on the year 1917, when he'd be out of prison at last, for that reason."

Warren cleared his throat loudly and said, "But what am I to say to those who want proof? My Superintendent, for example."

"We have more than enough proof. First, he tried to kill Penny tonight. She can identify him." He looked at Penny, sitting next to O'Reilly. "And others, like Sadie, can identify the body as the man in the Red Fox. Baldrik put the blame on Kane and called him 'Jack' when he was dying. He said Kane had used him as a diversion, throwing him to the police."

Darnell pulled out Heather Kane's photo and laid it on the desk in front of Warren. "Read the inscription on the back: 'To my husband, Galvin, with love. Heather.' That was in his bag." He opened the black bag on Warren's desk and pulled out two long, razor-sharp knives. "Look at his knives, stained with his victims' blood." He took out the calendars. "And this clinches it—these August through November pages from an 1888 calendar he had kept all those years, with dates of the killings circled. And this 1917 calendar with the same dates circled. His only failure was not killing his last victim, whom he wanted to be found the morning of November 9, just as Mary Kelly was found. And, God forbid, that would have been Penny."

Inspector Warren nodded. "When I present this to my father, I'm sure even the old Commissioner will agree with you. And he'll be relieved it's all over at last in his final years. I'm as certain as you are that the Ripper's lying in our morgue right now. Do you realize you solved both sets of crimes at once? Well done, John. Well done!"

Warren paused and rubbed his chin. "My only problem is, how do I tell the public it was actually him, that Jack the Ripper was stalking unsuspecting women in the streets of London all this time and I didn't warn them? No, my Commissioner will have to decide what to tell the press. He may have to tone it down."

Sergeant O'Reilly rose, and she and Penny came over to Darnell. O'Reilly took his hand. "I'm sorry I wasn't there, John."

"You were where you belonged." He glanced at his wife. "I'm not sure *Penny* was. But it's done now."

Inspector Warren said, "Don't worry about it, Sergeant. We understand everything. You did your part all the way along."

Chief Howard nodded. "Sergeant, you and Mrs. Darnell both deserve an honorary police badge, and a commendation. London can sleep in peace now.

Penny put an arm around O'Reilly's shoulder. "Stay with John and me tonight, Catherine. We have the spare room. And you shouldn't be alone. Not tonight."

O'Reilly nodded, but could say nothing.

Chapter Thirty-three

Friday, November 9

Newspaper headlines proclaimed the death of Galvyn Kane as he tried to escape from the police. He was dubbed the *"Whitechapel Killer"* by one newspaper, and Sandy Mac-Dougall of the *Times* called him *"The modern Ripper."* The word "copycat" appeared in articles time and again. But the name *"Jack the Ripper"* as such, was not associated with Kane. The Commissioner had put his foot down on that one, Warren told Darnell, and the files were then sealed. But all London now knew the name of Professor John Darnell, and knew the killings had ended because of his determination and planning, and his wife's courage.

At breakfast, with Catherine O'Reilly as a rare household guest, Sung surpassed himself with delicacies. Although O'Reilly's mood was dampened by thoughts of her mother's death, she found it helped to unburden her feelings through talking.

She told the Darnells about her mother, recounting some of her private memories of growing up in a village outside London before they moved to the big city and before her father joined Scotland Yard. At last she sighed and smiled at Penny. "Thank you for letting me stay here last night. I feel better now. I think I can eat. Mother would want me to go on."

After breakfast, they lingered over coffee in the sitting room, with O'Reilly continuing her own form of grieving by reminiscing about her mother. They insisted she stay for lunch, and she and Penny spent time together in the interim while Darnell kept busy on the phone to Warren and Howard.

Sandy MacDougall telephoned, congratulating Darnell,

but also berating him for failing to keep him informed. "I still think there's more behind this than you're telling me, John. But I know you'll never tell me."

The phone rang again, and George Bernard Shaw's voice crackled in the receiver, lively and crisp. "Congratulations to you, Professor, and to Sergeant O'Reilly! We did it, and I'm happy to have done my part. Now Kathleen has been avenged."

Darnell had a surprise for the playwright, however, and explained how Penny had taken O'Reilly's place. Shaw sputtered, "Well, I'll be damned! The understudy took the starring role."

Darnell said, "You trained both at once. And very well."

Shaw cleared his throat. "I'm sorry about the Sergeant's mother. I, ah, I'll be sending two tickets to my next play opening to you, John, and I'll send Sergeant O'Reilly—Catherine—two tickets, also. Front row, center. Tell both of the women that George Bernard Shaw considers them bloody good actresses."

Darnell sat back contentedly on the sofa and finished the small glass of sherry he'd been sipping. At last the final scene had been played out in this drama. But when an unexpected knock came at the door, he wondered, could there yet be something else?

Down the hallway, he heard Sung open the door, and heard a woman's voice, "We'd like to see Professor Darnell, please."

Sung said, "Come in, please."

In a moment, Sung stepped through the sitting room doorway and walked up to Darnell. He spoke in a low voice. "Six young women to see you."

"Six? What do they want?"

"I didn't ask, sir. They were smiling. I asked them in."

Darnell nodded. "I'll see them, of course." He stepped from the sitting room out into the entry and faced the entourage.

"Ladies, I'm Professor John Darnell. What can I do for you?"

The same woman who had spoken first, evidently acting as spokeswoman for the others, addressed him, smiling broadly. "Nothing at all, sir. We just want to present you with this plaque. We had it made this morning as soon as

we read about what happened last night." She held it out
to him.

Silently, John Darnell read to himself the words on the
gold metal insert on the mahogany plaque. But, when he
noticed Sung lingering a few paces back, and when Penny
and Catherine O'Reilly came in from the dining room, all
obviously consumed with curiosity, he smiled and read the
words aloud for them:

> "To Professor John Darnell, who saved Mary Kelly.
> From some of the other Mary Kellys of London. We all
> thank you. Mary Lou Kelly . . . Mary Anne Kelly . . .
> Mary Caroline Kelly . . . Mary June Kelly . . . Mary
> Elizabeth Kelly . . . Mary Kate Kelly."

When he finished reading it, the six women clapped their
hands, and the hallway filled with laughter. After they all
took their turns shaking hands with John Darnell and then
with Penny, the young women made a hasty, giggling depar-
ture and left Darnell standing in the entryway with Penny,
Catherine, and Sung. They all looked at one another and
laughed.

Darnell turned to Sung. "Bring me a hammer and some
nails, Sung. I'll hang this plaque in the sitting room right
now."

Sung nodded and turned to go.

Darnell called after him, "And when you do that, old boy,
bring that bottle of champagne you've been saving for a special occasion and four glasses into the sitting room." He
put an arm about Penny, and gazed on Sergeant O'Reilly
and Sung with a feeling of all-rightness in the world.

"Today is the ninth of November," Darnell said, "and
every Mary Kelly in London is still alive. I think that fact,
that simple, wonderful fact, entitles us to have ourselves a
small, private, and very well-earned celebration."